SHADOWRUN:
MAKEDA RED

JENNIFER BROZEK

SHADOWRUN: MAKEDA RED
Cover art by Peter Tikos
Design by Matt Heerdt and David Kerber

"#1 Ghoul" © 2016 by John Dillon. Lyrics published in all formats by permission of the artist.
"Fistful of Nuyen" © 2016 by John Dillon. Lyrics published in all formats by permission of the artist.

Published by Catalyst Game Labs,
an imprint of InMediaRes Productions, LLC
7108 S. Pheasant Ridge Drive • Spokane, WA 99224

DEDICATION

This is for my psychic twin, Bill Howard,
who once upon a time convinced me to watch Casablanca.

ACKNOWLEDGMENTS

Shadowrun is a wonderful, complex, and detailed game. I could not have written this novel without the help of other knowledgeable writers and fans alike.

Thank you to Sasha Morlock and Lars Blumenstein for excellent shadowrunner world advice and to Raphael Andres for nuanced Swiss-German insults.

Thank you to John Dillon for allowing me to include the lyrics of "#1 Ghoul" from Johnny Nuclear and the Meltdowns.

Thank you to Pongolyn and Ollietronic for being awesome about letting me fictionally do horrible things to them.

A huge thanks to Evan Louscher for being my on-call "Can I do *this* in Shadowrun?" guy (I like to keep one foot in the rules while I have my head in the clouds).

Thank you to Jason Hardy and John Helfers for editing me, making me seem that much more awesome, and keeping me on my toes.

As always, thank you to my beloved, Jeff, for playing out **Shadowrun** scenarios with me and always willing to be a sounding board. You make everything better.

ONE

It was too easy to get lost in the crowd of beautiful people, pounding music, and party lights surrounding her. Makeda allowed herself to be pulled along, becoming part of the whole. Blending in with her short green cocktail dress that slithered against her deep mahogany skin, she danced her way across the room toward the ramp that would let her board the Brussels2Rome Party Train. She felt every pounding beat cascade through her, driving her to dance.

"You're on the clock, Makeda." TechnoGalen broke the spell of music and lights as he murmured in her ear. *"Don't have too much fun."*

Sometimes, she hated having her team in her head through her internal comms, but when one was on the clock, duty always came before pleasure. Makeda let her head drop as she raised her arms, still dancing. "Don't rush me," she subvocalized. "I haven't seen the target yet. May have to look for him on the train."

"Roger that. Security is tight. Can't even get an eye on things."

She raised her head and let her gaze roam the party people. It was a who's who of the world's novahot rich and famous. Over there was a pack of Arabic royalty, famous for being famous. Next to them was a pair of top-rated ork urban brawl players. They were dancing with a trio of elven trid stars. Makeda lingered on the elves. She liked her men lanky and her women blonde. All three of them qualified.

"On the clock," she reminded herself. She pulled her eyes away and let herself stop seeing the individuals. Instead, she watched the crowd as a whole and found what was out of place. Sprinkled throughout the lounge were official Party Train security personnel. About half of them were in classic uniforms and wires. These were stationed on the outside of the dance floor—visible to one and all. The rest moved through the oblivious dancers, discreet and professional.

Makeda had to admire their calm, cool efficiency. One of the humans dancing near the current trid "It" girl, SKYLAR!, got too close. Her security man moved in, sliding between them with a dance move worthy of a stage performance. He executed a couple more dance moves that shifted the interloper back an acceptable distance. The whole time, no one around them knew what had happened.

She eyed the Japanese security man for a moment longer, appreciating his form and his ability to do his job. Makeda pondered the idea of flirting with him just to see what he'd do. Then the hair on the back of her neck stood up.

Someone was watching her as closely as she'd been watching SKYLAR!'s man.

Moving back against the crowd, Makeda shifted as close to the lounge's temporary wall as she could. She stood across the way from the ramp that led onto the Party Train. The hosts had set up a small gate with an electronic sensor. Two train station security personnel stood on either side of it. Through the gate was a short ramp into a longer covered tunnel that hid the train station from the partygoers and the elite from anyone who might be in the train station for other reasons. The door onto the actual train was at the end of the tunnel.

The way the lounge was set up, it was hard to imagine that this room, with its tables, chairs, and couches, didn't exist in the normal day-to-day operation of the train station. Makeda fanned herself and looked around as if trying to find the bar or the restroom. She wanted to know who was watching her. It was probably harmless. She was in a tiny cocktail dress that made her look divine, after all. Still, one could never be too cautious.

Makeda found the person watching her. The two of them locked eyes. There was no hiding that gaze from across the room.

Standing next to the bar, he was the most beautiful human she'd seen in a long time. With mint-colored hair, high cheek bones, and a slender face, he would've been considered "elven" if elves didn't already exist in the world. His matching mint suit—slacks, vest, jacket thrown over the chair he stood next to—would've looked garish on most people. On him, it fit like it was meant to be. She could tell he had dark eyes, but she couldn't see much more from this distance. Makeda wanted a closer look, and she was going to get it.

Despite her returned scrutiny, he didn't look away. Instead, he lifted his glass in toast and invitation. *Come drink with me, come dance with me, come here and be with me,* the gesture said.

Makeda was more than happy to oblige.

The music shifted from the wordless techno into the industrial pop song "#1 Ghoul" by the hottest indie band featured on the Party Train: Johnny Nuclear and the Meltdowns. A cry went up and the dance floor surged as the revelers gave themselves over to the beat.

"Got my arm candy onto the train," Makeda subvocalized. She let the music take her back into the heart of the dance floor. She gave the beautiful man a beckoned invitation as she did.

He put his drink down, held his arms behind his back, and sliced through the crowd like a man on a mission. By the time he got to her,

Makeda was sure her new crush had had some sort of defensive-arts training. He was able to bend around and move through the mass of dancers without interrupting a single one.

Makeda faced him as he stepped in next to her. He matched his dance moves to hers and bent in close, "I'm Imre..."

The song gave her the answer she needed for this moment in time. She sang along with it to him, dancing close, letting her arm and hip bump against his. "'...but know that I don't care. / You've got me dead to rights / 'cuz I'm addicted to your 'ware.'"

Imre got the hint, shut up, and just danced. He was as good as Makeda had hoped. Bowing her head again to cover her subvocalizing, she ordered, "Galen, get me everything you can on this guy."

"Get me a good full-face look."

Makeda peeked at Imre. He wasn't much taller than she was, but he carried himself like he was well over one hundred eighty centimeters. She was only one hundred sixty-seven and was almost eye-to-eye with him. Imre gave her a rakish smile but kept his hands to himself. He appeared content to let her take the lead.

This time, she raised her hands and ran them through his hair, letting her internal eye cameras get a good shot of his face. She gave him a broad smile as she realized he'd gone way old school with his looks tonight. There were hints of dark brown roots; Imre had bleached his hair, then dyed it mint. Part of her wondered what he'd look like without the eyeliner and with his natural hair color.

Her internal comms came to life as her hacker gave her the download. "Imre Dahl. German. Address in Hanover, Germany. Occupation: Casino Hanover VIP relations. That means he's on call for the whales. Don't know how far up the food chain. May be a good guy to keep in contact with after all this is done."

It explained a lot about her new acquaintance: his ability to afford this trip, his skill in moving through the crowd without disturbing anyone, his good fashion sense, and his apparent ease with strangers. He *might* be a very good person to keep around. She gave him another smile. Or to keep close in the short term.

Galen interrupted her prurient line of thought, "Saladin says to remind you that while you can have fun, you're on the clock. It's less than ten hours to Lucern and the call to your ride out of Switzerland. Find the target, then nail Imre to the furniture."

Makeda spun away from Imre, making him chase her across the dance floor as the song wound down. "Shut up, Galen." The fact that her team would be in her head if she did decide to have some carnal fun put a wet blanket on things. It came with the territory, though— you never shut your team out when you were on a run. Even if it was a simple extraction with a willing target. There was too much money on the line.

The crowd rushed to the bar after "#1 Ghoul" was replaced with a lighter rock song, one Makeda didn't recognize. Imre's left-behind jacket allowed them to get a seat at the bar. He gestured for her to take it as he stepped to the side.

"Do I get to know your name?" he asked as she sat.

"Maybe."

"Or do you want to be my #1 Ghoul?"

Makeda laughed and glanced at him from under the veil of her eyelashes. "What's a ghoul anyway? Is it a vampire?" She, of course, knew the answer. Every shadowrunner did. She wanted to know if he knew. From the smoothing of his expression into something neutral, hiding a grimace, he did.

Imre shrugged. "It's actually not very nice. I had to look it up when the song became popular. They're, well, undead cannibals, really. Not in control of themselves for the most part. I suppose that's the attraction. Powerful but not responsible."

She made a face and shook her head. "Oh. That's not very nice or sexy. Then again, people turned Nosferatu into a romantic lead. In that case, I don't want to be anyone's #1 Ghoul. I'm already powerful. And I like being in control."

Imre gave her a lascivious smile and gestured to the bartender, "What may I get you, my black beauty?"

"Taéngelé."

"A woman after my own heart." He ordered two glasses of the elven liquor and leaned against the bar. "Do I get to know your name? Or shall I make something up?"

"If I tell you what it is, what will you do with it?"

"I will whisper it in your ear at the most inappropriate times."

His purr made Makeda shiver, and they both laughed. She shrugged. "Makeda. Just Makeda." Behind him, she watched as small groups of people began to enter the train. First was a Japanese man in leather pants, a leather jacket, and no shirt—though he was adorned with bloody scratches that appeared to have come from his retinue of Japanese cat girls in identical vinyl bodysuits. Each one tapped their Party Train band to the electronic sensor as they entered.

"Ah, the lovely queen of Saba—better known as the queen of Sheba. Powerful, indeed."

She gave him a bright, surprised smile. "Most don't know that. Yes. My mother has big plans for me." Makeda sipped her drink, savoring the bite of the anise. "In time. Just not now. I have my own plans. My own ideas."

The next group included an aging dwarf couple. They tried to get on the train without tapping their bands to the sensor, and security had a very quiet, smiling word with them. Both dug through their clothing for their Party Train bands and scowled as they were made to tap them to the sensor and then put the electronic bands on.

Makeda touched her own Brussels2Rome band. It was her ticket onto the train, her wallet, and her identification wrapped up in one. She couldn't get it off once she'd put it on. She'd tried all of the manual, conventional methods. The band was too strong to break, too small to slip off, and sealed itself upon closing. To remove the Party Train band, you needed a special electronic pad to unlock it—or a very good set of tools. Fortunately for her, she always came prepared.

Imre followed her gaze and shrugged at the dwarves. He shifted the cuff of his sleeve, revealing his own band. "Security is tight."

"It needs to be. It's very exclusive. It's the place to see and be seen at the moment." A foursome of orks and trolls approached the gate. Sportsmen from the World Wrestling League and urban brawl. Security was just as polite and professional with them as they had been with everyone else.

"What do you do for fun?"

Makeda pulled her attention back to Imre. She had to trust that everything was going to go as expected. If not, she would use this man in front of her to get what she needed. "Whatever I want. Right now, travel. This was a good way to get to Rome. What about you?"

"When I'm not working? I like to travel, too."

"You work?" She touched his vest, feeling the soft suede under her fingertips. It made her want to pet him more.

Imre nodded. "I do. Is that a problem?"

She shook her head. "No."

"Good. Because, lovely one, I would like to spend more time with you, but I want you to know what you're getting into."

She widened her eyes. "What's that, working man?"

"I'm going to make the most of this trip because I've got reality to get back to in a couple of weeks. That means I want to party like tomorrow will never come."

"I think I can handle that." Makeda leaned in close, whispering in his ear. "I'll tell you a little secret, Imre...I work, too." This close, she could smell his cologne, something with lavender, cloves, and amber. It smelled as good as he looked.

He put a hand to his chest, "Be still my beating heart. What do you do?"

"Organize fundraisers for orphanages. Right here in Belgium." She grinned at his surprised look. "No, really. I do." She shrugged. "What good is money if you can't use it to help people who really need it? My parents are simultaneously proud of and aghast at my actions."

"I'm particularly proud of that background," TechnoGalen interrupted. *"Also, head's up. Get on the train. Time's wasting."*

Makeda glanced over his shoulder and saw the dance floor and lounge clearing out with remarkable decorum. Various security personnel moved in a coordinated sweep to bring the guests from their spots to enter the train without making anyone wait too long.

"You surprise me," Imre said, "And I might be able to help you with fundraising in the future."

"Oh?"

Imre didn't get a chance to answer before a tall ork woman in a train station security uniform appeared at their side. "Excuse me, the train will be leaving soon. May I escort you to the ramp?" Everything in her tone was polite and diffident, but both of them heard the command within the request.

Imre gestured to Makeda, allowing her to go first. He murmured, "I hope you keep surprising me...and I hope to surprise you."

Makeda glanced coyly over her shoulder at him then followed the security woman. Holding her head high and her shoulders relaxed, she waved her Party Train band at the sensor. This was the moment it would all come together or fall apart. Either her cover would hold... or it wouldn't.

Without waiting for the accepting beep, she was already turning to Imre, gesturing for him to join her on the ramp. If it went bad, she'd let the tears come and have him deal with it.

The sensor turned green.

Imre grabbed her hand and touched his band to the sensor with his other arm at the same time. Laughing as the sensor went green again and the train security personnel muttered welcomes, the two half ran up the ramp that led to the train.

Just inside the tunnel, Imre pulled her close, hovering his lips to hers, asking without words if he could kiss her. Beneath the cologne the scent of his sweat—woody and clean—enticed her as much as his body language.

She answered by kissing him, long and lingeringly, tasting his cologne and him as she did so.

An alarm blared, and the lights in the hallway went red. The doors on either end of the ramp hallway slammed shut.

"What?" Makeda looked around, not panicked, but curious. Like someone who didn't have anything to hide. Inside, her heart hammered in her chest. Something had gone wrong. Already, she was working through the problem, coming up with solutions. Everything from collapsing in a fake faint to taking Imre hostage.

Imre looked at the closed doors. He took both her hands in his. "I'll take care of this. Don't you worry."

She nodded, trying to keep her eyes wide and innocent. As soon as he moved to the train side of the hallway, she walked to the other door. "Galen, what's wrong?"

"Working on it. Someone's SIN tripped the shutdown."

She knocked on the door. "Hello? Hello? We're locked in here." She knocked again. "Me?"

Galen took too long to answer. *"No. Not you. Not your arm candy either. Someone just behind you two."* He sent her the security image of an elf with his hands up.

Makeda didn't recognize him. The lights went from red to white and the door in front of her opened just as she was about to knock again. A very large troll in a Party Train security uniform stood before her. On his chest was the name *Jarvis*. She opened her eyes wide and let some of the fear of being caught leak through. "We were locked in here."

"I'm so very sorry, Miss Makeda." The troll stepped forward and started herding her toward the other end of the tunnel, where Imre waited. "We take security very seriously. We thought it better to protect you and Mr. Dahl against the breach rather than subject you to possible injury."

Makeda nodded, then giggled. "Oh, I'll have such a story to tell my friends." She nodded to Imre. "When life does this, it's like a plot twist. It gives you something to gossip about at home."

Imre slid his arm about her waist as Security Captain Jarvis opened the door between the tunnel and the train. Makeda watched the captain's hand, and the code, with interest. She knew Galen would, too. It might come in handy in the future.

Nodding at her and Imre, the troll said, "Please accept our sincerest apologies for this minor inconvenience. I've let the hosts know, and they will make sure that something special is delivered to your sleeper suites. Please, have an excellent time on the Brussels2Rome Party Train."

"Thank you," Imre said. "We will."

Makeda gave Captain Jarvis a little wave as the two of them entered luxury incarnate.

TWO

The Brussels2Rome Party Train was a custom-built train designed to hold and entertain the world's elite. Everything from the floor to the ceiling had a designer's touch. From marble inlays to gilded tiles to polished wood, this first train car was as ornate as a five-star hotel lobby. Behind a small wood-and-marble podium stood a handsome Sikh man in a black dastaar and the Party Train uniform of black, white, and gold. Next to him was a map of the train.

Forty-five cars long, it showed everything from where all of the dance, bar, dinner, and lounge cars were—front of the train—as well as where the sleeper cars were—back of the train. Makeda noted that, while the graphic of the train appeared complete, there were at least five cars missing from it, including the engine, security, the kitchens, and the caboose. She also knew, from the team's previous investigations, that the train would be preceded and followed by double-car security trains. With this many of the world's VIPs looking to have a good time, security had to be tight.

Another colorful graphic showed a simplified version of the train's path through Europe. Most of these were not stops—just waypoints to be noted. The maglev track ran from Brussels to Köln to Greater Frankfurt to Stuttgart to Basel to Lucern (the location she was most interested in) to Zurich, then Innsbruck to Verona and from there to Rome. It was an ambitious train ride with almost too many dangers to count.

Least political among them was the Alpine Interdiction Zone. It was a pristine wilderness guarded by the Swiss *Gebirsjager*—mountain infantry. The train wasn't going through it, but it was traveling near enough that everyone was on guard. Lucern was the Party Train's only scheduled stop before Rome. It was a refueling station only. No one on or off.

Not too long ago, the Brussels2Rome Party Train would never have happened, no matter how much money had been thrown at it. Only the formation of the New European Economic Community, bringing in the fifteen biggest European corporations, allowed them to bypass almost all border controls. Only Switzerland still had some restrictions, and most of those revolved around metahumans. It was something Makeda didn't have to worry about.

"Where do you want to go first?" Imre gestured to the train map as he put his hand on the small of her back.

"I think I want to go freshen up after all that dancing." She moved away from him and paused at the sudden hurt look on his face. "Don't worry. We have twenty-four hours to enjoy. The party will still be here when I'm ready." She gave him a kiss on the cheek. "Go on. Have a good time. I'll find you."

As if by magic, a lovely brunette in the feminized version of the Party Train uniform appeared at the concierge's side. The Sikh man gave Imre a respectful nod. "I took the liberty of summoning one of our entertainment hostesses, Mr. Dahl. Again, we are so sorry you were locked in the entrance tunnel."

Imre looked at the three of them and laughed. "A hostess just for me? I'm honored. It is a vacation, after all." He glanced at Makeda. "I will see you soon, I hope?"

Makeda leaned forward and brushed her lips against his ear. "Count on it."

His smile returned. He stepped to the hostess and offered his arm. "Lead me to paradise."

She dimpled at him. "As you wish."

Makeda hoped Imre would have a good time. Good enough to forget her while she did her job. As the brunette led Imre away, the Sikh man came out from behind his small podium. "If you will allow me to escort you to your sleeper car, Ms. Makeda? Your baggage has already been placed within your suite." He offered her his arm.

Looking as amused as Imre, Makeda took his arm and allowed him to lead the way. She didn't say anything, testing to see if he was one of those who would chatter on about everything and nothing, or if he would remain as silent as those he escorted.

It seemed to be the latter as they walked through three sleeper cars. Each one appeared identical to the previous one, only reversed to keep the train's weight evenly distributed. The airlock between cars was obvious by its door system, but easy to navigate. With the thick, malleable walls, there was no danger of falling off the train. Makeda took note of the keypad next to each one. The rooms could be locked down.

The sleeper cars themselves were carpeted in deep burgundy that matched the curtains inside each of the sleeper car doors. Outer hall walls gave the impression of stone while the inner ones were a light rosewood with brass diamond inlays. Each door had a small window bracketed by interior curtains and a canted brass bar to help slide the door open. The doors' sensors were a smooth, matte black.

Glancing around, Makeda spotted areas where she would put cameras if she were designing security, but if cameras were there, they were well hidden. Luxury came with the illusion of privacy. Just as the train gave the illusion of old-world wealth while it floated on some of the best maglev technology money could buy. It was why there was almost no sense of movement.

When they stopped at sleeper car 9, her escort bowed his head and gestured to the door's sensor. "Only your Party Train band will open it."

Makeda tapped the sensor. It lit up green, and the door slid open a small bit. Makeda's escort slid the door the rest of the way open for her. Looking in, the sleeper suite itself was small but lovely. The size of a small office, three meters square, it currently looked like a living room with a small washroom. The scent of fresh citrus floated on the air. With a touch of a button, the whole room would transform into a bedroom with a queen-sized bed. It was the luxury version of an airport capsule hotel.

"Thank you." Makeda stepped into the room.

"If you need anything, please don't hesitate to ask. We are at your beck and call." With that, the concierge left her to the room, closing the door after himself. The door locked into place.

"Beck and call? That's new." Galen chuckled in her ear. *"Why do you get all the face time and luxury while I'm stuck here in the Matrix?"*

Makeda went to her small suitcase on the counter and pulled out her makeup bag. As she opened the foundation compact hiding a small toolkit underneath, she keyed the hidden switch on the side and set it on the counter. "Clear?"

"All clear. No bugs or cameras."

"I'm prettier than you. That's why." She said this aloud as she gazed in the mirror. She really did need to towel off and reset her makeup. "Besides, they'd have a fit over your wheelchair. You can't get on an airplane without setting off alarms, much less a train like this with a bunch of high mucky-mucks. You'd upset their delicate sensibilities by reminding them that not everything is perfect in this world."

"I may resemble that remark in meat space, but in the Matrix, I'm a fraggin' Adonis."

"I know. I've seen you." She meant that in the literal sense. While her Matrix avatar was a cheetah, his was of the statue of Adonis— naked and all. Somehow, he made the classic statue lascivious. No matter what he did in the Matrix, it was tinged with a sexual magnetism.

In meat space, TechnoGalen was a small Hawaiian man born without the bottom half of his legs. His parents, for whatever reason, had chosen to leave him without prosthetics, and he'd embraced this as his identity. Makeda suspected he also had spinal issues that precluded the use of prosthetics, but it wasn't any of her business unless he chose to tell her.

Galen was just as flirtatious in meat space as he was in the Matrix. Just as successful, too. When not on the job, he was a party animal. She rarely saw him without one of his three girlfriends—unless he was working. Like now.

Makeda wasted no time stripping off the cocktail dress and ducking into the washroom. She gave herself a quick wipe down to get the sweat off, then changed into black, hip-hugging slacks and a silky red top cut down to there, showing off her gold jewelry.

"Right, has HiddenPlath reported in?"

"Yes. She says the target entered the lounge not long after you did."

Makeda added the latest fashion—knee-high suede boots. For once, fashion had merged with the practical, and low heels were in vogue. This would probably last for about three more months. In the meantime, she was going to enjoy being able to move without pain and run without having to ditch her shoes first.

"Wearing what?"

"Skinny black slacks and a white, open-collar shirt. Long sleeves. Sending you an image."

Makeda paused as she gazed at the image. Not a bad-looking guy. The wrinkles around his eyes clashed with his youthful clothing. She shrugged. At least he was trying. "Doesn't look like much of a salaryman. Good. He'll fit right in."

"Still going to bring him back to your car for the duration?"

"That's the plan. I just have to find him first. I'm going to wring his neck for not meeting me in the lounge like he was instructed."

"What about Imre?"

She checked herself in the mirror one more time. *Yep, still stunning.* Everyone was going to be looking at her cleavage or gold eyes and likely wouldn't notice much more than a beautiful black woman enjoying herself on the Brussels2Rome Party Train. "I'm sure he's having a very good time wherever he is. I can hunt him down after the job is done. I know where he works." Makeda squared her shoulders, then let them relax. "Right. I'm going to find the target now. Going silent. If you see him before I do, let me know."

"Roger that."

Makeda slipped out the sleeper suite door and wondered where the target was now that he'd missed their rendezvous. Most likely in one of the bars in the open. At least, she hoped. Until she found him, there was nothing more she could do but a car-to-car search.

Crossing through the lobby car again, a new set of concierge personnel were on duty. They were attentive, but did not speak to her as she passed by. It was something of a relief. Having her face—along with Imre's—blasted to all train personnel as someone to be extra attentive to could make life hard in the long run.

Stepping from the lobby car into the first bar area was like stepping into another world. Gone was the old-world charm of wood and brass. In its place was a sleek, modern design of matte metal, clean lines, and muted pastel lights. The bar was to the right side, surrounded by people. The left had tables bolted to the floor but chairs that could be moved, and were. The music was soft rock, and the crowd had an older sense of age.

She strode through, glancing about. No sign of Tojo Isoshi. Makeda kept walking, shaking her head at invitations in the form of raised glasses and stroking fingertips. The party had just gotten started. Those who'd come alone were looking for playmates.

The next car was styled as a living room. It had a long table filled with finger foods and attendants ready to refill drinks. The music was low, but had a pulsing beat. Again, no Tojo, but Imre was here with several lovely young women. Makeda pretended not to see him. If he saw her, he decided to stick with his present company. She slipped out of that car as quickly as she could.

The industrial music hit her like a sonic punch to the face as she opened the next car. Johnny Nuclear and the Meltdowns were playing live, and the crowd was a mass of dancers, flailing about to "Fistful of Nuyen," another one of their hits. She scanned the room in a back-and-forth fashion, trusting that Galen would notice what she didn't.

While the target wasn't in sight, there were a couple of corp-security personnel against the wall of the car. They scanned the room like she did. By the patch on their shoulders, they appeared to be from Saeder-Krupp. That was not good. Makeda turned away as one of them looked to her.

"Is he here?"

"No. But there is a Saeder-Krupp exec over by the stage. Small Japanese man in purple."

Glad that her hacker was on the same wavelength, Makeda looked and spotted the exec. She made the mental note to stay as far away from the man as she could when it was time to exit the train. With that in mind, she slipped through the crowd, bouncing to the beat of the song. If she were on vacation, she'd just stay here. But duty before pleasure.

The next car was another bar car, almost identical to the first one she walked through. At the bar, drinking by himself despite being surrounded by people, was her target. Tojo stared at his drink, looking at the bottom of the glass as if it somehow could convey something meaningful to him.

He was a handsome man with a slight build and black hair. Now that she saw him in person, she could see he was older than she'd first assumed. Despite being designed for a younger crowd, his clothing suited him—even if it clashed with his current demeanor. She eyed him as if she were just a woman looking for something interesting.

Tojo was shorter than her. Makeda could tell that much from where she stood.

As she headed toward to the bar, she saw two more Saeder-Krupp security people standing in the corners; one near the bar, one near the opposite exit. The SK woman next to the bar straightened up as Makeda slid in next to Tojo. Not good. The target was under surveillance. Also, not good at subtlety.

Makeda ordered a cider and then leaned to Tojo, "For a man on vacation, you look like you've lost your last friend."

Tojo shrugged a little, not looking up. "I was supposed to meet someone. I missed them, or they didn't show."

"Life's too short to waste it on people who don't show up. Why don't you hang out with me? I'm by myself." She offered her hand. "I'm Makeda."

Tojo's head snapped up, his eyes wide. He started to bow. She stopped him. "I'm American. We don't bow. We shake hands."

"Makeda?" Tojo thrust his hand to her.

As she took his hand in hers, she squeezed a little tighter than she needed to, leaned in, and whispered. "We're being watched. So, now I'm whispering something naughty in your ear about dinner and then dessert and licking things off your body."

She pulled back, pleased to see Tojo blushing to the roots of his hair. It was exactly what she wanted to happen.

"Heads up, Makeda. Someone has flagged your SIN and is investigating."

That was the last thing she wanted to hear.

THREE

Makeda glanced around, waiting to see if either of the Saeder-Krupp security would move to intervene. She wasn't sure what she would do if they did, but something would occur to her. She worked best while under stress and improvising. Both guards stood their ground. The woman looked away as Makeda's gaze drifted in her direction.

"SIN being hit hard, but holding. No alarms."

Makeda smiled at Galen's report and tilted her head to the side, giving Tojo her full attention once more. "So, dinner?"

Tojo nodded with a broad, embarrassed but pleased, grin. "Yes. Dinner. And dessert."

She took his hand and led him to the exit next to the other Saeder-Krupp security person, a stocky dwarf. Though he stared straight ahead, she knew he was examining her. Just before she pulled Tojo out of the car, she paused to murmur in his ear, "We're going to have a good time, I promise."

Tojo nodded. "I hope."

Makeda smiled on the surface. That smile did not meet her eyes. With Saeder-Krupp security watching the target, this was going to be a bit more complicated than she thought. *Like every run ever.* It might involve throwing Tojo from the train and following after. She hoped it wouldn't come to that, but was prepared to do what was needed to get the job done. In the meantime, she knew she had to keep the target out of the public eye.

She mentally shrugged as they entered the next car—another dance car full of beautiful young people and techno pop music—it wasn't the first time she'd used her body to keep a target safe and pacified. It wouldn't be the last. The two cut through the crowd. As they exited the dance car, the Saeder-Krupp security woman entered. Makeda knew she was going to have to do something about that. She just didn't know what. Not yet, anyway.

The next car was exactly what she was looking for: one of the dining cars. They were met by a Party Train host and led to a booth in the middle of the room. Makeda gestured for Tojo to sit first. She slid in after, right next to him. At first, he looked startled, then his blush returned. Makeda gave him a coquettish glance. The more he was distracted by her, the less he would give away to their observers.

They both ordered the shabu-shabu hot pot and wine. As soon as the server left, Makeda murmured to him like a lover, "Tell me, my little *okurimono*, why would your soon-to-be former employers have watchdogs on you? What aren't you telling us?"

He shook his head. "I don't know. I'm nobody. I don't have an important job."

She waited until the dining car's din rose to answer. "No one pays this much money to extract someone ordinary, and Saeder-Krupp wouldn't spend watchdog resources on a nobody. What do you do?" Based on all her team's research, she already knew that Tojo worked for Krupp Specialist Engineering. A talented developer was worth poaching, but having security personnel assigned to a salaryman on vacation? There was more to this story, and she needed to find out what it was fast.

Tojo shrugged. "I'm just an engineer." He paused, tapping his fingertips on the table as he thought. "I've never taken a vacation before?" He offered up the suggestion like a sacrifice.

"Have you been talking about being unhappy?"

He shook his head.

"Recently broken up with a girlfriend? Closed any accounts?"

Tojo started to shake his head then shrugged. "I consolidated my credit cards into one account last month. Paid off a lot of debts."

Makeda pondered this. "Anyone close to you died or committed suicide recently?"

He blinked at her, surprised. "No." He thought some more and shook his head. "No," he repeated.

"But you changed your routine and booked the Party Train." She gave him a slow smile, then leaned into his lips and murmured "You caught their attention as a flight or suicide risk." She kissed him before he could protest her assessment. She let the kiss linger, tasting him. *Not bad at all.* When they came up for air, she ducked her head. "I'll take care of it...and you. All will be well. That's what I'm paid to do."

They looked up as the meal arrived in a series of fresh vegetable dishes and thinly sliced beef on a tray. Another server brought a boiling hot pot of soup. The meaty, savory smell of it wafted close, making Makeda's mouth water. She gestured for Tojo to put the vegetables into the bubbling broth and gazed around the dining car. The Saeder-Krupp security woman was nowhere to be seen. Then the back of a familiar head, exiting the dining car in a rush, caught her eye.

Imre Dahl had seen her kissing Tojo and appeared to be making a hasty retreat. Makeda rolled her eyes at the implied high-school antics. In truth, she would have rather been with Imre, but she had a job to do. She was going to do it and do it well. Imre could be contacted later. She glanced at Tojo. He wasn't going to be bad company. Just complicated.

"Tell me about you? Your job? Your home?" Makeda took a pair of chopsticks in hand and selected a slice of the raw beef to swish into the hot broth. She might as well keep Tojo talking about himself while they ate. It would keep him from asking about her. Also, it might give her a bit more insight into the Saeder-Krupp guards and why they were following him. Most people knew when they were important enough to warrant extra protection.

She ate as he talked, cooing at just the right moment to keep him talking. "That sounds hard..." or remarks to that effect were all she had to say to re-invigorate the conversation. Part of her studied the rest of the diners. Part of her kept an ear on Tojo's monologue.

"—Have you ever tried to make an elevator go sideways? Not as easy as it seems." Tojo flourished a bit of bamboo at her before popping it in his mouth. "Up and down are easy. There's only two directions. Sideways, not so much. There could be any number of directions."

Makeda turned her full attention to Tojo. He looked pleased with himself. "Make an elevator go...sideways?"

Tojo nodded, scooping fragrant rice and vegetables into his mouth. "It's going to be the next big thing. Elevators go up and down. But think about arcologies. They want—need—something more adaptable. The problem comes when you want the elevators to go north or south or east or west as well as up and down. Or any approximations of the four cardinal directions." He grinned. "Then again, some don't want straight lines. Some like curves. Like an airport tram, but in elevator form."

It was rare for an idea to bring a new perspective that was so weird and so outlandish that it had to work. It was much like the vaunted doggie door. Weird in conception, but once you had it, you wondered how you could've lived without it. Makeda considered some of the arcologies she'd "visited." All of them would benefit from elevators that moved sideways. She eyed her target. Things were starting to make more sense.

Tojo worked in Krupp Specialist Engineering. Thyssen-Krupp, a Saeder-Krupp subsidiary, was responsible for most of the world's elevators. If he was part of the team working on these sideways elevators, he was more than a nobody. There was a lot of proprietary information that could be worth millions in his head. Maybe. Perhaps that was why he was being extracted, and why Saeder-Krupp security was keeping an eye on him.

"I'm amazed at this idea. It's not something I would've ever thought of." Makeda smiled, truthful and worried. It was more important than ever to get him tucked safely away in her sleeper suite until they escaped the train.

"I know." Tojo's eyes lit up, warming to the subject.

A lovely blonde woman in one of the Party Train uniforms sat down in the booth across from them. "Good evening. May I join you?"

Makeda started to say "No," but Tojo answered before she could. "Yes, of course. It's good to see you again."

Makeda looked between the woman and her extraction target. First, Saeder-Krupp was watching him. Next, he was inviting strange women to eat with them. This was getting better and better. Maybe she should just drug the drek out of him and make him sleep until they got off the train.

The woman offered her hand, "I'm Beauty, one of the Party Train entertainment hostesses."

Makeda paused before she shook the woman's hand. "Hello."

"This is the hostess who made sure I got on the train all right when I missed meeting up with you." Tojo's cheeks flushed a hectic red that was more than the wine they were drinking.

Beauty smiled and glanced between them. "I had to check in on Tojo and see who this lovely lady was. He was so upset at missing you. We absolutely cannot have that on the Party Train. It's against the rules. I've been assigned to do anything—*anything*—I need to help our guests have a good time. We'd like to make this an annual event. Happy partiers are repeat partiers."

Makeda chuckled. "I think we have our entertainment well in hand. Thank you."

"What do you suggest?" Tojo blinked at the woman like he'd been drugged.

Makeda realized he was trying to flirt with her. She was all for Tojo having a good time while they were here, but with Saeder-Krupp nosing around, she'd rather they kept things low key and private.

Beauty leaned forward. "I have a private suite at my disposal. I would love to entertain you there. She locked eyes with Makeda. "Both of you."

"We'd love that." Tojo nodded like a teenager. He leaned to Makeda. "Please?"

It was all Makeda could do to keep from slapping him upside the head for destroying her neatly laid plans—again. She glanced at Beauty. The woman did match her name—and that lovely blond hair...

Makeda considered her options. Being occupied by official Party Train entertainment would keep the Saeder-Krupp security personnel off their backs. Also, it was private. It could keep them out of trouble for a bit.

She tilted her head and gave Beauty a thoughtful smile. "I think... perhaps...I would enjoy that. You said you have a room?"

If TechnoGalen said anything, Makeda swore she was going to reach right through the Matrix and throttle him. He must have sensed something, because he remained silent.

Beauty nodded. "I do. I'll have dessert delivered." She raised a hand and got their attendant's attention. After a couple of quick words, the server smiled with a glance to Makeda and Tojo then disappeared again.

"C'mon. Everything's set." Beauty slid out of the booth. Makeda and Tojo did likewise. Beauty directed them away from the sleeper cars and up through the rest of the train Makeda had not yet seen. When Makeda gave her a confused look, Beauty moved in close and whispered, "Staff get their own sleeper cars for entertainment in the front of the train."

"Lead the way." As soon as Beauty turned, Makeda grabbed Tojo by the shoulder. "We're going to have a talk about this."

Tojo smiled like a kid with a secret. "Trust me. It'll be fine."

Makeda smoothed her face into something pleasant and followed the two of them. She noted that there weren't supposed to be sleeper cars in this direction if the graphic of the train in the lobby car was even remotely accurate.

Makeda lagged behind, watching Beauty lead an apparently besotted Tojo through the train cars. "Galen, get me everything you can on Beauty. Is she who she says she is?"

"Working on it. Have a good time. I'll take pictures and rate them later."

"You're going to pay for that."

"Worth it."

Beauty dodged through the crowds like a pro, stopping from time to time to help Tojo navigate the dancing, drinking people. Her help was more to allow Tojo to cop a feel than anything else. From time to time, she gave Makeda a sly smile that promised the world. As much as Makeda wanted Beauty to be exactly what she seemed—an entertainment hostess hired to do whatever the guest wanted—it was more likely that the woman was a thief, a prostitute, or both. A joygirl was fine. A thief was not.

Then again, as they passed through half a dozen cars, none of the other entertainment hosts and hostesses gave her more than a passing glance or a brief wave. "Tell me you got something, Galen," she muttered as they entered a sleeper car and Beauty smiled, gesturing to an unmarked door.

FOUR

"Security is tight. I did find a 'Beauty Morel' on the public Party Train hostess list. Still digging, but she looks legit so far. I'm going after her HR file."

They stopped at the unmarked sleeper car suite. Beauty used her own Party Train band to open it. Another interesting tidbit. Makeda hadn't realized that the woman's bangle jewelry hid the same electronic security the guests wore.

Inside, the sleeper suite itself was identical to the one assigned to Makeda. Only this one was already in the bedroom configuration, and there was a tray of champagne, strawberries, whipped cream, and chocolate dipping sauce on the counter. A light musky scent perfumed the air—most likely filled with pheromones.

In short, it was an undisguised seduction in waiting. Makeda wondered if this was standard fare.

Tojo voiced her question. "Wow. Are all of the hostess suites set up like this?" He moved into the room to examine the bottle of champagne.

Beauty closed the door behind them. "Only if a guest avails themselves of the offered...amenities. We signal to the concierge, and they make certain all is ready."

The woman's slight French accent slipped through her cultured diction, adding an exotic undercurrent to her words. Partially aroused and completely suspicious, Makeda couldn't help herself. "Do you get paid extra for this?"

"Only if you want to tip me." Beauty gave her that sly smile again and trailed a finger down Makeda's arm. "This is part of my job and my pleasure. I'm paid well, and I *choose* how I entertain our guests." The two of them locked eyes as she continued, "I only want to do what you want to do. You can watch. You can join in. This is your party."

The explosion of the cork leaving the champagne bottle broke the moment, and both women jerked as if shot. Makeda saw Beauty's hand move to her thigh in reflex as if to grab a weapon. Then she straightened. It was quick, but Makeda was sure the woman had some sort of defense hidden under her short skirt.

A defense and a weapon, Makeda thought with a small leer. Maybe duty and pleasure were going to happily coincide for once. She let her eyes linger over Beauty and Tojo. Of the two, she was more attracted to the hostess than her extraction client. Together, they could make quite the threesome that would eat up the hours—and keep Tojo out of sight. Makeda felt the rush of blood through her body as she considered it.

"*Suimasen.*" Tojo laughed and put his hand over the top of the bottle to keep it from making too much of a mess. "I'm sorry," he repeated. Then flushed as the two women laughed. "Champagne?"

Beauty winked at Makeda. "Of course, but let me do that..."

She walked over to Tojo, giving her hips an exaggerated sway, and took the champagne from him. Winking again at Makeda, she drank a couple of swallows straight from the bottle then licked the edge of it to catch any drops. Beauty poured three glasses, handing off two of them. Makeda continued to watch, playing with the stem of her glass.

Tojo drank half his drink in a single gulp and chuckled. He let Beauty take the glass from him. She did so, pressing her body to his and offering a kiss. He accepted it, but slow and sensual. Not at all like Makeda had expected. Until this point, he'd acted like an inexperienced teenager. Apparently, that had been nervous anticipation. Once it got down to brass tacks, Tojo knew what he was doing.

Watching them, Makeda sipped her champagne and licked her lips. It was good. Really good. For a woman who usually drank synthahol, all this real alcohol was spoiling her. She smiled and swore one day she would have the real stuff, whiskey, whenever she wanted it.

Beauty guided Tojo to the bed, still kissing him. He let her lead the way, sliding backward until he was almost to the headboard. They grinned at each other as she fumbled with the hidden buttons. She pulled open his shirt with a dramatic flare and laughed as buttons went flying, then turned. "Makeda..." she made the name sound like a purr, "...would you hand me the chocolate sauce?"

Makeda couldn't help but smile. It was going to be a mess, but my, what a fun mess. She did as requested, thankful Galen was keeping his mouth shut. *Oh, to have some real privacy right now.* The idea of throwing all caution to the wind grew. But she didn't turn off her internal comms. It was the one rule she had when running point on a job. There was no privacy. Everyone heard and saw what she did.

Still...Makeda licked her lips, mimicking Beauty, who tasted the chocolate before she turned back to Tojo. She could almost imagine the taste of it. Her eyes traveled up the curve of Beauty's thigh to where it disappeared under the black skirt and wondered what else was hidden beneath it—silk or lace or a combination of both?

Makeda stepped back, drinking more of her champagne. She watched Beauty dab the chocolate onto Tojo's chest, then lick it off. He was lean and more muscular than she'd expected. Tojo was a man who liked to work out. Beauty teased one of his nipples, making him groan. He pulled her up for a rougher kiss.

Taking a breath, Makeda took another swallow of the champagne. She was surprised to find the glass empty. She licked her lips, her cheeks flushed from both the alcohol and just how much she wanted to be part of what was happening before her. *Well*, she thought, *it's one way to keep the package safe until the hand-off.*

Tojo and Beauty looked at her as she put her glass down. Beauty rolled off Tojo and stood in a smooth motion, revealing just how excited he was.

"We'd love you to join us." She walked to Makeda and looked up at her. "If you want..."

"I do." Makeda gazed at Beauty and, for a brief moment, saw another lovely blonde woman. An elf. One she hadn't thought of in months. She shook away the phantom of her past and concentrated on the gorgeous human woman before her.

Beauty offered Makeda a hand. Makeda took it and let herself be pulled toward the bed. Moving slow and watching Makeda's face, Beauty slid in close, slipping her hands under Makeda's silky shirt. She lifted her face up and offered a kiss. Makeda, never good at denying temptation, took it.

Letting the kiss blossom into something slow and deep as their lips explored each other, Makeda couldn't help but notice while Beauty's left hand was fully on her back, only two fingers of Beauty's right hand were touching her. It was a strangeness that made her pull back from the kiss and reach behind her for Beauty's hand...just as Galen's voice exploded in her ear.

"Makeda, get out of there. Just got into Beauty's file. She's a brunette, not a blonde–"

Frag, Makeda thought, her eyes widening as Galen's voice continued its alarmed warning in her head.

Beauty, her eyes shifting from soft seduction to something cold and calculating, pulled Makeda close—this time using all of both hands and pressing something to Makeda's back. "Too bad. You could've been fun..."

Even as Makeda tried to pull away again, she fell into darkness.

Makeda hit her head as she ducked into the escape tunnel, following Zaria. The elf mage moved fast, crawling over the same dirt and rock that scraped skin from Makeda's hands and knees. They were deep behind enemy lines, and corpsec was shelling the drek out of their hiding place.

She paused, trying to remember where she was and why she was here. Zaria looked back. "Move it, woman. Unless you want to be dead." Makeda moved. A deeper part of her knew this was a memory—one she didn't want to remember—but was helpless to do anything but follow.

Minutes later, they broke out into daylight as the escape tunnel collapsed behind them. "Why did we get involved with mercenaries again?"

Zaria threw up a wall shield as another missile struck nearby. "It was your idea. It's just a courier job, you said. It'll be a cake walk, you said. It's easy money, you said."

Makeda surged forward and grabbed Zaria by the waist. She propelled the smaller woman behind a large rock as automatic fire came from both sides of the line. Apparently, instead of waiting for intel and just providing cover fire, one of the mercs got caught or trigger happy or both. Now it was an all-out war—with them stuck in the middle.

"Remind me never to do that again." She looked around. There. The jeep. One man, keys in the ignition. "That's our way out."

The jeep stood next to the house where they'd received the info they needed to get back to Mr. Johnson to get paid. A hundred meters away, the barn that had been their makeshift camp was tinder. The acrid smell of gunpowder filled the air as dust rained down. The man in the jeep was armed, but looking the other way.

"Now!" Makeda and Zaria sprinted to the jeep. The merc in their way sensed something and turned at the last moment. Makeda's enhanced reflexes kept her from getting shot as she threw herself at the man. With a quick disarm maneuver, she twisted the man's hand and pulled the pistol from it then lost the weapon as he headbutted her. She punched him twice before stabbing him in the chest. He died trying to choke her.

Zaria clambered into the passenger seat as Makeda shoved the dead man from the jeep. They both buckled in. "Keep your head down." Makeda didn't look at Zaria as she started the car and shoved it into gear. The blond elf didn't say anything, and Makeda took this for agreement. She focused on getting the two of them out of there as quickly as possible.

Weapons fire whizzed all around, and the jeep tanged and clanged with ricocheted bullets. But they escaped through the trees and onto the dirt road. It took many kilometers and minutes for them to leave the battle behind.

"Are we safe?" Zaria's voice was soft.

Makeda pulled the jeep into a copse of trees. "As safe as we can be for the moment."

"Good. I have a problem." Zaria, who had hunkered over as instructed, sat up just enough to reveal the bloody bullet wound in her side.

Makeda was out of the jeep and on her side before she could finish saying, "Oh, fraggin' hell, you should've told me."

The elf shook her head. "No. We needed to escape."

Unbuckling her, Makeda lifted Zaria from the jeep. "Spells?"

"No more energy. I'd pass out if I tried."

"Right. There's got to be something in the jeep that can help." Makeda laid her on the ground and turned to the back of the jeep, digging through it, looking for a medkit or even a clean enough cloth.

"Makeda!" Zaria's scream was weak and filled with fear.

Makeda looked back to see Zaria being pulled into the bushes. She dove for the elf, catching her feet. Zaria continued to struggle and cry out for help as something pulled her deeper in. Makeda couldn't wrestle her away from the monster's grip. Her face hit the dirt as Zaria was pulled into darkness, still screaming her name.

"Makeda! Wake up. Dammit. Makeda!"

Saladin shouted in her ear and the blare of her internal alarm greeted her as she clawed her way out of the drugged sleep and induced nightmare. Makeda shook her head. Zaria being hurt had happened, yes. But there'd never been a monster. There'd been a farm house and a kind person. When Zaria disappeared, it'd been from their hotel room in Mons, Belgium. Not in the middle of the woods. There'd been no monster and no explanation. Makeda hadn't seen her go, and still didn't know what had happened to her.

"Makeda!"

She forced herself to the here and now. "Fraggin' son of a slitch... I'm awake." She turned her alarm off and surged to her feet, grabbing for weapons she didn't have. She took a step and fell face first onto the sleeper-suite bed. For once, a tiny room worked in her favor. Everything was numb—part drug-induced, part sleeping on the floor for hours.

"Are you all right?"

Turning over and sitting up, she did a quick assessment. Nothing broken. Nothing hurting. Her gold bracelet was missing, but her Party Train band was still there. "Fine. Bruised ego. Missing bracelet." Her fingers searched for, found, and peeled off the tranq slap patch from her back. She looked at it: a generic patch with the sleep icon on it. She dropped it to the ground.

"That's going to work in our favor."

"I know. All of it is tagged." Makeda took a breath, still trying to clear her mind and figure out what happened. "What time is it? Where are we? And where's TechnoGalen?"

"You were out for about six hours. You've just crossed the Swiss border. Galen's napping. He figured you'd need him more when you were awake.

Not much time. She needed to figure out a plan. Makeda nodded. "Smart. Is Beauty just a thief? Or something more?"

"I think you'd better listen. They didn't know we could hear through your comms."

"Play it." Makeda closed her eyes to imagine the scene as it happened around her unconscious body.

"Makeda?" Tojo's voice sounded far away. "Is she all right? What happened?"

"You didn't follow orders, that's what happened." Beauty sounded angry and cold.

"I don't know what you mean. I did what you asked. I put it in a safe place." Tojo's voice got louder as he came close.

"Tu es completement débile!" Beauty took a breath. "You put it in the safe. You were supposed to put it in a place I didn't need to break into. Especially not with your palm print. A place I could leave a credstick."

"The safe is the safest place in the sleeper suite." Tojo sounded petulant and confused. "I did what you asked me to do."

"Tu es betes comme tes pieds." Beauty's voice faded as she moved away from Makeda. "C'mon. Get dressed. Let's do this."

"What about her? We can't just leave her like this."

"Who is she? Earlier, you said she promised you a date on the train. Is she more?"

Tojo was quiet for a long moment. "Just a rich and beautiful woman who thought I might be fun to party with. We met buying Party Train tickets, waiting in chat. She's the first person to actually meet me in the flesh after, ah, chatting with me. She's even pretty in person."

"For Christ's sake." Beauty paused. Her voice got far away. "Give me her bracelet. We'll just let her think we robbed her and that's all this was. She'll be too embarrassed to tell anyone."

"Are you sure?"

"Sure as I can be. As rich as she is...? Would you want to report being robbed by someone you met from online for a date?"

"I guess not."

Saladin's voice came back on. *"That's it. Not much, but telling."*

Makeda's blood ran cold. That had been very close. Too close. Where Tojo had gotten the wits to make up the story about getting a date from chat, she would never know, but it probably saved her life. Makeda shook her head. "Beauty, or whatever her name is, is a runner. What the hell is Tojo doing with another shadowrunner?"

"Seems our little salaryman isn't as naïve as he's been saying. He didn't give you up. That speaks to his favor. Also, he lied convincingly to both you and the other runner. Though either he doesn't speak French or he doesn't mind being insulted. Repeatedly."

These were all things to think about. The one thing that would keep her from treating Tojo as an unwilling extraction from this point on was the fact that he didn't reveal who she really was or what they were doing together. She still wanted to throttle him, though.

Beauty, on the other hand, needed a sound thrashing...or an award for best actress. Makeda had to admit she'd been caught hook, line, and sinker by the runner. It wasn't just that Beauty had addled her hormones, she'd done a fine job of convincing everyone that she was who she said she was. Even the other entertainment personnel were fooled. That took a bit of doing. It spoke of foresight and planning.

She replayed the recording of the conversation between Tojo and Beauty. Whatever Beauty was, she wasn't corpsec and she wasn't interested in Tojo as a client or package or a wetwork target. She'd been interested in something he was supposed to sell her.

"Makeda?"

"Yeah?"

"Are you all right?"

"Yes. Fine. Like I said, bruised ego." Standing, Makeda tested her balance. It was back. "How long until the Lucern stop?"

"About two hours. Bern in about one. You want to get off the train between the two stations. The train won't stop at Bern, but it will at Lucern. If you aren't off by then, you're going to have to take your chances during the refuel. You really don't want to do that with corpsec tailing him."

An hour to find Beauty and have a word with her before finding Tojo and throwing him from the train. "Right. Wake Galen up. We might need a couple of EMP bursts soon. Have him and our drones on standby. Also, give me directions to where the bracelet is now."

"Drones are a no-go. All of the paparazzi drones have been shot out of the sky with no warning. The net is screaming bloody murder at the lost resources and lost opportunities. We can't get a drone within two kilometers of the train without risking them. No EMP bursts for you."

"Drek and double drek. Do you have any good news?"

"I can tell you where your bracelet is."

"Right. Let's do that first."

Following Saladin's instructions, Makeda returned the way she'd come, through the various dance, bar, and dining cars, through the lobby car to the sleeper cars. Along the way, she kept an eye out for Tojo and his Saeder-Krupp watchdogs. She didn't see either and neither did Galen, who had taken over as run operator once more. This worried her. She hoped to hell Tojo was in his own suite and not dead in a closet somewhere.

Six hours in and the party showed no signs of slowing down, though there were less people. Makeda assumed they'd retired to various sleeper suites for more intimate parties like the one she'd been offered. People still danced, drank, and ate. More sat and cuddled. A couple reached out to Makeda as she passed by. She gave them a smile, a shake of the head, and kept going.

Stopping in at her suite, Makeda checked her makeup and hair. She still looked good, if a bit tired. That was to be expected on a twenty-four-hour Party Train. Makeda slipped a collapsible baton into one boot, the compact tool kit into the other, and checked that everything else was in place. She planned to come back to this room, but she was willing to leave everything else behind if necessary.

"The bracelet is two cars down and hasn't moved in four hours. My bet is that she's laying low."

"Or she ditched it. Sleeper car?"

"Probably. Yes. At least, the map from the lobby says so. Though we already know it lies. I think I've managed to upgrade your band. It should see you as both 'Ms. Makeda' and one of the entertainment hostesses."

"Good to know. Let's go have a conversation with Beauty Morel... and maybe Tojo as well." Makeda checked her pants pockets for the slap patches she had hidden there: two sleep and three stim. She made sure one of the sleep patches was on top before she gave the room a final look and walked out the door.

No one passed her as she moved through the next sleeper car. There were more doors in these. Instead of two suites, there were four. Makeda suspected that they were as good quality as the previous suites but not as large. More space, more money.

Makeda just about jumped out of her skin when the last door before the opposite exit burst open and two laughing men—one human, one elf, both handsome, black, and chic—came tumbling out. She smiled at them as they gave her a guilty look.

"Sorry...was occupied," the human started.

"With each other," the elf continued. He waggled his eyebrows in a playful manner.

"But there's always room for one more," the human finished. They had the kind of look that tabloids loved: gorgeous and just disheveled enough to say they'd been having a very good time. She vaguely recognized them—actors, perhaps—and wondered if Galen was getting pictures or video to sell to the celebrity sites. She needed to remind him to split the profits.

"Thanks, but I've got another appointment to keep."

They pouted at her, then moved aside. "If you change your mind...come find us."

"I will. Promise." She left them half in and half out of the communal restroom. That explained the number of doors. None of these sleeper suites had a private washroom.

Makeda paused between sleeper cars. "Where in this car is the bracelet? Front, middle, or end?"

"Close to the front where you are."

"I'm going in hot. I'll use my ring. If the jammer sets off any alarms, use your best judgment on turning it off."

"Roger that.

Makeda readied herself and moved into the sleeper car. The smaller sleeper rooms had no windows in their doors. That was both good and bad. Good because Beauty couldn't see her coming. Bad because Makeda had no idea what waited for her within. If it all went pear-shaped, Makeda mapped out the straight path to her own room, then a secondary path to the first car past the lobby car.

She waved her Party Train band at the door's sensor. It blinked green and slid partially open. Makeda pulled it open just far enough to slip in and close it behind her.

FIVE

Beauty, sitting alone on the couch, looked up then dove for her bag on the counter. Makeda triggered her ring then threw herself at the woman, knocking the bag and Beauty to the floor. The bag, filled with all sorts of interesting things—zip ties, a small knife, Makeda's bracelet, a couple of credsticks (one silver, one gold)—scattered across the carpet.

The two of them rolled over and over, wrestling for the upper hand until Beauty kneed Makeda in the stomach. She grunted and gasped for breath as the two of them scrambled back. Beauty popped to her feet and punched Makeda as she stood. Makeda returned the punch, knocking the blond back. Beauty staggered against the far counter.

"We need to talk." Makeda dodged the thrown glass. "Just talk."

Beauty grabbed everything she could and threw it at Makeda—knick-knacks, glasses, bottled water, and silverware. "Get out," she shouted. "I don't want you here!" She grabbed the silver tray that had held the glasses and water and wielded it like a shield.

Makeda knew there was no reasoning with her. If she wanted to know where Tojo was, she was going to have to force the issue. "I've had enough. We're going to talk." Her wired reflexes helped carry her across the room before Beauty knew what had happened. She punched the woman's face twice, took the tray from her, and whacked her over the head with it.

Beauty stumbled forward and fell to her knees. While she was dazed, Makeda grabbed two of the zip ties that had spilled from Beauty's bag. She got one around both of Beauty's wrists and finished binding her to the couch leg bolted to the floor. Then Makeda backed off, feeling every ache and pain as Beauty regained her senses and surged to her feet.

Or tried to. The zip ties held. Beauty glared at her. Makeda glanced at the mirror, half-expecting another assailant. Her own battered face looked back. She had a cut on her neck, and her cheek was already swelling. In the reflection, she watched Beauty's glare fade into something frightened, then morph into neutral determination.

"Good. I see you can't use your comms. I don't know how long it'll take your team to discover that you're out of contact, but I figure I have long enough to get what I need." Makeda turned to her. "Where is Tojo Isoshi?"

Whatever Beauty thought was about to happen, that question wasn't it. "Tojo?" She blinked a couple of times and shook her head.

Makeda wasn't sure if it was a denial or an attempt to clear her head. "Yeah. The third to our threesome?" When Beauty didn't answer, Makeda gave an impatient huff. "Look, I know you needed his palm print. That's the only way to open the safe in his sleeper suite. I couldn't care any less about what you took from him or he sold to you or whatever. I want to know where he is."

"You're his bodyguard?" Beauty eyed her with suspicion and speculation.

"Something like that. Time's wasting. I really don't want to hurt you—professional courtesy and all that—but I will if I have to." Makeda pulled her baton from her boot and snapped it open for emphasis. "One last time. Where is Tojo?"

Beauty shifted as far away from Makeda as she could. "He's fine. I swear. I just dosed him with a special concoction one of my buddies made. A little bliss. A little zen. Some stuff I don't know. I tried to leave him in his suite, but he wanted to go meet up with you. He insisted on leaving to go to a bar. I let him. He's drunk, a little high, flying. He won't remember anything. He's fine, I promise. I've been on it, and it's a good trip." She shrugged. "It's not like he could go very far. We're on a train, after all."

Makeda groaned silently. Now the target was high and wandering. The question she couldn't ask was: Would it make him talk? "Which bar?" She thought she already knew the answer but asked anyway.

"I don't know. One of them. Probably the first one with an open seat. I'll bet he's still there, petting the carpet or something." Beauty shifted from scared to sexy in the blink of an eye. She relaxed her muscles and cocked her hip. That sly smile returned. "You know, I really did want to stay with you two. It would've been good. But we all have our jobs to do."

Makeda couldn't help but return the smile. "Yeah. It would've. Maybe in another life." She closed the baton and slid it back into her boot. She looked around the suite. "So, this isn't Tojo's room?"

"No, it's one of the assignation rooms." Beauty smiled a little wider and licked her lips. "Still can be. It's not like I'm going anywhere..."

Makeda crouched down next to her, keeping half an eye on the woman's feet, looking for another attack. Even though Makeda had proven herself faster, a runner never gives up. She stroked Beauty's cheek. "Yeah," she breathed. "Maybe in another life." With her other hand, Makeda pressed the sleep patch to the blonde's neck. "Would've been spectacular, but I'm on the clock."

Beauty's eyes went wide, then closed as her body went limp. Makeda took the time to cut the woman free and laid her out on the couch. She wanted it to seem as normal as possible. Then she gathered all of the spilled stuff from the bag and stuffed it back in—with the exception of the credsticks and her bracelet. The credsticks got stuffed into Makeda's pants pockets before she put her bracelet back on. Time is money, and Beauty had wasted a lot of Makeda's already. The broken glass got kicked under the couch, and she straightened everything as best she could in quick order.

Makeda checked the time. It was ticking down too fast for her liking. She turned off her ring and subvocalized, "I'm fine. Questioned Beauty. Looking for Tojo now. Report?"

"All is quiet. Get anything good?"

She opened the door and peeked out. No one was in the hallway. "She was a runner, but more of a lover than a fighter. She left Tojo drugged. He's probably in a bar now. She didn't know which one, and if he's drugged, no reason for him to stay put."

"What'd he sell her?"

"Don't know. Didn't ask. It's not like it was on her. Gonna ask Tojo when I find him." She crossed into the next sleeper car to find a couple of people deeply involved with each other. As long as it wasn't the Saeder-Krupp guards, Makeda didn't care. She squeezed by them muttering, "Open washroom at the end there."

"What's the fun in that?" the girl asked.

Makeda shook her head. To each their own. She opened the door between the train cars and ran smack into Imre.

"Makeda!" The pleasure was plain on his face. "I've been looking for you."

Oh, he looked good. His mint color hair was tousled and there were sweat trails down the sides of his face, but that eyeliner was still perfect. He had changed clothes. Now he wore a pair of black pants, a white flowing shirt, and a sleeveless red duster with padded shoulders. She wondered where he'd got it. He was handsome, like a comic-book pirate come to life. Also, he still smelled divine—the clove, amber, and lavender mixed with his own personal scent. At any other time, she'd yank him back to the dance floor. Or into a private room. But now was not that time. Pity.

"Imre. Hi. Having a good time?" They swayed together in the airlock between sleeper cars. It was quiet and very private. Except for the obvious cameras above the doors.

"Yeah, but I was hoping to spend...holy crap, what happened to you?"

Ah, his eyes had reached her face and seen her bruised cheek. It was amazing how long it took most people to actually look another person in the face. Most of the time, they looked around the person, at their body, or at things in their hands. When you had visible bruises on your face, it brought this small fact of life to play in a big way.

Imre reached a hand toward her and then stopped as she pulled back. "You're bleeding, and your cheek—did someone hit you? I swear, if they did..."

"No, no. The only thing that happened was me hurting myself. I fell in my suite and cracked myself a good one. I didn't realize I was bleeding. It can't be that much." She turned to look at herself in the door's glass. The reflection was faint, but the scratch along her neck was weeping. She touched it and hissed at the sting.

"We've got to get that looked at." He moved up close behind her. "Seriously, what happened?"

She licked her finger and rubbed at the scrape, ignoring the pain. She did that until it had almost disappeared into her dark skin. "It's fine. And like I said, I fell in my room. It was clumsy and dumb. It's why I'm in my boots now." She watched his face, looking for his belief or skepticism. Imre looked away for a moment. He appeared to make a decision. Makeda guessed he didn't believe her, but chose to ignore that for now.

Imre shifted closer, not quite touching her with his body. "Well then, let's go get a drink. We can have a good time. Make the ache go away." He whispered this in her ear.

Makeda wanted to in the worst way. The scent of him was driving her mad. Pheromones. The man had to be using a pheromone cologne, and it was working. She had to get away. "You're all charm." She shook her head, her face neutral.

His smile faded. "But?"

"But, I kinda promised I'd look after this one guy...a favor to a friend."

"The guy you were kissing in the dining car?"

Makeda looked away. "You saw that?"

"I saw that." He shrugged, disappointment written in the slump of his shoulders. "I had hoped to see you again."

"What about after the Party Train? In Rome?" She wanted to kick herself at the hopeful look on his face. *Breaking hearts everywhere I go.*

He nodded. "Maybe. What happened to your...guy?"

She shook her head. "Part of the problem. We got separated. He isn't good at following directions. You know how it is. It's why I've got to find him."

"Find him soon. Your time is ticking down. Bern in thirty-five. Ditch the pretty boy. On the clock."

Makeda kept her face still at Galen's interruption, but Imre saw something change in her eyes. "You really like him?"

"I really need to find him." She shrugged. "We'll have Rome. Or, if not Rome, I know where you work." She leaned forward and gave him a brief kiss. "There are some duties I can't shrug off, as much as I might want to."

Before he could say anything, Makeda whirled away and exited into the next car. She needed to escape that confused, hopeful look on his face.

It didn't take long for Makeda to find Tojo. He was in the same bar she found him in the first time, in almost the exact same place. Though a quick look around showed that his watchdogs were nowhere in sight. She wondered why, but that was a fortunate mystery for another time—like never. She slid in next to him at the bar.

Tojo, as before, was looking down at his drink. He drew patterns in the condensation on the glass, then the bar, and back again. He didn't look sad. He looked dazed with a myriad of expressions crossing his face. First a smile, then a frown, then confusion, then pleasure, then sleepy dazed again.

Makeda didn't know what he was on and she wished she'd questioned Beauty more, but now she needed to get him to a safe place. "Tojo, it's time to go."

He blinked up at her and smiled, then the smile disappeared. "Are you mad at me? I didn't know she'd do that. I didn't know I'd see her again. We did the deal, then she was gone. I liked her. I thought she liked me. I thought that's why she came back."

"We can talk about that later." Makeda slipped an arm around his slender waist. "C'mon."

"No." He shook his head. "I'm sorry. I really am. I thought we were going to have a good time."

Makeda looked around. No one was watching them, yet. Of course, in a mostly drunk and high crowd of partiers, they could probably strip naked and barely get a glance. "We can still have a good time. Let's go back to my place."

Tojo hung back. "You forgive me? I really need money where I'm going. Say you forgive me."

What was it about men and their insistence that if they thought, or knew, they'd done wrong, you *had* to forgive them, whether you actually forgave them or not? All she wanted to do right now was strangle him or hog-tie him. Makeda nodded and forced a smile to her lips. "I forgive you. You were being smart."

She tightened her arm around his waist and pulled him from the bar stool.

"Really smart," he agreed, going with her. "I modified the data chip to look like something else."

"I'm sure you did. Very smart." Makeda pulled him along back towards the sleeper cars. She didn't listen as he continued mumbling about a data chip. She looked around for the Saeder-Krupp security guards. If she were them, she'd have her hacker looking through the security cameras for them. If that was allowed.

As she escorted Tojo through to the next car, she thought she saw the black uniform of security enter the car from the other side. Going back would be too obvious. They had to hide. Now.

"C'mon. We've got to hurry."

Tojo raised his head as they pushed through the crowd. "Why? What's wrong?"

"Your guards are back." Makeda saw the blocky, black-clad shapes pushing towards them. Makeda didn't think they'd been spotted through the dancers, yet. She half-lifted Tojo over to one of the corners a trio of trolls had taken over. She pushed her way in between the large metahumans. Pulling Tojo with her behind the trolls, she put a finger to her lips with a *shhhh* that couldn't be heard over the music. But the gesture was clear.

The three trolls turned to them, hiding them from the Saeder-Krupp corpsec as they moved through the car, looking at everyone.

"What's going on?" the largest male asked. The female troll tilted her head and whispered something to the third troll at her side.

Makeda giggled and shrugged. "We're hiding. It's a game." She more mouthed the words than said them.

"Who's playing?"

"My guards," Tojo answered, his drugged voice slurring. "They're watchdogs. Don't want me to have any fun."

Again, Makeda wanted to smack him. All she could do was nod. "It's true. Stick-in-the-mud family. Tell me when they've gone?" She winked and prayed the trolls would play along.

The trio of them laughed, closing ranks around them even more. "We like fun," the huge troll said while the female troll gestured her hand in a downward motion.

Makeda didn't hesitate. She dropped to the floor and pulled Tojo with her. He landed hard and burped. Then laughed at himself. That laughter turned into tears. "I'm sorry. I'm so sorry. I didn't know she'd do that. I need the money. I'm sure it's going to be fine, but I need it just to be sure. Life's crazy. Crazy things happen."

Of all the things she brought, something to make the target sober wasn't one of them. Makeda wished she had. Not that she knew which of the drugs Tojo was on that caused these wild mood swings. "It's okay. I'm fine. No blood, no foul. I just slept. You see I'm fine." She muttered these things in his ear, hoping he heard over the music and talking.

"You're not mad at me?" He wiped at his face.

"No. But we can talk about this more in my room. Everything's going to be just fine." She glanced up at the trolls. They were talking with each other, but keeping an eye on the Saeder-Krupp guards as they moved through the room.

"My room...I need to get my nuyen!" Tojo tried to stand up.

Makeda pulled him back to the floor. "Stay down. We'll go there next."

"Promise? I need it. I did all this to make sure I was safe. My future's bright. Probably."

She nodded. In truth, more money was always a good thing. In any other circumstance, there'd be a good chance Tojo would've been robbed of both his paydata and his payment, but Beauty, and whoever else she was working with, was stuck on the train. It was in everyone's best interest that Tojo had gotten paid and not stiffed. If he'd raised an alarm, there'd be all kinds of trouble.

The huge troll bent down. "They're gone. They went back the way they came. Toward the sleeper cars." He offered Makeda a hand up. She accepted, then helped Tojo off the floor.

"Thank you. You were brilliant." Makeda kept a tight hold on Tojo's hand as he pulled her, intent on getting to his room and his money. She had to reign him in. It was a nice change of pace, instead of having to drag him around. However, the guards were where they wanted to go. She'd have to be careful.

"Stay and drink with us. We like fun!" The smaller troll grinned at her and laughed.

Makeda patted his arm. "Maybe in another life. For now...we're off."

SIX

She slid her arm around Tojo's waist again and let him pull her into the joint between train cars. There, she held him back. Tojo looked at her. "What? What's wrong?"

Makeda pointed into the next car. Saeder-Krupp corpsec moved before them with slow deliberation, their heads on swivels, looking at everything around them, their faces flat and grim. "Your watchdogs. We've got to go slow now."

Tojo stuck out his bottom lip like he was going to have a temper tantrum, then shook his head. He squeezed his eyes tight. "I think I'm drunk."

"You were drugged. It's okay."

As more people entered and left, she watched the black-clad guards move through the car ahead of them, examining every face and every corner. When they left that car, Makeda led Tojo into it. She wondered again why the guards didn't just patch into the train's security system and look through the cameras for them. That's what she'd have Galen do. The Party Train security must have that on lock down.

"Which sleeper car is yours?"

"Sixteen."

A couple of cars past hers. That meant it was one of the smaller suites with the communal bathroom. Good to know. She pondered the idea of stopping at her suite before going to Tojo's, then decided against it. He might throw a fit. She glanced at him. He had that dazed expression painted all over his face again. That was one hell of a concoction Beauty hit him with. Her annoyance and anger faded. Worry crept in. What would the comedown be like?

Once they got to the sleeper cars, Makeda watched the watchdogs knock on every door. When doors opened, they talked with the person and showed them something on a datapad. For the rest, they waited about thirty seconds, then moved on. After they left each sleeper car, she and Tojo would enter. It became the world's slowest train chase, one Makeda was determined to lose.

She pulled Tojo into the last airlock before his suite and watched the guards do their thing.

He pulled out of her arm and hugged himself tight. "You're mad at me."

Makeda blinked at him. "What?" If this was a good trip, she didn't want to know what Beauty thought was a bad trip. The sooner she got him behind closed doors, the better.

Tojo shivered, his chin quivering as he hugged himself tighter. He looked like he was trying to hold it together. It was already a lost battle. "You're mad at me. I'm sorry. I thought everything was going to be okay. I mean, all shadowrunners are friends. I've seen it on the trids. And Herr Schmidt said it'd be fine. I mean, he set it all up, didn't he?"

She froze. "Herr Schmidt?"

It was what they called Mr. Johnson in Germany. Her mind spun up, moving from the immediate danger to consider a much wider, overall danger. The Johnson she'd dealt with to get this run had also been Herr Schmidt. Too many questions popped to mind. The first of which was whether or not Tojo's "Herr Schmidt" was the same one she worked with to get the run. He probably was. It was too much of a coincidence not to be.

Tojo nodded. "He's the one that helped me find you. He also said that paydata would help me get settled in the new place."

Same Johnson. What in the hell was a Johnson doing setting up two runs with the same salaryman on the same train? That was a recipe for disaster.

Mr. Johnson. Or Ms. Or Herr. Or Doktor. Or whatever title the Johnson chose. When corporations hired deniable assets for a job, they did it under the cover of a generic name. Johnson in North America. Tanaka in Japan. Wu in China. Schmidt in Germany. Jones in Britain, and so on. This left the shadowrunner in the dark as to whom she was working for—the person and company.

A fixer was the known go-between. They matched corps and runners to work together. Sometimes, the fixer was integral and part of every negotiation and meet. Sometimes, they did nothing but make introductions and leave each party to their fates. They always got paid. Makeda's fixer had been the latter. It was supposed to be a cakewalk, after all.

A good Johnson was worth gold in both nuyen and consistent work. A bad one would get you killed. All Johnsons worked for themselves and their corporate masters. You worked with them knowing they cared nothing about you except the end results of the run. When it came down to it, all Johnsons were bastards. It seemed that Herr Schmidt was more of one than expected.

"I needed it." Tojo belched and turned away.

"I know." Makeda nodded, not really paying attention to him. Her mind was half on the guards before her and half on the problem presented. She considered the ramifications of Schmidt and the two runs—one an extraction, one for paydata—as she watched the corpsec duo move from suite to suite, knocking on the door, and talking to the people within, showing them something on the datapad.

"I feel sick." Tojo touched her arm with a sweaty hand.

She brushed it off. "Tojo, please shut up. We can talk about this in the suite. I have to think."

His answer was to throw up in the corner of the airlock. The pungent smell of vomit filled the small space, making Makeda gag. A quick look told her that the guards weren't done with the sleeper car ahead. She opened the previous door and backed out of the airlock with her hand to her mouth. "Tojo!"

Makeda opened the bathroom door, thankful her Party Train band worked on it. Tojo stumbled toward her. She pointed to the toilet, pressing back to keep from touching him. He rushed in and vomited more into the waiting receptacle. She closed and locked the bathroom door.

"What a fraggin' mess," she muttered.

"Bern in fifteen," Galen warned.

"Son of a trog." How had time slipped away so fast?

"So, Herr Schmidt had two runs involving our target, eh?"

Makeda turned away as she subvocalized, "Yeah. Shitty business practices. Look into it more if you can. Be careful."

"Always."

As Tojo got sick again, she focused on her face in the mirror, concentrating on not getting sick herself. She didn't look too bad, but the bruise and swelling of her cheek was obvious now. Beauty'd had one hell of a right hook.

She rinsed one of the washcloths and handed it to Tojo once it looked like he had stopped throwing up and was just panting on the bathroom floor. With any luck, this will have gotten some of whatever Beauty dosed him with out of his system.

Tojo hauled himself to his feet and stumbled over to the sink. Makeda moved to the bathroom door and looked out the peephole—partly to give him some privacy, partly to watch who was going by. At least this was going to give the Saeder-Krupp guards a lot of time to get ahead of them.

"Drek. I liked this shirt." Tojo wiped at the white shirt with the wet cloth and proceeded to make a bigger mess of it. He tried to button it, but half of the buttons were missing.

Makeda glanced over her shoulder then back at the peephole just in time to see a large black mass fill it. She jumped back from the door to Tojo and put a hand over his mouth just as the pounding began.

"Anyone in there?"

Makeda kept a tight grip on Tojo as he jerked in surprise at how fast she moved and the sudden noise. She murmured, "Calm, chummer. We're all good here."

The pounding came again. Makeda counted in her head. At thirty-five, the pounding came a third time, but it was faint. They'd moved on to the next suite. Makeda let out the breath she didn't know she'd been holding. She looked at Tojo and he nodded. She let him go. "Sorry. Guess they came back."

She wondered at the doubling back. The guards weren't moving in a logical pattern. Start at one end of the train and go to the other end. That made sense to her. Then again, if corpsec missed their target on the first pass, it would take that much longer to find them. Maybe there was a logic to it. Their lack of a visible, logical pattern made things difficult.

Tojo shrugged and repeated, "It's all good." He took a breath. "Can we go to my room now?"

"Two minutes. That should be enough time for them to knock on all the doors in this car." She eyed his gray skin and sweating brow. "You going to be sick again?"

He shook his head. "I just want this to be done. I want to get my nuyen and get to my new home."

At that moment, he looked every bit the salaryman he was. Makeda nodded. "Soon. There'll be some rough going, but soon. You look a lot less fuzzyheaded. Why don't you wash your face?"

Tojo dropped the dirty washcloth into the waiting receptacle and grabbed another one. He washed his face and swished out his mouth with the provided rinse. He washed his hands in water hot enough to steam. When he was done, he patted his hands dry and took a steady breath.

"I feel...embarrassed and queasy, but better." Tojo gazed at the floor, not meeting her eyes. Then he bowed low and held it. "I'm sorry." It was a simple apology for everything.

"Accepted. It's what happens after you're drugged." Makeda eyed him as he straightened up. He looked better. Less gray. More in control. His shivering was gone. She listened at the door, then looked out the peephole. Nothing.

"I—I didn't know she was going to drug you."

"Hold that thought. We'll talk about it in your room." She glanced at him. "I promise. I will listen. You can explain it all then."

This time, he was quiet. They stood there in an uncomfortable silence for the next minute. Makeda didn't care. What she wanted was control of a space, where she could make sure there was no one watching or listening in. If the target was uncomfortable now, he'd be really uncomfortable in a corporate cell. Or dead.

After what seemed like forever, Makeda opened the bathroom door and looked out. The sleeper car was empty. She offered Tojo her hand. He accepted it, and the two of them went to the airlock. It was open on both sides, and a man in a Party Train concierge's uniform was cleaning up the spot where Tojo had been sick. He nodded to them as they passed by. Makeda ignored him. Tojo blushed to the roots of his black hair.

When they got to car sixteen, she let him open the suite door. The two of them entered. Makeda closed and locked the door with a sigh. Tojo had already stripped off his shirt and thrown it in a corner. As he looked for another shirt to put on, Makeda slipped her compact out of her boot and pressed the hidden button on the side. She spun in a slow circle.

It was a small suite, designed more for a single person than two, but two could make it work. While all of the furnishings were of high quality, they didn't have the same lushness her suite had. No marble or brass accents. The couch bed was a double instead of a queen. No washroom, but there was a small sink and mirror. It was a nice, if less opulent, room.

"Oh, there's nothing here. Beauty already checked."

"He's right. No bugs of any kind," TechnoGalen confirmed. *"Ten minutes to Bern."*

Makeda clicked her compact off and slid it back into her boot. "Put on your warmest shirt. You have a coat, right? We're going to be out in the cold for a bit." That was what she'd forgotten in her room. A coat. They would have to go back to get it. Plus, the window was wider in her suite. She needed that to help him out of the window.

Makeda smiled to herself. The train was moving fast but smooth. It would probably terrify Tojo to go out the window. She admitted a little fear herself, despite having the enhanced reflexes to land in relative safety. Part of her was thrilled. She'd never had to jump off a train before. She lived for new experiences.

Tojo slipped into a long-sleeved button-up shirt. He didn't say anything as he dug through the small closet, pulled out a leather jacket, and tossed it to the bed. Then he went back into the closet.

Makeda heard a soft beep and Tojo sigh with relief. "It's here. She didn't stiff me." He showed her a matte black credstick with gold bands, then clasped it in a fist.

"Is that full?" Gold credsticks could hold up to 200,000 nuyen. She saw it was certified, but didn't see how much was listed on the small display screen.

He shook his head. "Half." Tojo laughed. "I still don't understand what's so important about maintenance codes."

"Right. Tell me about this second deal that Herr Schmidt set up. What did he say?"

Tojo's face crumpled again. "You *are* mad at me." His voice was resigned and depressed.

"No. I'm not. But every time you say that, it pisses me off. Stop it." Makeda crossed her arms. "Just answer the question. I need to know what you agreed to. I have to work it into my plans. Multiple runs with the same—" She paused. She'd almost said "salaryman." She didn't know how he'd take the insult. "With the same person is unusual. Especially on a train like this, where no one gets on and off except at the end points."

Tojo sat on the bed and shrugged. "After the whole extraction thing got set up, Herr Schmidt called me back and asked me if I could get a copy of the elevator maintenance codes before I left. That it was worth a lot of money to the right people. I told him it was no problem, and he offered me 100,000 nuyen for it. Said the money would go a long way in my new home."

"And he set it up to happen here, on the Party Train?" Makeda rested her chin in her hand and considered it.

"Yeah. It's as private as you can really get. The rich don't like to be spied on." He gazed at the credstick. "I don't understand why anyone would want the codes. I mean, who wants to muck about with a shut-down elevator anyway? Besides engineers, that is."

Makeda shook her head and furrowed her brow.

"The codes only work when the elevator is turned off. That's when you do maintenance." Tojo shrugged. "I do a lot of development for how the elevator works and takes care of itself. What it senses when it's moving and when it's not. Maintenance is one of the biggest challenges to the sideways elevator."

A light went on in Makeda's head. "What kind of maintenance?" She hugged herself to keep her voice even.

"Uh..." He paused and thought for a moment. "Speed tests, stop tests, alarm tests. Some emergency tests. That sort of thing. Edge cases."

"You mean, you can make an elevator move even if it is locked down?"

"Yeah. Or powered off. All elevators have emergency power packs now. You've got to be able to test that they work."

She uncrossed her arms and stepped to him. "What elevators do these maintenance codes work on?"

Tojo tilted his head. "Well, all of them. It doesn't make sense to have a maintenance program that works on only some of the elevators. It's hard enough to take care of one program as complicated as this. Why would you want to keep track of more than one?"

Makeda sat down next to him with a *thump*. Backdoor keys into every Thyssen-Krupp elevator—the most ubiquitous elevator manufacturer in the world—was worth a lot more than a mere 100,000 nuyen. No wonder Beauty had slap patched her.

"That's, uh, interesting." And that was the understatement of the year. Hell, Makeda could make money just selling the knowledge that those codes existed.

Tojo nodded. "I know. But I couldn't just walk out with data chips. The company frowns on that sort of thing, so I made it look like one of these. But really, it's just a data chip." He held up the credstick. "On a train like this, no one's going to say anything about people running around with gold credsticks."

Makeda's heart stuttered in her chest. It took all her willpower to not look at the credsticks she'd taken from Beauty. There was a very good chance that she had a copy of the maintenance codes. "That... that's brilliant." She meant it. In another life, Tojo could've been a decent shadowrunner. "You just put the faux credstick in a datajack to download them?"

"Yeah. That's it."

She took a breath. "Right. I'm going to use the restroom. You pack a small bag with whatever you can't leave behind. Be ready when I get back. But pack light. You're going to have to carry it for a bit." Makeda didn't wait for an answer as she peeked out the suite door, then hurried to the communal restroom at the end of the car.

Once inside with the door locked, Makeda took the two credsticks from her pocket. Both had the same flat black-matte finish, but one had silver bands, the other gold. The one with gold bands was larger and had a larger display. The display didn't show a number, but it had a word: *Isoshi.*

"You are so sharing that with us," Galen said, his voice soft with awe.

"Yes, but not a word. Technically, we're stealing from another runner team, and that's not going to sit well with anyone. So we don't do anything with this. Not until this job is done. Don't even sniff around for buyers until we test the codes." Makeda lifted up the short curls at the base of her head and slotted the faux credstick. "I mean it, Galen. Not a word to anyone. Not Saladin. Not Plath. Not anyone. This is too hot, in the best and worst sense."

"So ka."

Her headware went to work and asked for the passcode. She entered *"Isoshi,"* and the files unlocked. She made two copies of them. One for her own personal use that she locked down under double encryption. One in data storage, encrypted and ready for transfer. She made sure the data chip was completely empty before she pulled the fake credstick from her datajack.

Without thinking about what she was doing. Makeda stomped the small device into pieces. She picked out the data chip and stomped it again until it was also in pieces. Then she put some of the pieces into the trash and some in the toilet. After she relieved herself, she flushed the other bits to parts unknown.

A *bing* sounded in her head. Makeda jerked in surprise. She flushed hot with guilt and her stomach flip-flopped. "What? What is it?"

"Ah, we've just passed Bern. You need to get a move on, Makeda. Get off the train now. You'll meet your contacts in Lucern…. Or nearby."

"Right. On my way." She squared her shoulders and walked out of the bathroom like she owned it. Makeda did not think about the mega-lucrative paydata sitting in her head. She had a client to extract, and that had to be her main focus right now.

Using her Party Train band to get into Tojo's room, she wanted to sigh at the way he didn't react. He just smiled at her and hefted his small bag. He didn't think it was strange that she could get in and out whenever she wanted to. He may have shadowrunner leanings, but he didn't have the right mindset. It had to be those drek trid shows about shadowrunners and the corp security who tried to catch them— succeeding only when it was convenient for dramatic purposes.

"Here's the plan. We're going to go to my suite, get my stuff, then go out the window." She continued on through his double-take. "It might hurt a little when you hit the ground. It's important that you do two things: First, don't roll too far away. You won't hit the track. They're elevated. You'll get a little bruised, but you'll be fine. Second, try to keep an eye on where I come out. Head in that direction. I'm going to try to jump with you so we don't get too separated. Clear?"

Tojo nodded in slow motion. He looked afraid and unsure. "What if I get hurt?"

"Don't think that way." She saw the stubbornness creep into his expression. "We'll burn that bridge when we come to it." She took him by the arm. "Look, this is your freedom we're talking about. You wanted this. We've got a lot of kilometers to go before we get you there. This should be the roughest part. We can do this."

"We can do this." The repeated words were hollow. He tried to smile and failed.

She ignored it. "That's the spirit. We *will* do this." Makeda opened the door. "No more stalling. Time's wasting." She led him out of his room and down the hall. To his credit, Tojo didn't look back.

There were more people in the sleeper car hallway now. For some, the party was winding down. Others were just looking for a place to rest or recharge before they returned to the bacchanal. Either way, Makeda and Tojo needed to step over and around people sleeping, making out, or passed out.

As they entered the sleeper car with Makeda's suite in it, Party Train personnel were checking on their guests and trying to get them moved to more comfortable, less trafficked places. Makeda opened her suite and stopped in her tracks as the two Saeder-Krupp security guards turned to look at her.

Makeda saw that they had gone through all of her belongings— her bag was dumped on the bed, its seams ripped open. Her scant clothing also had their seams opened, and even the bed had been torn apart. She had no idea what they were looking for, but she knew her cover was blown. No corpsec in their right mind would destroy the personal effects of someone as rich as her background suggested. Either that, or they were so far lost on leads they were willing to risk a royal reaming from someone rich enough to do it.

Either way, she was in trouble.

Makeda backpedaled and took off the way she'd come, dragging Tojo with her. He'd gasped as he saw the guards barrel out of the suite. Then she didn't have to drag him at all.

The two of them bolted down the hallway to the exit. As soon as they got through, Makeda smashed the control with her elbow. It hurt like hell, but she hoped it would lock the door behind them.

"Galen. Trouble. What's at the end of the train?" Panting, she didn't try to hide her whispered words.

"Sleeper cars and storage, as far as I can tell."

"Windows?"

When Galen didn't immediately answer, Makeda pushed a drunken couple behind them and into the path of the oncoming Saeder-Krupp guards. This time as they moved from car to car, she used her other elbow to smash the control plate. It wasn't slowing the guards down much, but it did something.

"Can't tell from my eyes in the sky, but alarms are going off in the cars you've been in."

"Yeah. Breaking the door sensors."

"It's helping. Sorta. Confusing things, anyway."

They burst into the next sleeper car. It was the farthest car Makeda had visited. She had no idea what was beyond. At the end of the car, the exit door looked different. There was a punch pad instead of a sensor. They sprinted to the door. Makeda typed in the code she saw Security Captain Jarvis punch into the pad when she'd been locked in the train ramp. The pad beeped green, but as she moved to open the door, it gave a deeper *blat* and went red. Makeda had no idea what that meant beyond the fact that they were trapped.

"Everything is going into lockdown. Comms are going insane. I don't know why. I don't think it's you."

Makeda moved to the communal bathroom and waved her Party Train band at it. The sensor went green. Thank God it still worked. The door slid open just as she saw the Saeder-Krupp guards bust into the sleeper car.

"Help!" Tojo yelled at them as Makeda grabbed him and threw him into the bathroom. She followed behind, closing and locking the door. This time, she held onto the door handle and braced herself with her back to one wall and a foot to the other.

"What the hell, Tojo?" Makeda growled the question at him as she set herself for a fight to keep the door closed.

He shook his head. "I can't let them think I went with you willingly. I'm sorry. If they do catch us, I want plausible deniability. I've been drugged. I can say I didn't really know what was happening. I thought it was a game or something. Until you wouldn't let me go."

Makeda snarled, but she found no fault in his logic. For a salaryman, he had some weird pockets of street smarts to go along with his general naivety. "Fine. Get over there and get that window open. We don't want them to catch us. Even if Krupp Specialist Engineering lets you back in, they'll never trust you again."

Tojo stopped messing with the window and looked at her. "What do you mean?"

"I mean, I'm sure there's a log somewhere that you downloaded those maintenance codes. It's possible they were even watching you through the security cameras make your fake credstick. If they didn't before, they're probably going to go through their videos now."

They both jerked at the pounding on the door. "Open up!" The voice was female. "Open up before we're forced to fire."

"I've got it," another unfamiliar voice said.

Tojo turned back to the window and fought to get it open. Makeda braced hard against the wall as there was a *click* and the door unlocked.

"Oh, hell," Galen said. *"Brace for impact."*

Makeda had no idea what he meant. She didn't have time to figure it out. The train jerked in a downward angle it should never travel, and Tojo went flying into the shower. Makeda's head bounced off the wall hard, making the world go black as metal screamed.

SEVEN

Makeda opened her eyes. The world was upside down, and emergency lights glowed a faint green. She lay on her back, trying to make sense of what she saw. She hadn't been knocked unconscious—the screaming of torn metal still echoed in her ears—but the blow to the back of the head had rattled her. The door was open and bright white light streamed in. Turning her head, she saw Tojo sprawled on the ceiling of the shower. His eyes were closed, but his hands twitched like he was fighting to regain himself.

"Galen, what happened?" Her voice was a whisper. No answer. "Galen? Galen?" Fear and panic welled up, suddenly large and overwhelming. She did what she always did in a crisis: shunted all the panic to the side and began to work the problem. Time enough for a breakdown later.

Checking her headware, she found it was intact. But when she tried to access anything in the Matrix, there was nothing. Total blackout. Jammer or just a lack of signal, she couldn't tell.

She fought against the fog, but her brain didn't want to work. She wanted to stay where she was and sleep. Sleep for days. Let someone else deal with whatever this was.

She heard Tojo moan. Makeda realized that, without her connection to the Matrix, she was the only help she and Tojo had—and *something* had crashed the train.

Galvanized by this, and the memory that Saeder-Krupp security was on to them, Makeda sat up, shook her head, and got to work. Corpsec wasn't beating on the door. Wasn't bearing down on them with guns drawn and cuffs ready. That was one immediate problem gone. Makeda blinked away the fog, clearing her mind. A plan. She had to have a plan.

Something had crashed the train. Why would they crash the train? That couldn't be good for anyone. Were they in the AIZ? Makeda shook her head. The train route wasn't supposed to get that close.

She realized the panic had gotten in after all. That's why all the useless questions crowded her mind. She needed to focus on the immediate.

First things first. Get rid of the tracking devices. No use running if there was a corp GPS tag on them. She pulled her compact out of her boot and opened the toolkit. A couple of small screws later, and she was free. Makeda crawled to Tojo and removed his wristband, too. She stuffed both in her pocket.

Tojo blinked his eyes open. "What happened?"

She shook her head. "Train wreck, I think."

"You?" His eyes got very wide.

Makeda shook her head again. "No. I was going to throw you from the train. Remember? Not blow it up."

She got to her feet and wobbled until she put a hand on the wall. Standing on the ceiling was disorienting. Nothing was where it was supposed to be. She looked up and to the left. The toilet hung above her, already empty of water. Turning her back on the weirdness of it all, Makeda gazed out the bathroom doorway. Across the hall, through the broken glass, she could see snow and sky. "Can you stand?"

Tojo checked himself over. "I think so."

"Good. Follow me." She stepped to the doorway and looked out. There were screams in the distance and the groan of metal still settling. The hallway was twisted, the metal ceiling rippled with the damage of landing upside down.

"I'm hurt. I'm bleeding."

Makeda didn't look at him. "We all are. Move."

Her mind was in overdrive. Was her extraction client important enough to crash a train to get at? To injure or kill fifty or sixty of Europe's richest people? No, probably not. Were those backdoor elevator key codes worth all this damage? Maybe. Probably. With Tojo dead, no one would know they'd been leaked, and *that* was worth millions, considering how many Thyssen-Krupp elevators were in use. Had this been part of the plan all along? Get the codes and murder the wage slave making a run for it? If she were a ruthless shadowrunner and into wetwork, definitely.

Makeda rubbed her mouth, thinking about the amount of damage done in the name of a job. She did this in an abstract manner, considering what kind of resources it would've taken to pull off, rather than the horror of the limbs maimed and lives lost.

She'd been ruthless from time to time, but she would never take a wetwork job. That meant the team she was against was already one up on her. Two, if you counted the crashed train.

Down the hallway, the corpsec guards did not fare as well as she and Tojo had. When the train crashed—Makeda really wanted to know how it had happened—she had been braced to hold the door closed, and Tojo had been thrown to the other side of the bathroom.

The guards, on the other hand, had been thrown to the far end of the half-crumpled sleeper car. They lay jumbled on top of each other.

Icy wind blasted in through the broken windows, and Makeda shivered. She hadn't gotten her coat from her suite. Judging by the mangled door at the end of the car, she wasn't going to.

Neither Saeder-Krupp guard moved.

Makeda walked down the ceiling to the guards, careful not to step on any of the glass from the windows, wincing at every noise the train made. Once she got to the guards, Makeda knew both were dead. The dwarf had a piece of metal jammed through his chest. The woman's neck was bent at an angle not designed for the human spine. She checked for a pulse on each of them anyway.

Nothing.

Another blast of cold wind reminded her why she was here. The woman's coat. Light armor and a damn sight warmer than nothing. Makeda struggled with the body until she got the coat free. Before she put it on, she pulled the Saeder-Krupp corp patch from the arm, turning the coat from corp property into generic military fashion in a single rip of Velcro.

Makeda shrugged it on, cutting off the wind from her shivering flesh. The guard didn't have a visible weapon, but in her fight to get the coat off, Makeda found a holdout, a Walther Palm Pistol, at the small of the guard's back. She took it, along with the sheath. The sheath refused to work with her pants. They were too loose and fine for the thick leather. She abandoned it next to the body and shoved the pistol into one of the coat's interior pockets. A quick search of the armored jacket came up with nothing but a package of Buzzbuzz and a NutraSoy Energy Cake. Neither had been opened.

"Makeda?" Tojo stood outside the bathroom, looking pale and shaken. "What do you want me to do?"

She stuffed the stimulant and food back into the coat's pockets. "Stay put. I'm coming." As she hurried with careful steps back to Tojo, she subvocalized across all her comms. "TechnoGalen? HiddenPlath? Saladin? Code Black-Three."

If they were receiving and she just couldn't hear them for whatever reason, she'd let her team know that the plan had had a bad turn, but she was going to press on to the next phase of the operation on her own. That meant getting in contact with the Lucern people to get evac'd out of Switzerland on her own. They could meet up with her at the next port of call in Spain.

Tojo had a towel pressed to the back of his head. It came away bloody when he looked at it, but not too bad. However, the sight of blood made him go grey. Ignoring it and the blood, Makeda took the towel from him and tossed it into the bathroom.

"You have your bag. Good." Makeda looked out the broken window. Mountains, trees, and snow as far as the eye could see. All of it was filled with the debris of the train crash. She eyed a piece of the maglev track. An explosion. That was the only thing she could think of to cause this amount of damage. A definite attack.

"Right, let's go. Mind the glass. Don't cut yourself." Makeda climbed out the broken window, wishing she had warmer pants. Once in the snow, she threw the first of the Party Train bands as far forward as she could. The other one, she threw over the top of the train. That would separate them from everything else. Maybe.

"Makeda..." Tojo stood half-in and half-out of the window. He held to the side of the train while dabbing his foot to the ground as if it were water. He shook his head and reached for her.

Makeda grabbed his hand and helped him out. Tojo wobbled next to her. He must have taken one hell of a shot to still be unsteady. That was going to make moving through the mountains difficult and slow. She pulled him with her as she stepped back from the train to get a good look at their situation.

It was a disaster. The more she looked, the more damage Makeda could see. All of the train was off the track. Beyond the main train, the security cars had been launched into the air and come down hard on a rocky hill. The two cars had rolled down the hill and crashed into a copse of trees. There was no movement from either of those two cars.

The front four Party Train cars were tumbled on top of each other, with more than half a dozen slammed in behind at odd angles. The middle set of cars were on their sides, jammed together, with one car deeply indented. The last third of the train had rolled and was twisted, with the cars at the back rolling 270 degrees from where they had started. Not a single car was undamaged, though the end of the train had fared better than the front by a long shot.

Behind the Party Train, the following security car had used the back end of the train like a ramp. It had flown forward and landed on top of the Party Train, then rolled off. The middle car it had landed on had buckled almost in two. As Makeda looked back and forth over the shattered train, it was the only scenario she could come up with.

She realized she was on the edge of panic again. Makeda turned to what was moving. This was where the greatest danger was.

Among the debris, bodies lay bleeding, moaning, or still. It looked like some had been thrown out of the train through the windows. Some had crawled out. People stumbled around, screaming and crying. All of them were stunned and panicked. Even the Party Train personnel.

Makeda forced her mind into work mode. None of this mattered. None of it was important unless it was a danger to her or her client. Where was the danger?

No one was looking at them. No one watched them in particular. They were not important, and that was the way Makeda needed it to be. She scanned the tops of the trees and then the line of the train's single rail.

The maglev track was twisted and broken. Scorch marks traveled up and down the trestle. Either someone had set off a bomb or shot the track with a missile. Makeda didn't know enough about demolitions to tell which was true, but from the amount of damage, whoever had caused the explosion meant business—business she didn't want any part of.

A helicopter flew overhead.

Makeda ducked her head as she watched it go by. Panic welled again, and again she shunted it into the background. The rational side of her recognized the cross of the DocWagon symbol. That gave her an idea.

"Do you have a DocWagon contract?"

Tojo frowned at her, confused.

"DocWagon? Crashcart? Any medical contract?"

His face brightened with understanding. "No. Never needed it. Never was sick or anything. Plus, we had local corp clinics."

Makeda nodded. "Good. Stay here."

Tojo clutched her hand, shaking his head. "No. I'm not leaving you."

She resisted the urge to slap his hand away or to roll her eyes. Then again, if he stayed with her, she could continue to protect him. Safety over expediency. "All right. Just keep your mouth shut and go along with anything I say. And keep up."

A second helicopter flew overhead. She didn't recognize the symbol on it. Could be the Swiss version of Crashcart. Could be corpsec. Could be an assassination team.

Makeda took off as fast as she could over the uneven ground and snow, pulling Tojo behind her. It wasn't much more than a fast run. She headed toward the middle of the train, where most of the people were. As soon as she hit the first knot of people, she grabbed a dwarf man by the arm. "Run, they're still coming for us!" She pointed at the circling helicopter.

Dazed and already panicked, the dwarf ran to another dwarf, a woman. "Run!" he cried, grabbing her hand. The two of them took off toward the nearby forest.

A bloodied elf woman looked between the dwarfs and Makeda. She pointed at the helicopter. The woman stumbled as she looked up and almost fell. Then she, too, took off running. Three more people followed as the herd instinct kicked in.

Makeda hurried to the next set, a group of Arabic men next to the Japanese man and his pack of cat girls. "They're coming for us. Get out of here! Run!" This time, she pointed at the fleeing dwarf couple and the elven lady. Not stopping, Makeda pulled Tojo with her to the next group of people. Behind her, there was a smattering of Arabic and Japanese, then they, too, were fleeing into the forest.

As more and more people headed toward the forest—running, limping, stumbling—more followed. No one knew where they were going, but with so many people heading in the same direction, it made sense that someone did, someone in charge, and that was where they all needed to go.

The next set of people all wore Party Train uniforms. They milled about in confusion. Some watched the mass exodus into the forest. A couple tried to check on some of the injured, but most were crying and hurt. Makeda grabbed the arm of an Indian woman in a concierge's uniform who seemed dazed but uninjured. "Please, they've cut us off. We can't call for help. They're still attacking! We've got to get the people away from the train."

Two large black drones, Strato-9s by the look of them, buzzed the train. The already-dazed train wreck victims, primed by Makeda's warning, panicked. A cry went up, and those who could run, did.

The concierge nodded. "I've got this, ma'am. Run!" She turned to the rest of the uniformed train personnel and gave orders to evacuate everyone who was still alive—carry them if they had to.

Pleased, Makeda also ran in the direction of the forest, but she moved in a diagonal pattern, away from the crowd of panicked and hurt passengers. Tojo hurried alongside her. "Why did you do that?"

As soon as they hit the tree line, Makeda slowed them to a fast walk. "Two of us running away from the train would be found immediately. We would be under suspicion of causing the crash. A hundred and fifty of us? Some really hurt while we're not? Not so much. I wanted to cover our tracks for as long as we could. Crashcart and DocWagon will go to the most hurt first. The local law enforcement will tap into the Party Train bands for the GPS to find the rest."

Tojo stopped and touched his wrist. "Mine's gone." He blinked at her in wonder. Panic hovered on the edge of his eyes.

Makeda paused, working to catch her breath. "I know. We don't want to be found. We need to escape the train and whoever attacked it." She didn't say that she thought Tojo had been the target of the attack. That probably would have broken him.

They continued to move away from the train and the mass of people as they moved through the forest. It was mostly even with an uphill angle, covered in dead leaves and soft ground. There was less snow but more branches to deal with—both on the ground and at eye-level. Makeda kept an arm up in front of her face to protect herself as she pushed through the foliage.

Tojo stumbled over a tree root. Makeda whipped around and caught him before he hit the ground. She lifted him up and gave him a smile. "Okay?"

He nodded, breathing hard. "Yeah. Didn't see it."

Behind them, a voice yelled, "Makeda, wait! Take me with you. You have to."

Both of them turned to see Imre, mint-haired and bloody-faced, weaving through the trees, closing in fast.

EIGHT

Makeda pushed Tojo behind her and yanked the Walther out of her jacket pocket. "Back the frag off, chummer." She put her shoulder to the tree next to her, ready to dive for cover if needed. Her eyes darted all around, looking for the other attacker. The man in front of her was obvious to the point of distraction. If this was an attack, that was his job.

No one else was near them. To the right, the sound of crying and shouting people. To the left, nothing. Makeda heard the drones and helicopters. They were also to the right. Flashes of color appeared and disappeared through the trees more than five hundred meters from them.

Imre stumbled to a stop, leaves kicking up, his hands up as she pointed the pistol at him. "Wait, no. You've got to help me. I know what you are. You're a shadowrunner. You told me. I want to hire you."

Makeda narrowed her eyes. "I didn't tell you anything." What was his angle? All around them, the forest was still empty of people. She'd be able to hear them for a long time to come, but Imre was the only one to follow her and Tojo. That made him dangerous.

Imre nodded so hard his hair flopped in his face. "You did. Where do I work?"

"Hanover Casino. VIP services." She looked for the trick.

"Right. I never told you that. I only told you that I was a working man. I never said where or what I did." Imre kept his hands up. "You know that because of what you can do. I want to hire you to get me away from here."

Makeda thought back to the previous conversations with the man. Flicking through her memories, it was Galen who had told her what Imre did for a living. Then she'd made the amateurish mistake of saying she knew where he worked. Stupid slip.

If she were the murdering-in-cold-blood kind of runner, the man—handsome or not—would be dead. Makeda shook her head. "No. I already have a job. Move on."

"I'll pay you 100,000 nuyen. Certified. Right here, right now." He jabbed at his duster pocket with his chin. "I've got money. I've been trying to get free for years. You're my best hope now. Please. I'm begging you. Please."

Makeda couldn't decide if this was another one of Herr Schmidt's plans or not. Or if it was an assassin's ploy to make her trust him. Then again, 100,000 nuyen was nothing to sneeze at. "Tojo, do you know this man?"

Tojo stepped around Makeda and looked at Imre. "No."

"You didn't make a deal with him? You've never seen him before?" Makeda kept her finger off the trigger, looking for a reason to not kill Imre. Beyond the fact that weapon's fire was a sure way to get people's attention, she hated killing. Especially in cold blood. She couldn't trust Tojo to put a sleep patch on him or to not get himself hurt or taken prisoner in the process.

"I swear. I've never done anything with him. But I did see him in the bar. Once. He was drinking with a pretty brunette woman. His hair kinda sticks out." Tojo watched her and the gun, his eyes wide and frightened.

"You don't understand," Imre begged. "Once you work for the casino, that's it. You're theirs for life. Especially VIP services. They'll kill you before they let you go. You know too much about their operations and too much about the whales—their tastes, their schedules, all of it. I had my arm broken the first time I went looking for another job. The second time was worse. I was told if there was a third time, that was it for me. Please. I have money. I even have a safe place to go. I just don't know how to get there from here."

Tojo reached a hand out to Makeda, but was smart enough not to touch her. "They saw me with you. They had to have called it in. Saeder-Krupp will be looking for two people. Not three. Maybe it wouldn't be so bad to have him with us?" He glanced at Imre. "He says he has money and wants to hire you. Also, we kinda need to hurry."

Makeda frowned at Tojo. "You want him with us?"

He shrugged. "I don't see why not. We're all running away."

She glanced between the two men and sighed. Tojo had shown some savvy moments and an ability to adapt. Also, he had a point. They did need to hurry. Makeda gestured to Imre with the pistol. "Which pocket?"

Imre blinked at her. "What?"

"Which pocket is your nuyen in?" Makeda motioned for Tojo to move back.

"My left one."

"Then use your left hand to get it out."

It was awkward, but Imre dug into his inner duster pocket and pulled out a certified credstick with two fingers. It was the discreet black matte and had platinum bands on it. He looked at the display. "That's the wrong one."

"How much is on that one?"

Imre grimaced. "Two-fifty."

"Two hundred and fifty thousand?" Makeda gave him a slow smile. 250,000 nuyen was worth a bit of risk and danger.

Imre nodded.

Makeda gestured to Tojo. "Toss it to him. That should be enough to cover my fee, keep the three of us hidden, *and* get us to where we need to go. All that takes money." When Imre hesitated, she shook her head. "Not a negotiation. You need us more than we need you. You'll still have the hundred thousand. I'm sure that'll take you far wherever it is you're going."

He tossed the credstick to Tojo. "Eventually? Morocco. But Spain is where I need to go next."

Makeda felt her cheek twitch, and she gripped the pistol tighter. Spain was where she and Tojo needed to go. It could be coincidence. It could be more. Spain was a good jumping off point for a lot of the world. Light security in and out. Main international airport. No extradition treaty. There were a lot of reasons to move through Spain. Clenching her jaw to keep from asking about Spain, she watched Imre. He watched her as carefully has she watched him.

Tojo caught the credstick and handed it to her. The display showed ¥250,000. That would do. "Turn around."

Imre hesitated, fear crossing his face for the briefest of moments before disappearing again. "You're not going to shoot me in the back, are you?"

Makeda snorted. "Not yet. I am going to pat you down though. Understand?"

"*So ka.*" He turned around and put his hands on the top of his head, palms down. "You have my permission. I have a small utility knife at my belt."

Makeda walked up behind him and put the pistol against his back. She kept her finger off the trigger but said, "I have enhanced reflexes and my finger on the trigger. Twitch at all, and I will shoot you. It'll happen even before I realize it. If you want to live, you'll stay very, very still."

Beginning with his left side, she moved her hand around his neck and over his chest. In the pocket, she counted two more credstick-sized items, and his inner pocket held a datapad. Makeda found the multi-tool at his waist. She repeated the motion on the right side after shifting the pistol to her left hand. This time, she found a handkerchief, corp scrip, and smart glasses in his pockets. She slid her hand over the flat of his back, down to his rear and to the inside of his thighs. She had to push his duster out of the way to make sure he didn't have any other weapons.

As she was finishing up, Imre murmured low, "This was not how I'd imagined you first touching me. It's not unpleasant, but it could've been so much more."

Makeda smirked. "The day isn't over yet." Stepping back with the Walther still leveled at him, she raised her voice. "Turn off your comms, datapad, and smart glasses. Anything that could ping out your location. Sleep mode, private mode, or all the way off."

"Can I turn around?"

She stepped back to Tojo's side. "Yes."

"You'll help me?" Imre fiddled with his smart glasses before returning them to an inner pocket. He repeated the motion with his datapad. "Get me to where I need to go?"

Makeda looked at Tojo again. He was the client. "Your choice. You're paying."

Tojo didn't look at her as he turned off his datapad and AR glasses. "Yeah. That's fine."

She gave Imre a considering look. "I can get you a flight to Spain once we reach my contacts. It'll be expensive, but doable." The sounds of people faded, but the crisscrossing pattern of the drones and helicopters had not. "Either way, we need to make it to a cave, and quick."

Makeda put the pistol away and zipped up her jacket. "Welcome aboard. Keep up. This first part is going to suck."

She knew she was going to have to keep a close eye on Imre. But for now, he seemed to be exactly what he said he was: a wage slave looking for a way out. Unlike many, he'd had the smarts to make plans and could adapt. Mostly because he'd been exposed to some powerful people who didn't have to play by the rules. Sounded like a shadowrunner in the making to her.

All of this was just conjecture, of course. Makeda recognized the wishful thinking and admitted it to herself. Either way, she was looking forward to finding out the truth.

Imre lowered his hands and nodded. "Yes, ma'am." He buttoned the top couple of buttons on his duster and moved up next to her. "The plan?"

She looked through the trees toward the sloping rock. "We go up. You see anything that looks like an opening, you let me know. You see anyone following, you let me know. You see anything that makes you blink twice..."

"I..." Imre glanced at Tojo. "*We* let you know."

"Exactly."

The three of them moved through the trees as one, with Makeda in the lead. All of them were fit, but Tojo kept slipping and stumbling, unused to the extended physical exertion. As the trees thinned, the fog rolled in. It wasn't cold, but it obscured the view. Every time the sound of something flying came near, all of them hurried their steps. They climbed upward. Even Makeda panted for breath.

Tojo tripped on a rock and fell hard. He stifled his cry of pain. Makeda returned to him. His pants were ripped, and one knee bled. Not a lot. Enough to speak of the stinging pain he must be in. She moved him to one of the few trees that grew on the trail. "Hold on."

He did as he was told. She examined his knee, manipulating it. Nothing broken. Imre handed her his handkerchief. She cleaned the scrape while Tojo grimaced. "Put weight on it."

Tojo did as told but slid a bit on the slick rock. He steadied himself and nodded. "I'm good."

Makeda realized the problem was Tojo's shoes. He had smooth-soled shoes designed more for a dance floor than hiking in the mountains. There was nothing to do about that now. Without being asked, Imre stepped to his side and helped him. Something about Imre's smooth confidence rang alarm bells in Makeda's mind, but she couldn't put her finger on what bothered her.

"Step like this..." Imre showed Tojo how to test his footing and keep his balance.

It was exactly what Makeda had been about to do. "Been hiking long?" She tried to keep her voice light and devoid of her sudden suspicion.

Imre kept his arm out for Tojo to clutch at when things got unstable. "When the client, who has never gone skiing, decides he wants to learn how but doesn't want to go alone, it's up to VIP services to make sure they have a good time and come home safe."

It was an answer. Just not an answer to the question Makeda asked. She wondered if that was on purpose, or if he'd been trained to answer the question he thought the client was actually asking. It was an interesting trait in someone who'd catered to the rich and famous. It was also something she did all the time.

Maybe he'd like to run the shadows once he was used to being out from under the company's thumb. A man had to eat, and he needed to work to get the nuyen to do that. No matter how much he had stashed up for his escape, it wouldn't last forever. She wondered what he'd do then. She wondered if he'd even thought that far ahead. Possible. After all, he had to anticipate his client's needs.

They all looked up as the sound of a drone got closer.

"Imre, help him move faster." Makeda scanned the tree- and rock-filled hillside. Less trees. More bushes. Nothing stuck out. There was no convenient hole to hide in. They'd have to get over the ridge and into the clear to see what was on the other side. Thank goodness for the obscuring fog. The only other thing in their favor was the fact that no one was specifically looking for them—yet.

Or maybe they were. She made an abrupt halt. The men stopped short of ramming into her. "Imre, you still wearing your Party Train band?"

He shook his head as he pulled up the sleeve of his shirt to show his bare wrist. There was a large bruise under his thumb joint. "No."

"How'd you get it off?"

"I beat on it with a piece of the marble counter that broke in the crash."

Makeda eyed him. "How'd you know you needed to get it off?" This time, she didn't hide her suspicion.

Imre raised his hands in a surrendering gesture. "How do you think we know where our whales are in the casino? The less they have to think about money, the more they lose. We know everywhere they go because their band gets them into the VIP areas. Their stats tell us exactly what they want when they get there." He glanced behind and looked through the trees. "Look, you're free to interrogate me all you want, but you're the one who said we needed to find a cave. I'm not sure why, but we should move."

He had a point. "It'll mask our heat signatures. And you're right. We can talk later."

Makeda started up again, scrambling over rocks and using the bushes for leverage. She found what looked to be some sort of small animal path worn in the dirt. She followed it, concentrating on keeping the three of them moving at a good clip—never mind how much panting she was already doing. Despite the fog giving an eerie feeling to their flight, she was thankful for its ability to hide them from possible—probable—searchers.

They walked and climbed in silence for a good twenty, twenty-five minutes before Tojo asked, panting, "What is a whale? I mean, I know what a whale is, but I don't know what you mean when you say it."

"Big spender in the casino. Rich people who don't care how much they lose. Whales. They get whatever they want. We make losing money a pleasure."

Makeda smiled at Imre's words for two reasons: First, he unconsciously used the word "we." Being part of the casino was ingrained in his head. It spoke to the truth of his story. Second, she'd played the whale once in a casino run. It had been a lot of fun. Someday, she'd do it again. Casinos really did everything they could to keep their big spenders happy.

Her smile faded as she clambered up to the top of the ridge, gasping for air. Nothing but mountains, trees, and the valley lay before her. Hell of a place for a city girl. No wonder she didn't have Matrix access.

Scrabbling down the other side in a half-walk, half-stumble, she looked back to see how Tojo and Imre were doing. Tojo looked scared to death, but he was following Imre's lead. If the mint-haired German hadn't been here, that would be her right now. She turned back around, trusting the men to follow. This side of the mountain held more promise of a place to hide.

Makeda found the hole, hidden by a thin layer of snow, as her foot broke through the ice.

Falling about two meters and crashing to the rocky floor below, she landed on one foot and her butt. Makeda curled into a ball to minimize the damage as she rolled a meter to the side and bumped against a wall of dirt and rock. A quick assessment said that she was alive and mostly unharmed.

Flicking her vision to thermal, she gave the hole a once over to make sure she hadn't fallen into an animal's lair. Did the bears in Switzerland hibernate? Were there even bears in Switzerland? Makeda had no idea. To her relief, there were no living animals in sight. The hole was more of a cave or tunnel at about two meters high, two meters wide, and five meters long.

Outside, she heard both Imre and Tojo calling her name as they scrambled down to reach her. Looking up, she couldn't see their heat signatures through the earth, and that was what she'd been looking for.

"I'm fine," she called. "Be quiet!" Makeda pulled herself to her feet and walked to the opening. Imre and Tojo looked in at her. "I found our hidey-hole for the moment. Come on down. Not quite sure how we'll get back out, but I'm sure we'll manage."

She gave them a confident smile in the face of adversity. They weren't as far away as she wanted them to be, but this would do. It was cold outside, and it would only get colder as the afternoon became evening.

Imre helped lower Tojo down. Makeda stood back as he dropped, ready to catch him if he stumbled on his hurt knee. Tojo winced a bit and hopped on one foot. Then he waved her off.

Imre dropped through the hole and stayed crouched as he looked around. "We alone?"

Makeda rolled her eyes. "Nope. There's a bear over there in the corner. I thought we could kill it for its fur and meat."

He stood. "Sorry. I deserved that. I couldn't see." He pulled out his smart glasses, then gave the cave a quick look over.

"This will do until morning." Makeda nodded to where Tojo now sat. "We'll stay on that end of the cave, away from the opening. It'll keep us warmer and hide us from the eyes in the sky."

Imre nodded and joined Tojo. Makeda eyed the hole. There was no way to close it up. She shrugged and turned her back on it. That was one problem she couldn't solve. Time to move on to the next one.

NINE

The problem with waiting is the fact that it takes a while and time slows to a crawl. Once Makeda got everyone down and hidden, there wasn't much to do except talk. After a couple aborted conversation attempts by Tojo, everyone lapsed into a distracted silence.

Makeda considered their situation. No backup. No contact with the Matrix. They were going to miss the Lucern connection—most likely. She had an extra passenger. She had no idea where they actually were, but she knew it was someplace between Bern and Lucern. Closer to Bern. Either way, it was going to be a few klicks walk in the correct direction over mountains and through the forest. That was going to take more time than she wanted it to. More time than she had.

But all was not lost. They were well hidden, the cave was much warmer than in the open, and it provided shelter from the wind and any other inclement weather. They had light from the cave entrance, but that would not last. She would watch the sun go down and figure out which way they needed to go when she decided it was time to leave.

She considered her clients and wondered when the last time either of them had spent a night in the complete darkness of the wilderness. Never mind that it'd been many months for her.

Tojo. He was far out of his depth, but he trusted her to get him to where he needed to go. For now, he was content to sit with his back to the earthen wall and rest his arms on his knees. He was awake, staring at the wall opposite him, his face devoid of emotion. She could see he was tired, but he still seemed optimistic despite his small injuries.

Imre. He sat against the back wall of the small cave with his knees up, resting his forehead on them. He was still enough that he could've been asleep. Makeda listened. His breathing was easy, but she didn't think he was actually asleep. Either he was also lost in thought or he was listening hard. He tilted his head before raising it and met her eyes. Then he gave her an unsure smile.

Makeda nodded to him. Both men seemed well. That was going to change with their escape. It would be hard going over the mountains. Still, it was enough that they were both fit and in decent spirits.

In the meantime, she took stock. On her, she had her baton, her small toolkit, a lot of certified nuyen, a pistol with four bullets, two stim patches, two sleep patches, a package of Buzzbuzz, and an energy cake. She had no way to turn the snow into water, nothing to start a fire with, and very little in the way of food.

This was a good way to get them all killed.

"Right. Everyone empty your pockets and bags. I need to see what kind of supplies we have on hand." Her voice was loud and sudden in her ears after the long silence.

Both men stared at her for a long moment, confused at the command. "Really?" Tojo asked.

"Yes, really. Whoever blew up the maglev track also blew my nice, neat plan to hell. I need to know what I'm working with." She beckoned with both hands. "C'mon. Let's see what we have."

"Even our money?" Imre asked. His face was unreadable in the fading light disappearing too fast from the cave entrance.

Makeda was tempted to say yes, but right now, money wasn't the issue. Survival was. She shook her head.

Imre started at the top of his duster and pulled out a multi-tool, the bloody handkerchief, a datapad, his smart glasses, and an ampoule of a drug. He pulled a small wad of corp scrip from one pocket and put it back. "That's it." Then he snapped his fingers and pulled a lighter from his left boot. Makeda had to admire his taste in footwear. It was a high-quality Amina brand with rubber soles. No wonder he hadn't had any problems in the snow or mud.

Makeda pointed her chin at the ampoule. "What's that?" She had missed it in her hasty search of his body. That was a mistake that could've gotten her killed.

"Long haul." Imre shrugged. "I got it from a client who liked to party very hard and wanted me to keep up. I thought I'd be on the run by myself once I hit Rome. I figured that if I could keep moving for three or four days, I'd shake loose anyone looking for me."

"Hell of a drug. Knocks you out for hours on the come down." She turned to the other man. "All right. Tojo?"

Tojo had nothing in his pockets, but he had his shoulder bag. In it, he had a full set of clothing, a toiletry bag that included a collapsible cup, a liter bottle of water, a holo of a green dog with multiple tails, a datapad, AR goggles, and a roll of toilet paper. When she gave the toilet paper a double glance, he'd scowled. "I have no idea how civilized the washrooms will be on our trip. Better safe."

Makeda raised both hands in surrender. She suspected they would all be pleased at Tojo's sensibilities by the time they were done. "If you're cold, put the second shirt on now. We're going to be here a bit, and I don't want to have a fire tonight. Smoke will bring the search parties."

Tojo put the rest of his clothing back in the shoulder bag before he added the extra layer.

Makeda put the bottle of water, the collapsible cup, the lighter, and the multi-tool to the side. To it, she added the energy cake and the Buzzbuzz. "This is the sum total of our usable emergency gear. I don't recommend the long haul, and as we're not trying to get rescued, the rest isn't needed. However, pull the batteries on your datapads. At least for now. I don't want those giving us away. Especially if you've got things set to automatically log in whether you're in private mode or not."

Imre made a face and popped the battery out of his datapad. "Never occurred to me..." The rest of the stuff, he put back in his pockets. He touched the lighter. "Do you want to carry that?"

Makeda shook her head. "It's yours. I just wanted to know what we had. Now I know we can have a fire tomorrow if we're not out of the woods by then. However, I'll keep these for now." She grabbed her stuff, the water, and the collapsible cup. "In a couple of hours, we'll eat. In the meantime, you should see if you can sleep."

Imre slid the lighter back into his boot.

Makeda stopped him as he went to put away his handkerchief. "You've got a cut on your face."

Touching his forehead, Imre's fingers came away tacky with drying, flaking blood. He grimaced and used the handkerchief and saliva to clean away the blood as best he could.

Tojo didn't say anything. He replaced his things in his shoulder bag. He lingered over the picture of the green dog for a moment, then shoved it in and looked away.

Makeda didn't want to ask. She had the maternal instinct of an angry jackal, and crying upset her. She didn't know what the dog meant to him, and didn't want to know. Personal details forged complicated bonds between a runner and a client. It also opened Tojo up to remembering the good parts of the life he'd left behind. This was not the time for him to get second thoughts. Plus, who has a holo of a virtual pet anyway? She shook her head, then cleared away some of the rocks from the spot she planned to nap on.

As she settled in, wishing she could wear Tojo's extra pair of pants—they were way too slender for her hips—Imre asked, "Tell me about your dog?"

Makeda sighed inwardly. She was going to find out after all. Despite not wanting to know, she listened. There could be useful information in the telling.

For a long time, Tojo didn't say anything. It was long enough that Makeda, curled up on her side facing the guys, resting her head on her arm, thought Tojo was going to ignore Imre's question. Then he spoke, keeping his voice low. Makeda realized Tojo didn't want her to hear what he had to say. This kept her mind alert even as her body relaxed. She kept her eyes almost closed and listened hard.

"Kiriko. That was her name." Tojo rummaged through his shoulder bag until he found the holo. "She was my first virtual pet. There were others, but she was my favorite. I raised her from nothing. At first, I even did the thing where I fed and walked her every day, so she'd grow. When I got bored with that, I set it on automatic, but I never got bored of her. She was my best friend for the longest time."

"What happened to her?"

Tojo stared at the holo. "I had to prove I was willing to leave everything behind."

Imre shrugged. "I don't understand."

"Herr Schmidt told me I needed to prove that I was willing to give up everything for my new company. That I was willing to sever ties with everyone and everything I knew." He put the holo back in his shoulder bag. "Since I don't have family, I had to delete her. Everything that she was is gone."

And that is why you had watchdogs on the train, you idiot. Makeda kept her thoughts to herself and wished he had told her about the virtual pet when she was questioning him about recent deaths or suicides. Then again, he was probably embarrassed by his love of the digital creature. It was a private part of him. Or so he thought. Clearly not.

Imre shifted, scraping against the rock and dirt. "No backups?"

Tojo shook his head in small, slow arcs. "The new company had ways of knowing if I did." He gazed up at the dirt ceiling. "I could remake her...when I get to my new home. But it wouldn't be the same. It wouldn't be my Kiriko. I'd trained her to do so many things that I forgot them all. Sometimes, she'd surprise me with an automatic response to something I did. She was the best code buddy I ever had."

Makeda watched them with slitted eyes. Imre didn't say anything. He gave Tojo's forearm a squeeze. Tojo continued to look at the dirt ceiling. Silent tears rolled down the sides of his face, making tracks in the dirt on his cheeks.

She wondered what kind of company would make you sacrifice the thing you loved most to prove your willingness to leave your job. Then again, people who didn't have vibrant online lives didn't understand people who got emotionally invested in their digital ones. They often thought the digital existence wasn't worth as much as a meat body one. Makeda knew a score of people who could refute that assumption.

Be that it is may, Herr Schmidt was a bastard to make Tojo delete his only friend.

She pondered the Johnson. Schmidt had done a couple of unusual things where Tojo was concerned. Two runs with him on the same train without letting the runners know. Then again, Schmidt could've had her get the codes off Tojo when she extracted him. That made more sense. It would've been safer and cheaper. Less chance of the runners clashing with each other. It was almost as if Schmidt either wanted mistakes to be made or he didn't know what the hell he was doing. In both cases, he was a danger to the entire operation.

After a few long minutes, Imre glanced around the cave as the other man wiped at his face—a polite way of not seeing the tears. "So, tell me about this new company?"

Makeda made an effort to not react. This was a good test of Tojo's ability to keep his mouth shut. It would tell her what kind of a talk she needed to have with him later.

Tojo shook his head. "I can't."

Good boy. It was better than she'd hoped for.

"Oh, I understand."

"You don't. I don't know who I'm going to be working for yet. I just know it'll be better than where I was. I won't be stuck in a go-nowhere, do-nothing-new job."

Makeda's pleasure at Tojo's denial turned to disbelief.

Imre sat back and stared at the smaller man. "Ah, isn't that a bit, ah, dangerous?"

That was putting it politely. If Makeda had been part of the conversation, she would've asked, "Are you stupid?" Instead, she filed all the information away and planned not to tell Tojo anything important.

"It is a risk," Tojo agreed. "But that's why I made the deal to sell the paydata. I have money if everything goes wrong. I'm willing to take a risk to get my freedom, but I don't trust everything I hear. Especially not from a recruiter. Then again, if even half of what she said was true, I'm going to enjoy life a lot more. If not, I have enough money to help make life enjoyable wherever I end up."

"Paydata?" Imre sounded very interested, if a bit bemused.

"Yeah, I..." Tojo paused. "I don't think I should talk about it. You're not a shadowrunner, and I think Makeda would be upset if I said anything."

"Wait, why?" Imre sounded more mystified than upset. "Because I'm not a runner, and she is?"

Makeda didn't move except to breathe in slow, even breaths. She could feel them both looking at her. It seemed Tojo had picked up some of her caution, but not enough. Still, he stopped when he should have and before she had to pretend to wake up. It was a really good thing that no one knew she had the only copy of the paydata—as far as she knew.

Once more, she wished for her team to be in her head. Runs were supposed to be fast and clean. Extract, escape, deliver. She admitted she was more upset at the lack of information than the lack of back up. She was good on her feet and specialized in improvisation. But she couldn't be effective without knowledge. That was what her inner control freak was really upset about.

"Yeah." Tojo shifted his shoulder bag, getting more comfortable. "You don't have the same code of honor shadowrunners have unless you are one. I saw it on *Breakout: A Shadowrunner's Story*. It was a really good show."

"I'm not sure how real shows like that are. But all right, we can talk about something else." Imre sounded like he was considering whether or not Tojo was off his rocker.

Makeda wanted to laugh. She also made note of the show. She needed to see what the wage slaves were eating up as a "real" shadowrunner's story.

"What did you do before this?" Tojo reached for the right words. "I mean, *really* do. I heard what you told Makeda, but I still don't understand what that means."

"I worked at Hanover Casino as one of their top VIP service people." Imre sighed. "It was a wonderful and terrible job. The short version: I did whatever the VIP wanted me to do. Fetch and carry, act as a companion, be a secretary, tour guide, and entertainment specialist. That sort of thing. If they wanted joygirls or -boys, or drugs or a private card game, I arranged it for them. It didn't matter if I liked them or not. What mattered is if they liked me."

"It doesn't sound so bad."

"You try explaining to a spoiled brat that they can't do novacoke on the casino floor because it's against the rules and get backhanded for it, then smile when they tell you to go clean yourself up because they can't have you making them look bad. Or drive a beaten joyboy back to his pimp and pay him an extra fee for returning damaged goods. Or have to smile again when that same client comes back and requests you personally because you give such good service...and no, you can't say no."

"Wow." Tojo's voice was low and awed. "That really happened?"

"Yes. And worse. The rich are bastards. Every last one of them. They never do anything because it's the right thing to do. There's always an angle. They always get something out of everything. Any rich guy who says they're doing it for altruistic reasons is a liar." Imre's voice thickened with suppressed emotion. "The ones who say they're doing something because it's the right thing to do are the worst of the lot. They're the ones who find the orphan to have a picture or trid with, then they leave them behind like an abandoned doll."

"And I thought being a maintenance dev was bad."

Makeda wondered who had hurt whom to make Imre hate the rich so much. It was personal. Very personal. With the amount of loathing in his voice, it was a testament to his acting skill that he hadn't sneered at her when she told him her background story of doing charity benefits for orphanages in Belgium.

"Bad is what you make of it. Suffering is suffering, no matter where you are or what job you do." Imre shifted in his spot. "I think I'm going to follow Makeda. I'm gonna rest. I may not be a runner, but I understand how much mountain climbing is going to suck hoop in the morning."

Makeda listened to the two of them get comfortable and waited until both of them were breathing slow and deep before she let herself follow suit.

Hours later, Makeda was on her feet with the Walther in her hand before she realized she was awake. In the back of the cave, Tojo and Imre slept back-to-back curled up in tight, protective balls. Tojo used his shoulder bag as a pillow.

She looked around, seeking the source of her sudden wakefulness. Bright moonlight shone in through the cave opening, illuminating the cave enough for her to see.

There was no immediate danger in sight. Makeda cocked her head and listened. Far away or high above, something with rotors flew. A search team. That wasn't a surprise. Even if they had found the rest of the scattered Party Train passengers, they were missing three.

But search teams didn't work at night. Not usually. It had to be a heat-seeking drone. Makeda pondered this. She didn't think the local authorities would operate at night, though with the caliber of people on the Party Train, it wouldn't surprise her if private security forces had gotten involved.

Laying back down, Makeda continued to listen for sounds of people getting closer to their position. The night was quiet except for the sleeping noises of those in the cave. She wondered how far out the search teams would look.

Then again, the ones searching might not be part of the official rescue party. Makeda considered the two sleeping men. If Tojo had been the target, the assassin was not going to give up so easily. She grimaced. It would've been so much easier to kill him on the train. Why blow the track? Why so much collateral damage?

Answers, much like sleep, eluded her for the rest of the night.

TEN

"Why didn't you remind me that we hadn't eaten?" Makeda broke the energy bar into thirds and passed two pieces to Tojo and Imre.

Tojo chuckled as he accepted his tiny meal. "And wake you up? No. Not me."

Imre agreed as he ate his piece in a single bite. "I've learned not to wake a woman up unless she says to." The two men exchanged conspiratorial glances and grinned.

Makeda rolled her eyes and finished her meal in two bites. As she did so, she poured a cup of water for Imre. Each cup held about a hundred sixty milliliters of liquid. "Drink it. This is all we have until we can find a safe source for water." She poured herself a cup and gulped it down.

Tojo, who had been nibbling on his piece of breakfast, pointed upward. "What about the snow?" He stuffed the rest of the energy bar in his mouth and made a face.

"No. Eating snow can dehydrate you. Your body has to work too hard to break it down. Plus, it's cold. Hypothermia. Not to mention, you don't know what kind of little beasties live in the snow." Makeda poured him a cupful of the water. "We'll be okay with this for now." She gave him a confident smile she did not really feel. "So drink up."

Leaving the cave was harder than Makeda thought it would be. None of them had realized just how much the earth had protected them from the cold and wind. As soon as she was boosted out of the hole, Makeda knew they would have to find shelter before nightfall. If they didn't, they would require a fire to keep from freezing.

Imre boosted Tojo out next. "Holy hoop. It's fraggin' cold out here."

"You'll warm up as soon as we get moving. Help me." She and Tojo pulled Imre from the cave with a bit of effort.

"*Ach du meine Güte*," Imre muttered and shivered. "Did it snow last night? Is it supposed to snow in the spring?"

Looking back the way they'd come, their tracks, still somewhat visible, were covered in a fresh layer of obscuring snow. "Yeah. Good and bad for us." Makeda rubbed her hands together. Last night, she'd used the sun to figure out which way was north—and civilization. "C'mon."

The clear morning and dwindling trees made for easier hiking, but it did nothing for Makeda's nerves. With fewer places to hide if a vehicle flew overhead, they'd be spotted in a minute. Moving from the higher snow-covered areas to the grassy vales helped a little. The red in Imre's coat and her shirt didn't stand out quite so much, and there were large boulders and juts of rocks to hunker next to if needed.

By midday, it had warmed up enough that Makeda tied the armored jacket over her shoulders like a cape and Tojo had shifted to carrying his jacket, though he kept both shirts on. Imre opened his duster, but didn't take it off. When they rested in the shadow of a huge boulder, Makeda broke open the Buzzbuzz and gave out the caffeinated candy chews. Each of them ate it and drank the last of their bottled water with mingled regret and relief.

"How far to get to where we're going?" Tojo's face was red from exertion and the sun. It was clear he'd never gone on a hike like this before.

Makeda eyed his shoes, wondering how many blisters he had. She didn't ask. She had at least one growing at the base of her left big toe. It was just as well he hadn't told her about them if he had any. There wasn't much she could do about them now. "I don't know. I figure it can't be more than ten kilometers before we hit civilization. Or, hopefully, a signal."

"Haven't gone this long without checking the news or my e-mail or forums in like...ever." Imre stretched. "Or gone so long without food."

Makeda snorted. There was a man who'd never had to scrap for his piece. She wondered what it would've been to have a childhood like that. Golden handcuffs. That wasn't her story. Growing up as a poor military brat had trained Makeda to watch for opportunities, mistrust authority figures, and go hungry in silence. Her parents had worked hard for what they had. It was never enough.

"Me, either." Tojo brightened. "But I guess I'll have some war stories to tell my new friends over drinks."

Somewhat amazed at Tojo's optimism and naivety, Makeda stood. "Come on. If we're lucky, we'll find either shelter or a signal before dark. Pray for the signal. My team will be here to pick us up as soon as they can find us."

She led the way again, setting a fast but not overly aggressive pace. She didn't feel the least bit guilty about lying to them. She had no idea if her team was even still in Switzerland or if they'd moved on to Spain already. Part of her hoped they were still around and within helping distance. TechnoGalen had contacts everywhere. As soon as she got a signal, he'd be able to help. But she couldn't say any of this to her clients.

Makeda still hadn't put her finger on what, exactly, it was about Imre that her gut didn't like, and Tojo didn't need to lose his optimistic spirit. That would keep him going for a long time. Though it was true that a signal would be more help than shelter. The question was, what kind of Plan B had her team put together once the train had been attacked? Did they leave anything behind for her?

The fog crept back in by late afternoon, and the temperature dropped enough that everyone bundled back up. The sun shone in scant lances through the low-lying clouds and deepening fog. The smell of loamy earth rose around them. Every fifteen minutes of their impromptu hike, Makeda checked her comms with a subvocal update. "Still walking. It's foggy. Where the hell are you? Galen? Saladin? Are you reading me?"

She was just about to call a halt when a stranger called it for her.

"*Sluta. Vem är du? Vad gör du här?*" The creaky, feminine voice came out of the fog to the right. She sounded irritated.

Makeda stopped with her hand inside her coat. She waved the other two back. "Excuse me?"

"American," the unseen woman spat. "Take your hand out of your coat slowly. I have you in my sights."

Makeda obeyed, shifting her cybereyes to thermographic vision. A short, squat woman with a rifle pointed at them stood in the shadow of a tree, becoming part of it. She looked like a dwarf with old style cybergoggles. "We're just passing through. Looking for a road or signal."

"That doesn't tell me who you are or why you're here on my land." The rifle, a Remington 900 from its silhouette, didn't waver.

"There was an accident. We're looking for help. Please." Makeda shifted, making sure she put herself between Tojo and the gun. "We're hungry and thirsty."

"We can pay," Imre added. "I have corp scrip."

The dwarf ignored Imre. "What's your name, *schwarze*?"

Makeda winced at the slur, then pushed her reaction away. It wasn't like she'd never been insulted by bigots before. "Makeda. My name is Makeda."

"You with the men? Willingly?" The tip of the Remington shifted towards Imre.

Makeda relaxed half a touch. If the woman was concerned with whether or not she was a prisoner, it was possible they were going to be able to get out of this without anyone dying. "Yeah. I am. I'm the one leading them out of the mountains. You might say they're my wards."

"You step forward, Makeda." The rifle remained on Imre.

Tojo took half a step toward Makeda, lifting a hand to clutch at her. He froze at the *clack* of the Remington being cocked. "Makeda, no..."

The rifle now pointed at her and Tojo.

Makeda waved him back. "I'll be fine. Don't. Move. Don't." She pointed at each of them. "There's a Remington 900 pointed at us. It can do a lot of damage." She turned back to the dwarf woman. "I'm coming. Please don't hurt them."

As soon as the short woman came into sight through the fog, Makeda shifted to normal vision and was surprised to see how old the dwarf was. She couldn't have been more than a meter high, her iron hair hid what color it had been in more youthful days, and her face was a mass of wrinkles—both smile and frown lines. Makeda was shocked at how old her tech was. The goggles were almost welded to the woman's face with scar tissue. Keeping her hands up, Makeda stopped about halfway between the two sets of people. She didn't say anything as she waited on the dwarf's pleasure.

"If the Jap or *Schwob* have you captive, now's a good time for you to let me know. I can leave them for the wildlife." There was no hint of remorse or regret in those words.

Makeda shook her head, almost surprised at such racist terms being used so casually. "No ma'am. They really are my wards. I'd appreciate you not hurting them." Even with her enhanced reflexes, she didn't think she could retrieve her gun and shoot the woman before the rifle did its damage.

"*Jaså.* A black woman in charge of a German and an oriental guy? I've seen stranger things, but not by much." The dwarf considered the three of them. "Heard there was a train accident yesterday a ways from here. You from it?" Despite the woman's apparent old age, the rifle never wavered in her liver-spotted hands.

There was no way to tell what answer would get them what they needed. Right now, that was more important, and the dwarf woman was calm enough. "We need to get help."

"Didn't answer my question. I think the answer is yes. You blow it up?"

Again, Makeda shook her head. "No." Part of her wanted to say a lot more. To beg for a Matrix connection and food and water. Self-preservation told her to keep her mouth shut. She kept her silence.

"You know who blew it up?"

"No."

The woman tilted her head. "You know *why* they blew it up?"

Makeda looked back at Tojo and shrugged. "I don't know." She thought she did, but wasn't willing to give this stranger that kind of information.

"I really don't like people on my property. There's gonna be more of you, I'll bet."

"Please. If you give us a little food and water and maybe a Matrix connection, we'll be gone as fast as we can go." Makeda shivered. The sun had dipped behind the mountain, and temperature dropped fast.

The dwarf lowered her rifle, letting the tip of it dip to the ground. "My name is Vasti. If you're fraggin' up the corps, I guess I can give you a hand. You wouldn't last another day out here in the mountains. Not with the mana storms coming and the incryptids running about."

Makeda sighed in relief. "Thank you. We appreciate it. We really do."

She would have said more, but Tojo took this moment to collapse to his knees, then face plant in the grass.

ELEVEN

Makeda hunched over, whirled around, and ran to Tojo as Imre dropped to the ground. Vasti took a knee and scanned the horizon.

Leaning over Tojo, Makeda expected to hear a shot or to feel the pain of a bullet in flesh. None of that came. She scanned him for injury. There was no blood. She felt for a pulse. Strong and steady. Makeda tapped his cheek.

Tojo blinked his eyes open. "*Ohayō*, pretty lady." He blinked again and sat up with a jerk. He almost smacked Makeda in the face with his head. "What happened? Where's the woman with the gun? Did she shoot me? Am I hurt?"

"No." Makeda frowned and touched his forehead with her inner wrist. "Did you faint?"

Tojo touched his chest and stomach, looking for a wound that wasn't there. "No?" He didn't sound sure of himself. "I just...I was standing, not moving like you said, and then I was looking up at you."

Imre, still on the ground, laughed. "You locked your knees, didn't you?"

Makeda rubbed her forehead and got up. "He fainted."

"Blacked out due to lack of oxygen," Imre corrected. "He locked his knees. I've seen it happen dozens of times in receiving lines."

Makeda eyed him. "In other words, he *fainted*. I use the words I mean."

Imre and Tojo looked at each other. Tojo shrugged. "Yeah. I guess so." He rubbed the back of his neck. "Are we all right?" He flicked a glance at Vasti, his concern obvious.

"Other than you fainting, you're fine. If you weren't, you wouldn't be able to ask the question." Vasti stood in a fluid motion that belied her age and hinted at internal cyberware. "Follow me. I'll get you some food and appropriate clothing."

That perked everyone up. "Thank you. We appreciate it." Makeda touched her equipment, making sure it was prepped out of habit before they set off—bottle, stimulant, and gun—and missed the dozens of other things she usually carried with her.

Imre touched Makeda's wrist, making her pause. "How do we know we can trust her?"

"We don't. But it's better than we have now." She gave him a humorless smile. "Unless you'd rather stay cold and hungry, facing Awakened beasties in the dark?"

"Well, when you put it that way..." Imre shrugged.

Makeda gazed ahead, watching Vasti's back, sure the woman was listening. "C'mon. Daylight's wasting, and we don't know how far we need to go. Make sure Tojo keeps up, yeah?" This last was phrased as a request, but they both knew it wasn't.

"Get a move on! Daylight's fading." Vasti didn't turn around as she called behind her, though she slowed her step for them to catch up.

Imre nodded. He moved to Tojo's side and took up the escort position as if born to it. Makeda felt that niggle of warning and doubt again, but didn't know why. Imre did exactly what she asked him to do. Nothing more.

Vasti's home was a rustic-looking cabin designed for a happy hermit. There was a tiny bedroom, a small washroom, and an open area that encompassed everything else—living room, kitchen, kitchen nook, and office. Everything was old school. Gas and electric and very little in the way of automation. Makeda thanked whomever was listening that the toilet was a septic system and not an outhouse.

As they made themselves comfortable, Makeda subvocalized a call out to her team. Nothing came back. The silence in her head was deafening. What had happened to her comms? Were they damaged? Maybe, maybe not. Either way, she was still on her own.

She leaned against the humming refrigerator, drinking the Joy Cola Vasti had given them. It was the nectar of the gods, sweet and bubbly.

Imre sat at the small wooden table and checked his smart glasses. "No Matrix connection?"

Vasti scoffed. "No. Nothing wireless. Not here. I've got jammers all over my property. I don't want people sending in drones or anything."

"Why not?" Tojo sat on the couch with his shoes and socks off, bandaging up his blistered feet the best he could.

"Look, *tobu*, it's clear you don't know what the real world is like, but you're going to get an education the hard way. I'm too old to have to deal with trespassers or to deal with people from my past who want one last hoo-rah. So, no wireless. It makes people lazy. If you're gonna make me leave my house, you're going to have to work for it."

The whole time Vasti grumped at them, she stood over the stove, frying up a mess of soy beefcakes. She checked on the rice from time to time. The beefy smell wafted through the small space. It was mouthwatering.

Makeda's stomach rumbled, and she swallowed a couple of times before she pulled her thoughts together. "You're helping us."

"The sooner I get you out of here, the sooner no one comes on my land looking for you."

Made sense. Makeda stepped to the counter to look at the beefcakes and get a better look at Vasti's face. "Or you could've left us to the storms and the monsters."

Vasti looked at her. "Maybe. No nuyen in that."

It was hard to tell what the old dwarf was thinking with those implanted goggles obscuring her eyes. Makeda knew from the twitch of a smile at the corner of her mouth that Vasti had dropped a couple of clues that she expected Makeda to pick up. She reviewed the conversation.

Hope surged as Makeda picked up what Vasti had laid down. "Nothing wireless, but you've got wired comms."

"Give the girl a prize." Vasti pointed at a cabinet. "Get out four plates. Set the table."

Makeda wanted to leap for joy. She was going to get to talk to her team. Her pleasure turned into surprise as she found herself reaching for a set of gorgeous blue-and-white porcelain plates. Makeda was almost afraid to touch them. "Whoa."

"Just because I live out in the boonies doesn't mean I live like a savage."

"Clearly." Imre came over to get the plates from Makeda and set the table. "Flatware?" Vasti pointed at a set of drawers. He looked through them until he found what he was looking for. Again, the flatware was of exceptional quality. With no napkins in sight, he set the forks to one side of the plates.

Makeda mulled over Vasti's words. *"No nuyen in it..."* She looked up and gazed directly into those goggles. "How much did you earn from finding us?" It was disorienting to ask her twin reflections these questions, but she was sure she was right.

"A couple thousand." Vasti's hint of a smile became a smirk.

She considered this, watching the dwarf work. "Well, we're not knocked out, and you wouldn't be telling me this if it was someone who was going to hurt us."

"Assumptions, girly." Vasti picked up the sizzling pan of beefcakes. She nodded at the pot of rice. "Bring it."

"Assumptions, yes. But you wouldn't have told me if you didn't get anything out of it. How much is he going to pay you to let me talk to him?" Makeda knew she was on the right track as she stirred the rice, then brought it to the table. She followed her hostess's actions and dished out equal portions of steaming food on those beautiful blue-and-white plates.

"The other half of the money." The old woman returned the almost-empty pan to the stove. She gestured to the pot. "Just put that on the table. Won't hurt it."

Makeda flicked a glance at her clients. Imre and Tojo split their attention between the conversation and the food. Tojo furrowed his brow, trying to keep up. Imre kept his face in that neutral expression of polite interest.

"I'll be able to talk to my team?"

"Yes. After we eat." Vasti gestured to the men. "Can't you see them boys are starving, but waiting for us? For *ussländers*, they got manners. So, sit and eat."

Makeda glanced around the table. Both Imre and Tojo sat in their assigned seats with untouched plates. She ducked her head as she sat and picked up her fork. That was the signal to dig in. For the next few minutes, the only sounds were forks to the plate and the *mmm*s of enjoyment. Makeda was no exception.

After eating and drinking so much real, rich food, it was a relief to get back to the kind of food Makeda was used to. Comforting, really. Going almost a full day of exertion without eating added to the enjoyment, but there was nothing like the tastes of home, and soy beefcakes were a favorite.

"I don't think I've tasted beefcakes this good before." Imre scooped more rice to his plate to sop up the leftover gravy and juices.

Tojo nodded with a "Mmm-hmm."

"There's plenty of water. All of you can get cleaned up. I think I've got a practical shirt you can wear—have—Makeda. The rest of you are on your own. I don't keep extra men's clothing around." Vasti shrugged. "Not a hotel or a hostel."

"Even if you can be hostile from time to time?" Makeda grinned at her. She was sure she had the dwarf's measure. Giving as good as she got was the right way to act with Vasti. Backbone and a thick skin were needed. She had no doubt that Vasti had once been a shadowrunner. Maybe even before they were known as shadowrunners.

Vasti grinned back. "If you had to deal with *pflock* like you, you'd be hostile, too." She cleared her plate and began to clean up the kitchen.

"May I help you with the dishes?" Imre stood and brought his cleaned plate to the sink.

"Nope. You can go take a shower. You smell like a gym locker." Vasti wrinkled her nose for emphasis.

Imre bowed his head. "Yes, ma'am." He stepped outside to take his boots and socks off before he returned and headed to the bathroom.

Once the shower started up, Vasti tapped Makeda's arm. "You got a datajack, yeah?"

Makeda nodded.

"I'm gonna let you talk to your guy, TechnoGalen, but I'm going to monitor the conversation. Make it quick." She looked toward the bathroom. "I don't trust *Herr Döufu*. Germans. You can't trust them. They've always got a second reason for everything they do."

Makeda nodded. "He's holding his cards close. Even so, if everything is wired, he's not likely to overhear the conversation."

"No, but he can decide to do something stupid while we're both plugged in." Vasti took Tojo's cleaned plate from him and saw the expression on his face. "Don't look so shocked. People lie. All the time. There's no altruism in the shadows. Just money, the run, and the victims."

Tojo looked between Vasti and Makeda. "But...he's running from his corp, too." His eyes begged Makeda to back him up. She didn't respond.

"Maybe. Maybe not." Vasti scowled. "He's too nice. Too polite. Anyone that nice is hiding something."

Makeda chose not to address this, even though doubts about her client continued to plague her. "Lemme talk to my team. The sooner I do, the sooner we can all part ways."

Vasti beckoned her over to the computer setup—a clunky, Frankenstein-esque mishmash of old and new tech. "You'll have to sit on the floor. This is built for me." She pulled a datajack from a tangle of wires and offered it to Makeda as she made herself comfortable.

"Thanks."

"Plug in and wait."

Makeda gave Tojo a comforting smile—at least she hoped it was comforting—before she jacked in. Instead of an AR room, Makeda found herself looking at a text chat window—black background, green text. There were already two people in the room: RealAdonis and Perchta.

Perchta: My guest will get to talk when the nuyen is in my account.

RealAdonis: sent

Perchta: Received. I'm monitoring this and will keep a log. The log will be destroyed on the last payment. Got it?

RealAdonis: yes

A virtual keyboard appeared in Makeda's line of sight. She changed her name from Guest2945 to Makeda. It was a strange, archaic setup, but it worked.

Makeda: Real old skool.

RealAdonis: Prove yourself

Makeda: I know what you do in the shower with the duck.

RealAdonis: Damn good to hear from you.

Makeda: Prove yourself.

RealAdonis: I know what you mean when you say, "You're not on the bike."

Makeda: Heya Galen.

RealAdonis: Status?

Makeda: Alive. Fed and getting cleaned up thanks to Perchta. Missed the meet in Lucern.

RealAdonis: No drek. What a mess. Lost the deposit.

Makeda: Plan B?

RealAdonis: They're pissed, too

RealAdonis: Plan B. Make it to Bern. No one there cares about foreigners. Go to the airport. I'll have a flight for you and the target. You'll be going to Málaga, Spain as planned. Might even be able to get you some alt IDs

Perchta: They care about metahumans in Bern, but they don't do anything about it. Remember that.

Makeda: Spain as planned. Right. Can the flight take 3?

Makeda: Thanks Perchta.

RealAdonis: ?? 3?

Makeda: Picked up an extra client on the run. Paying client. He needs to get to Spain, too.

RealAdonis: !! What the hell? You can't pick up every stray out there!

Makeda: It's Imre.

RealAdonis: Ditch him! I don't care how hot he is.

Makeda: Paid 250,000¥ for the escort.

Perchta: I get my 5%.

Makeda: 1

Perchta: 5

Makeda: 0

Perchta: That's not how this works, girly. But I'll go to 4%.

Makeda: 3% and you have a deal.

Perchta: Deal.

RealAdonis: That's out of your cut.

Makeda: We'll talk about that later. I need 3 on a flight out of Bern to Spain. I'll cut him loose after that. The extra seat comes out of that 250,000¥.

Perchta: 242,500¥.

Makeda: Whatever. How far from here to Bern, walking, Perchta?

Perchta: With the wage slave? 2-3 days. He's slow. About 50 klicks. You might be able to catch a ride about halfway in. Maybe. Some of the trogs and orks don't like foreigners. Some do.

Makeda: 3 days then. Flight for 3 out of Bern. Private craft, no questions asked.

RealAdonis: Expensive.

Makeda: Don't care. This run's already gone pear shaped. I want it done.

RealAdonis: Ok

RealAdonis: I'll get it done

RealAdonis: When will you be back in wireless range?

Perchta: 15 km from here.

RealAdonis: I'll have info for you when you return to civilization. Good to hear from you, Makeda.

Makeda: You, too.

Perchta: Gonna cut off this chat before it gets mushy.

Makeda blinked as the chat room disappeared from her cybereyes. She pulled the datajack from its socket and rubbed her face. Tojo now sat on the couch. He watched them with a neutral expression. Checking her internal clock, not even four minutes had gone by. The shower was still running.

Vasti held out a certified gold credstick and a credstick reader. It had 5,500 nuyen showing in its display. "7,500 nuyen, please."

"You're a bandit." Makeda said without rancor as she pulled Imre's platinum credstick from her pocket and transferred the money.

The old woman smiled at the 13,000 nuyen when it showed up on the credstick display. "I prefer to think of myself as an opportunist. Not many ways for someone like me to make money these days.... And retired or not, I still need money to keep the homestead going."

"I know. I would've done the same thing in your place."

"Are we okay?" Tojo's question was soft and hopeful.

Makeda nodded. "I think we'll be okay. Got some traveling to do, but things are in motion." She watched Vasti as she answered Tojo.

Vasti shrugged one non-committal shoulder at Makeda's implied question. They both looked up as the shower cut off. Vasti pointed at Tojo. "You're next." She murmured to Makeda, "Don't worry. I got a tankless water heater. You'll be fine."

Makeda waited until Vasti had disappeared into her bedroom and both Imre and Tojo had showered and were settled before she decided what to tell them. She stood and paced the threadbare rug while they sat on the couch.

"Right. I've gotten in touch with my team. We still have some walking to do, but the plan is to get us to Bern. By the time we get there, we'll have a flight lined up.... Then all of us are going to Spain."

"Spain?" Imre tilted his head. "Thank you. I wasn't sure you'd be able to get me where I needed to go."

She shrugged. "As it happens, Spain is an excellent jumping off point to a lot of places in the world. We'll be going to the Málaga airport. You can get to Morocco from there on your own."

Imre frowned, but didn't say anything.

Makeda locked eyes with him, making sure he understood. "Once we're in Málaga, you go your way, me and Tojo will go ours."

"That will work." Imre nodded. "I understand."

She wanted to say more. Something about staying in touch, but this wasn't the time or place. Imre had a lot of skills she could use, but until she handed Tojo over to his new corp, that sort of stuff needed to wait. Duty before pleasure and all that. Also, she still couldn't tell if she could trust him.

Trust was a hard thing to come by in the shadows. Especially when you were working with an unvetted person. Imre was a puzzle. He was a client, but he also seemed to have the skills to make a good runner, and probably a good teammate. That's what also made him suspicious. Perhaps he'd learned such skills working at the Hanover Casino. Perhaps not. His former job sounded like a training ground for runners, but there was nothing and no one to vouch for him.

Even if there was, her gut told her that something was off with him, and she trusted her gut. Makeda just wished she could figure out what it was. Until then, his money did the talking, and he was just another extraction client. She just hoped it wouldn't end with his knife in her back.

TWELVE

Makeda opened her eyes to moonlight streaming in through the window. Tojo snored on the couch. He had offered it to her. She had refused. Her client needed better rest than she did. Not to mention that she was used to sleeping on floors, in vehicles, and other uncomfortable places.

She sat up, looking for Imre. He was on the other side of the couch, near to the kitchen. He wasn't snoring, but he looked like he was asleep, curled up in one of the comforters Vasti had given them.

Makeda slid her boots on and wrapped her comforter around her. She still wore the clothing she'd escaped the train in. They all did. She'd insisted they sleep in their clothes, ready to run at any sign of trouble. That was when she'd seen the first real crack in Tojo's brave face.

It was the littlest things that broke a person. The proverbial straw. In Tojo's case, it was the need for comfort, and that meant not sleeping in his clothing. It took her a bit to figure out that his brave face had cracked because they'd been helped by Vasti. She'd read once that prisoners could survive almost anything, but they were most likely to riot after things started getting better. That was when they realized just how bad it had all gotten.

That was where Tojo was. Having a real meal and a roof over his head after the train wreck, fleeing through the mountains, and spending a night in a cave made Tojo realize that the trip to his new home wasn't done. There was more to go, and it would suck. There was no comfortable car, plane, or train waiting for him. He already hurt—blisters, bruised knees—and he was tired, but there were many more kilometers to go. All of this was realized because she asked him to sleep in his clothes.

After a couple of quiet words with him, explaining why she wanted this—better safe than sorry more than the thought they would actually be attacked in the night—she'd allowed him to sleep in just his t-shirt and pants, hanging up the buttoned-up shirts to air out. It had been a safe enough compromise.

But now, she was awake, and she didn't know why.

Moving with silent steps, she walked to the door, unlocked it—even out here in the boonies, the retired shadowrunner couldn't let go of her locks—and slipped out in an exhale of breath. The cold night air caressed her skin, covering it in goose bumps. She pulled the comforter closer and enjoyed the silence. It was the first time in days she'd been alone.

From her vantage point on the covered porch, Makeda could see more than she thought she would. The cabin itself butted up against a couple of trees at the edge of a clearing. The sloped land gave way to rolling hills and rock. A dirt path that led to the north looked like a glowing river in the moonlight.

This was the path they would follow for at least a day. Once they returned to the wireless world, she'd be able to suss out the situation and make a more concrete plan than "go north, get to the Bern airport within three days."

The door to her right opened, and Imre slipped out with a quick step. She clutched for the palm pistol she didn't have on her, then relaxed as he shut the door. Makeda glanced at Tojo through the window. He was still asleep.

Imre hugged himself, wearing his sleeveless duster. "I saw your shadow. It woke me. The light, dark, light. You good?"

Makeda glanced in the window again and saw that her shadow indeed had played over the floor where Imre had slept. "I'm good. Just thinking about tomorrow." She moved away from the window to the other side of him. It was outside Vasti's small bedroom, but that didn't matter. Makeda assumed everything that happened in the cabin, and outside of it, was recorded. Especially with strangers in the house.

"You have a plan?" Imre rubbed his arms in an absent attempt to keep warm.

She nodded. "As good of a plan as I'm going to have for the moment."

He looked out at the view she'd been enjoying. "I have to admit, I'm going to be sad to part ways. I had hoped to spend some time getting to know you." He sighed. "Wishes and fishes and all that. We could keep in touch after Spain?"

Makeda didn't say anything. She watched his lips move as he spoke. She wished he had been her original client. Then, they would've spent most of the train ride in her suite, entwined in each other. She let images of their naked bodies linger in her mind, and she sighed. That would have been fun.

But getting to know him now was out of the question. Until the mystery of her doubt was settled, she needed to keep Imre at arm's length. She glanced at him again. At least, the emotional distance needed to remain.

"I mean, I've kinda gotten used to you being around. In charge." He hugged himself more, rubbing his arms against the breeze that danced about the cabin. "I really like you."

"Yeah?" She gave him a half-smile and an open gaze to tell him she liked him, too. Just because she needed to keep him at arm's length emotionally didn't mean she couldn't keep him close physically. After all, she was in charge and responsible for his well-being.

You are such a lech. She smiled all the more at her mental scolding.

He nodded, glanced at her, and bit his lip for a moment. "You...I mean, you're beautiful, but you're *smart*. And fearless. And..." He shook his head. "Capable. It's nice to see."

"Thank you. I use what I have to get the job done."

Imre turned to her. "Can I...? I'm serious. When all this is done, can we still keep in touch?"

"Keep in touch?" She kept her real cards close. Makeda let the smile play about her lips as she watched his face. He was handsome. Again, she wondered what he'd look like with his natural dark hair. "Keep in touch how?"

Catching onto her flirting, he returned her playful smile. "Oh, you know. By comm...or AR..." He stroked the back of his knuckles down her cheek. "When we're not running for our lives. When I'm all set up in Morocco."

"We're not running for our lives right this moment." She tilted her head up in an invitation. He accepted it, kissing her slow and lingering, letting their lips explore each other.

Makeda opened the comforter to wrap the two of them in it. She took a breath as the cold of his clothing pressed against her warm body. Kissing him all the more, she let him press her against the wall of the house, his hands roaming her sides down to squeeze her ass and pull her tight against him.

She pressed to him, feeling his arousal, thinking of where they might go for a quick bit of love making. Not inside. Too small. No privacy. Outside was cold. She gripped the comforter in one hand around his neck and used the other to unfasten his duster so she could slide her hand under his shirt, against his skin. Part of her wanted to wrap her legs around him right then and there, but the logistics of getting her pants off while keeping her boots on confounded her hormone-addled brain.

Sex on a run was pure adrenaline and sensation. There was nothing like getting naked when your life was on the line. More than once, she and Zaria had made time for love when there had been no time to spare. It was the best sex she'd ever had. Right now, there was no good place for what she wanted, but he smelled so damn good and was so warm...

A howl rose in the distance. It was joined by another and another. It sounded like it came from the valley just over the ridge. Not very far away.

It was an unwelcome reminder of where they were and how dangerous things had become. They both looked towards the sound, then each other. Makeda chuckled. "Oh, you are dangerous. Maybe we can find some privacy tomorrow when—"

Whatever else she was going to say died in her throat as the howling cut off with a high-pitched yelp of pain and the growling snarls of wolves fighting *something*. The yelping stopped, but the growls and snarls did not. The sound of breaking branches and the fight continued until there was a roar of victory and a fleeing of four-footed animals. Then a thick silence descended.

"What—?" Imre began, but Makeda put a fingertip over his mouth.

They both listened hard over the beating of their hearts. The sound of tearing flesh and cracking bone floated to them on the wind. Whatever was out there was eating its kill, and neither of them wanted to get its attention.

Makeda drew Imre to the door, ignoring the cold as she gathered the comforter to her. She showed him three fingers, then counted them down before she opened the door and both of them slipped back inside.

Imre walked to the kitchen as Makeda dropped the comforter at her spot on the floor. He handed her a glass of water as she joined him. The two of them drank in silence as they both contemplated the incryptid creature they would have to outrun over the next couple of days.

THIRTEEN

Dressed in the clean linen shirt Vasti had provided and full of oatmeal, Makeda felt ready to tackle the next part of their trip. If all went according to plan, in half a day they would have semi-regular Matrix access—or at least e-mail. Tonight, they'd find one of the rural barns to sleep in. Tomorrow, they would meet a real road. They should be able to thumb a ride into Bern from there—if they were lucky.

If not, tomorrow they'd walk until they found a place to rest and call for a taxi of some kind. Bern had an international airport, after all. The closer they got to civilization, the less chance there was of running into the beastie that had eaten the wolf last night. Whatever it was, that was something she didn't want to face.

Makeda eyed Vasti a couple of times, wondering if the old woman knew what was out there. She did. Of course she did. The question was, would she tell Makeda about it? If yes, how much would it cost? It looked like they had a lot of money now. But they didn't. Not in the grand scheme of hiring planes, buying fake IDs, and bribing border officials. She wasn't sure they'd have enough.

As Imre helped Tojo wrap his feet in anticipation of a lot of walking, Vasti beckoned Makeda to follow her. The two left the confines of the cabin in silence. Makeda wondered if something had changed overnight. Vasti checked the corner cameras of the cabin before leading Makeda down the dirt path until they were well out of earshot of the cabin.

The dwarf woman stopped in the middle of the makeshift road. "You're going to walk that way for a long while. The road is the easiest way to go, but there's no cover. Keep that in mind. The wires are lit up with at least a dozen missing passengers from the train. Rewards offered to anyone who finds and helps the survivors. Big rewards. So far, you aren't wanted criminals. At least, not for the train attack."

Makeda nodded.

Vasti turned those scratched chrome goggles on her. "I didn't bring you out here for my health. I saw you watching me. What do you want to say...or ask...out of earshot of the boys?"

Makeda blinked at Vasti's bluntness, used to people talking around a point for a while. Then again, she had been obvious about her desire to talk to Vasti, but she didn't want to warn Imre or worry Tojo. "Couple of things. First, If I don't contact you within twenty-four hours after we leave, I want you to contact Galen for me. Tell him to 'Do what needs to be done.'"

"What's in it for me?"

"500 nuyen now. 500 more when I comm you."

"No skin off my nose." Vasti rubbed the scar tissue around her goggles. "Deal. And the other thing?"

"I was outside last night."

"Not alone." She snickered.

Makeda ignored that. "There was something else out here. It attacked and killed a wolf. What was it?"

"Ah." Vasti looked around. "Where?"

Makeda pointed toward the northwest ridge.

"I don't know what he is. I've seen him, though. I call him Gregor. I think he was once a troll, but then Genom got to him. One of their experiments. He escaped. Or they let him go. Gregor was quiet and kept to himself. Smart. I'd see signs of him on my land. Then I think he got caught in a mana storm. That changed him. Now he's just big and mean and obvious. Heard rumors from the net that he has a particular hate on for trolls. Otherwise, he's just territorial."

"Why do you let him stay?"

"Why not? I don't like people. Gregor is a good deterrent for trespassers." Vasti shrugged. "Besides, why not let him live? Gregor has never bothered me in my home. I know he's gone by here. He doesn't like houses. Or maybe it's just walls he doesn't like. I don't know. I don't like messing about in the woods or messing with him. Live and let live."

Makeda nodded, adding the details to her plan. "What's the land like between here and civilization?"

"Abandoned farms, or people like me who want to be left alone. Most of them don't have the connections I have. They also really don't like foreigners. I'd stick to myself until I got into Bern. The city, by the way, is a poseur. A tarted-up jenny pretending to go to the opera. Everyone can see the cracks. Most people pretend they're not there." Vasti pointed a stubby finger at Makeda. "So don't be expecting real civilization. More like glorified slums with pretentions of grandeur. Just be glad it has an airport you can fly out of. It's not much of one, but it's serviceable. It says 'international.' What it means is that even a Cessna from Germany can make the commuter hop."

"Good to know." Makeda looked back at the house. Tojo and Imre watched them out the window. "It's been good to meet you, Vasti."

"Don't get mushy on me. Besides, you owe me 500 nuyen." She pulled her credstick and reader from her bag.

"And you need to give me a way to contact you." Makeda transferred the money. "Mushy or not, I appreciate what you've done."

Vasti snorted. "I appreciate the nuyen. Now I can get some upgrades."

For all Vasti's gruffness, it was clear she'd enjoyed the bit of company while it was here. Probably why she didn't just murder them in their sleep for their nuyen. Then again, TechnoGalen knew they'd been there, and Makeda could hear Vasti in her head saying, *I'm too old to muck about with murdering you. Too much blood to clean up. And then there'd be people wanting revenge. Pah!*

Vasti scowled at Makeda's smile. "What?"

Makeda shook her head as she pocketed the credstick. "Nothing."

"Good. Now get off my land. I need some peace and quiet."

With several bottles of water, some old MREs that Vasti had dug up, and an extra backpack for Makeda, the three of them walked down the road that was more dirt than not. Vasti had taken pity on Tojo and given him a set of hiking spikes for his shoes. Tojo looked ridiculous, but he walked with a much more stable step over the uneven ground. That improved his mood.

The fog rolled back by mid-morning, and the sun peeked out from time to time. The cloudy sky was a welcome change from the heat of the last hike, though the dark clouds behind them promised wet weather. That would be a problem later—hopefully when they'd already found shelter. For now, it kept things comfortable and a little brisk.

They didn't speak as they walked. Makeda kept an eye on their surroundings, looking for signs of predators—human and animal alike. The world felt both too quiet and too noisy. Unfamiliar bird song mixed with animals rustling in the undergrowth of trees. The trees around them were just strange enough to shift into uncanny valley territory. The green wasn't the right shade, and the trees weren't the right shape. It felt like walking through a dream.

She wished she could access the Matrix for information about the flora and fauna outside the city, just to be sure. Not to mention doing a bit of research about Bern and its denizens. Once she was back in the wireless world, she wasn't going to leave it again for a long time. She felt like part of her had been cut off. It was so easy to look things up, to play music or the latest trid. It bothered her when it was gone. What had once been taken for granted was now sorely missed.

Makeda scoffed at herself. *You've become spoiled*, she scolded. *Reliant on technology. There was a time you didn't have two nuyen to rub together, much less a constant Matrix connection to any information you wanted, whenever you wanted it.* The scolding carried a bittersweet sting of nostalgia, Then she relented. She'd earned the money for her headware—with hard work, blood, sweat, and tears.

Imre and Tojo walked together behind until Imre caught up with her. They walked in step until Makeda gave him a sideways glance. "What's up?"

"I think Tojo needs a break. He's trying to do the brave-face thing, but he's slowing down. He already has blisters. I'm sure of it. His gait is off."

Makeda nodded. "Not much we can do about that now." She'd get him healed as soon as they reached a place that it could be done. "But yeah. A break is called for." Makeda was ready for a rest. It was only a few more kilometers until she had a decent signal again. She gestured to the tree line across a small field. "There. In the shade. We'll rest and have a bite to eat."

Tojo sat straight-legged with his head down while Imre sprawled in the grass. The hiking spikes on the bottoms of Tojo's smooth-soled shoes still looked funny. She smiled.

That smile disappeared as she saw the bottom of Imre's boots. They weren't just the fashionable brand she thought they were. The height they gave Imre wasn't from lifts as she first thought. The boots had deep treads that made hiking across dirt and rocks and fallen branches a breeze. She hadn't realized that. She'd just thought them part of the current fashion of practical boots with rubber soles. But, no, these boots were designed with a specific purpose in mind: hiking.

Makeda looked into the forest, contemplating this, before she sat with her back to a tree. The forest was more of a copse with some undergrowth. Through them, she saw the roof of some sort of structure. It was weatherworn and old. Maybe a stable. Probably a barn.

She drank her water as she watched Tojo struggle to get into the ready-to-eat meal package. Imre sat up, pulled his multi-tool from his belt, and flipped open the knife. He offered it to Tojo. Instead, Tojo handed him the package. With an experienced flick of the wrist, Imre had the MRE open. He gave it back to Tojo. "Don't toss the spice bottle if you don't use it. Those are like gold."

Makeda, already suspicious with a sinking heart, froze. That was something a military man would say. Or corpsec. Someone who'd been through training. Or another shadowrunner. Someone who'd spent a lot of time in the field. Those two sentences crystallized it for her. From his boots to his multi-tool to his ease in the wild, Imre wasn't who he pretended to be. He couldn't be. Traceable SIN or not, Imre didn't work for a casino babysitting pampered guests. Or if he had, that was in the past.

Makeda felt her cheeks flush with anger and stared at the weatherworn roof. Anger at Imre for not being what he said he was. Anger at TechnoGalen for not figuring out that Imre's SIN was fake. Anger at herself because she should've seen it sooner. She'd known something was wrong. It'd been the fact that Imre had been too comfortable with everything that had happened, and she'd been too comfortable with him—treating him more like a team member than a client.

Calming herself with an effort, she stood, brushing dirt from her backside. "Imre, a word?"

"Are we leaving so soon?" Tojo groaned. He stuffed the rest of his cheese cracker in his mouth.

"Nah. Just want to consult with Imre for a moment."

Imre got to his feet, his expression asking what was up. He followed her deeper into the copse of trees. He stuffed his hands into his duster pockets as he met up with her. "What's wrong?"

Makeda turned her back to Tojo and moved in close. She slid her hand around Imre's belt and pulled the multi-tool from it. "When were you going to reveal yourself?" she asked as she stuffed the tool in her pocket. She kept her voice low so it wouldn't carry to Tojo.

He gave her an uncertain look. "What do you mean?"

"Why would an experienced valet wear hiking boots on a luxury train? Unless he expected to go hiking." Imre started to pull his hands from his pockets, but Makeda shook her head. "No. Don't move." She held the Walther at her waist. "Let's talk."

Imre relaxed his arms and eyed the pistol with concern. His face went neutral.

"Merc, corpsec, or shadowrunner?" She watched his eyes. They cut away from her on the last word. Shadowrunner. Better than the other two. "Ah, a runner. Did you, your team, blow up the maglev track?"

"Makeda..."

"*Don't* lie to me. I know you want to, but this isn't the time or place." She kept her voice even, hiding just how angry she was. She wanted him to have been a good guy. Now, she had no idea what he was, except a possible, probable danger to her and to Tojo.

Imre hunched his shoulders. "I didn't cause the train wreck."

Makeda scowled at him.

"I didn't. I swear."

"But you are a shadowrunner. What do you want? Why did you insist on coming with me? Are you a danger to Tojo?"

"Makeda—"

"Don't 'Makeda' me. Just answer the damn question. What do you want with us?"

Imre glanced over her shoulder and blinked in surprise. "Frag."

The word was a whisper of shock, designed to make her look. She wasn't going to fall for it. She wished she could cock the Walther to make a point. The holdout pistol didn't need to be cocked. "Dammit, Imre, I—"

"Makeda!"

Tojo's shout of fear cut off the rest of her words. Makeda threw a glance over her shoulder then turned, her eyes going wide. Across the field, from the direction of Vasti's cabin, the biggest, angriest creature she'd ever seen was charging at them. It seemed they had entered Gregor's territory.

And he was pissed about it.

"Oh, frag me. Run!" Makeda didn't have to tell him twice. Tojo ran to her as fast as he could. When he got there, he clutched at her arm. She shook him off and pointed at the roof top. "Run there. Get inside that building. I don't care if it's locked. Break a window. Go now!" She shoved him in the right direction.

Tojo did as he was told and ran, his shoulder bag slamming into his hip as he went. Imre backed up, but didn't run. Makeda aimed her Walther at the charging monster.

If Gregor had been a troll before, he was a troll's troll now. At least three, three-and-a-half meters tall, his mottled skin was the color of dying moss—yellow green into dead brown—and covered with branches. The more she aimed, the more she realized that the tree branches and vines actually grew out of the creature's skin. Somehow, he'd merged with a tree.

"I don't think that's going to work." Imre took another step back.

"Might slow it down. Run. Get to the building. Vasti said that it doesn't like buildings." Makeda continued to aim, then fired as it opened its mouth to roar. She hoped she could hit the brain through its unarmored mouth.

The creature's roar died in its throat. It stopped, shook its head a couple of times, then roared. The sound had a slight watery tinge to it. Then it sprinted at them again.

Makeda ran. Imre was at her side. They burst out of the trees as Gregor crashed into them. On the other side, in a small valley next to several large boulders, was the building Makeda had glimpsed. It was an older barn, sun-bleached until the paint was almost gone. There were no windows on the lower floor and a couple of boarded-up windows in the upper floor.

Tojo fought with the barn door, trying to break the rusted chain wrapped around the door handles. He kicked at the chain with the hiking spikes and then slammed his shoulder into the doors, trying to open them enough to break the chain. The chain creaked and bent but did not break.

Makeda skidded to a stop near one of the boulders. "Get that door open!"

Imre hesitated before sprinting over to the barn to help Tojo.

Watching the mutated troll-thing charge toward them was like watching a car crash in slow motion. There was nothing you could do to stop it, and it felt like time stretched out a thousand years.

As soon as Makeda realized that the creature had been attracted by Imre's movement, she yelled, "Gregor! Over here! Come get some, you giant lump of a monster." She waved her arms and jumped.

It was the best she could think of off the top of her head. It wasn't cool, but it worked. Gregor swung toward her, and his charge slowed to a lumbering run. She aimed the Walther at one of Gregor's eyes. It was a big, muddy yellow thing that never seemed to blink. She fired once, shooting true. The eye winked out, and a bloody mess took its place as the mutant creature rushed her.

He swung huge arms at her head. With her reflexes reacting as they should, Makeda dodged and dodged again. Gregor's fist grazed her hair. Part of her waited to hear the sound of the door crashing open. With agility she didn't see coming, Gregor kicked the meaty part of her thigh. She sprawled against the boulder, then ducked a claw swipe that left marks on the stone.

Makeda dove away from the boulder, and Gregor followed. She stumbled and hit the ground hard, losing her gun. She rolled out of the way of Gregor's fist as it slammed the ground next to her head. She kicked his shin. It gave a loud *crack*, and he howled. She grabbed the multi-tool from her pocket, snapped open the knife, and stabbed him in the wrist as he punched where her head had just been. Gregor reared back with a yelp, holding up the injured limb with the knife still stuck in it.

Scrambling away from the monster, Makeda had the vague sense of Imre moving fast from the side—faster than an un-augmented human could. He leaped above her. She grabbed the Walther and turned over. Imre pulled a monofilament wire from his sleeve and jumped for Gregor. Then he garroted him, with his knees pressed to the mutated troll's back.

Makeda rolled to a stand and dodged Gregor's flailing arms as he tried to get Imre off of him, the weapon slicing into his throat. Gregor's mouth gaped wide, gasping for air as the garrote cut deep. Makeda aimed and shot the monster through the roof of his mouth. There was no exit wound.

Gregor stopped flailing. He stood there for a long moment, bleeding from the mouth, eye, and throat before crumpling to his knees and falling over sideways. Imre rode the creature to the ground and leaped off it with a graceful hop. Makeda stepped away from both of them as Imre reached over and grabbed his multi-tool, pulling it from the troll's wrist. He had to twist the tool to get it free.

She turned her back on both of them and quick-walked to the barn. The chain lay broken on the ground. Part of the barn door was splintered. She opened it wider and stepped within. Tojo stood towards the back, hugging his shoulder bag. "You all right?"

Tojo nodded. "A little bruised, but fine. The monster?"

"Dead. Let's go."

Imre walked inside the barn and stood near the door.

Makeda shook her head. "There's no way you can claim to be anything but a shadowrunner or corpsec after that little display. You're not coming with us." She shifted until she was between the two men, protecting one from the other.

"We're not done talking. I'm not corpsec, and we didn't blow up the track."

It was a subtle shift, but Imre's entire demeanor changed from polite solicitude to polite command. Makeda gestured to his feet. "Then why are you wearing hiking boots? You expected to be out in the countryside."

Imre glanced at his boots. "Yes. But in Lucern. We were going to get off the train then. Escape into the city. Make like we'd been kidnapped."

"We. How many of you?" Makeda held up the pistol. "Never mind. I don't want to know. I want you to back away. You don't need us, and we don't need you."

He raised his hands. "You're not going to make this easy, are you?"

"Not in my job description."

"I need a word with Tojo."

Makeda looked over her shoulder at her client. He looked terrified and confused. "Why?"

"I'm not asking for permission." Imre tilted his head in a listening pose. "No."

"No what?"

"No, don't shoot her right now." He nodded to Makeda's chest.

Makeda looked down. A red laser dot danced over her sternum. "You fraggin' son of a slitch." She wanted to say so much more, but didn't dare. The person on the other end of that red dot could take exception to her insults.

Imre shrugged. "That's what some say. In any case, I would put your pistol down before Fatima gets antsy. Put it on the ground and kick it to me. We just want to have a conversation with Tojo."

She did as she was told. "Tojo doesn't know anything. Why do you want to talk with him?"

"Because we need the data we paid for." He picked up the pistol and put it in one of the many duster pockets. "Come on in, everyone. Richter, you're on watch."

"But I gave it to your team." Tojo frowned. "At least, I think I did. I gave it to Beauty. I watched her take it out of the safe." He

JENNIFER BROZEK

looked at Makeda. "You know. You saw. Well, you didn't see. You were unconscious. But I told you. I did what I was supposed to do."

Makeda nodded, her hands still in the air. She knew all right. She knew they were both in deep drek. Tojo had in fact handed over the paydata, and he had no idea she stole it from Beauty. Accidentally stole it—of course, details like that don't matter a whole lot in the shadows. How the hell was she going to get them out of this one?

FOURTEEN

Three more people joined them inside the barn—two humans and an elf. The elf woman, Pongolyn, was a hacker. Fatima was a street samurai, from the amount of weapons she had on her, and Ollietronic seemed to be a fixer or face of some kind. He was constantly on the comms after Pongolyn gave him the all-clear with a personal signal booster. Though it seemed like he was doing a lot more virtual typing than talking. Even with the booster, the Matrix signal sucked hoop.

Fatima stood next to Imre and kept an HK 227-X trained on Makeda. The last of Imre's team, Richter9.0—"*Because I'll rock your world, baby!*"—was the huge troll from the Party Train. He patrolled the outside. They'd been polite and firm, separating Tojo from Makeda to talk to him.

Makeda sat apart from the rest with her back to one of the barn's support poles. They'd stripped her of her external gear and credsticks. She was lucky to keep her coat. Imre made sure he collected all of the nuyen. They made Tojo sit against another support beam. He'd also been stripped of all his gear and credsticks, leaving him in a sullen state.

While Imre's team talked and glanced at her or Tojo from time to time, Makeda subvocalized, "Galen, got a problem here. Come in."

Nothing.

She checked her e-mail. Two new e-mails had downloaded, with more in process. It seemed there was just enough signal here to get text through in sporadic bursts and not much else. Makeda locked down all of her accounts except one. She shifted until she could tap her fingers on her legs and bent her head to watch them. She didn't want anyone to see her get that faraway look of a person working on the net.

She typed out and sent Galen an e-mail. <*Imre is a runner. We're in trouble. More when I know.*> An error message popped up, saying that she was unable to send the e-mail right now.

Trying not to curse, Makeda hit send again and waited to see if the e-mail would send or be rejected. It was slow going. While she hit send again and again, trying to get the e-mail to go through on the scant signal in the area, she listened to Imre and Tojo talk.

Imre hunkered down next to Tojo as he gave the man's shoulder bag back. Tojo made a show of emptying it, then folding his clothing as neat as he could before putting it back in the bag. "Are you going to give me my nuyen back? I earned it."

Makeda could've laughed at the question. It was something a person who lived in the light would ask, not knowing how futile it would be. Imre's answer surprised her.

"Yes. Once you give us what we bought. We make a deal, we stick with it."

"But I gave you the codes. To Beauty. I watched her put it in her bag." Tojo hugged his shoulder bag again. It was an unconscious gesture of fear, trying to put something between him and Imre.

"See, here's the problem. I found Beauty—LaFroideur—unconscious and bruised in her sleeper suite. There had been a fight. Someone had tried to clean the room. It was a rushed job. I woke her up. Just as the train crashed, she discovered her credsticks and the codes were missing." Imre doodled in the dirt with a slender finger. "I'm going to need those codes again."

Tojo shook his head.

"I'm afraid, I'm going to have to insist."

"I can't give them to you now. I don't know them. I just downloaded them. I didn't memorize them. I did what I was supposed to do. You're the ones who messed it up." Tojo scowled. "I earned my money. I did what I was supposed to do." He repeated the words as if they were a spell that would make everything right again.

"We need them." Imre's voice was low and soothing.

"I can't give you the codes." Tojo started to stand. Imre pushed him back into his seated position. Tojo's face crumbled into something desperate. "I didn't keep a copy of them."

Imre's team shifted around them, looking more and more unfriendly.

Makeda knew she had to do something. Quick. She racked her brain for an idea.

Fatima shifted her submachine gun from Makeda to Tojo. "Why are we keeping him alive again?"

Bad cop, Makeda thought. *Maybe*, she added. Fatima seemed overeager to commit violence. She couldn't be sure it was a tag team of bad cop, good cop going on.

Imre raised a hand to calm her. "Because he's the man with what we need."

Makeda saw her chance. It was a slim one, but when you lived on the edge, it was all you needed. "No, he's not." She stood in a smooth motion keeping her hands out. "I'm the one who has what you want. And you're keeping Tojo alive because *I* need him alive.

Also, because he really did sell you the codes. Too bad LaFroideur couldn't keep hold of them. Where is she, by the way?"

The HK 227-X swiveled over to Makeda again. Fatima bared her teeth. "She's dead."

Makeda flicked a surprised glance at Imre and raised her hands higher. "Not by me. I left her asleep and unbound—as she did with me. Professional courtesy." That explained Fatima's want to hurt someone.

"It happened in the train wreck." Imre stood and stepped between Fatima and Makeda. He leaned to his teammate and muttered, "Let me deal with this. That's my job."

She gave him a glare that could've peeled paint from a wall before she stalked over to Pongolyn and Ollietronic.

A firewall warning popped up as someone tried to hack into her PAN. Thanks to TechnoGalen's programs, everything was immediately shut down, locked up, and put into private mode. Makeda scowled and pointed at Pongolyn. "You stop that right now. Otherwise there'll be no deal. No codes. No nothing."

The elf's expression didn't change, but she looked at Imre. Makeda waited. Everyone tilted their head or dropped their eyes to the ground in that listening pose. Imre stood between Makeda and the rest of his team. A quick confab, or argument, over their personal comm system ensued. She wished she could be a fly on the wall of it to gauge their mood. Though by the looks of it, it wasn't friendly.

Tojo watched everyone with a wary, stubborn eye Makeda didn't like, but understood. He even glared at her a couple of times, confused at her role in all this. She was his protector. She also had his codes, and he didn't know how she'd done it or why she hadn't told him about it.

Imre nodded and relaxed, satisfied with the results of the conversation. He gave her a half-smile and gestured for her to follow him. Makeda did, not looking at Tojo. She felt his eyes burning holes in her back as she and Imre walked to just outside the barn.

The clouds had rolled in dark grey and heavy. They promised rain. A lot of it. Makeda hoped they wouldn't be walking in it. The way things were going, they would. Probably chased by a bear to boot.

"I need to know, do you actually have the codes? Or are you just trying to keep your client alive?" Imre stared at her with those big, dark eyes under a messy fringe of mint-colored hair.

It was a ridiculous situation. She covered her mouth and tried not to laugh. His unstyled hair clashed with his sober manner. She felt like she was watching a telenova. His party-boy look conflicted with the very real danger he posed and thrilled her to her toes. Makeda couldn't help it. She wished she had a holo of this moment with him looking so somber and ridiculous at the same time.

"This is serious," he continued. "They want to cut their losses and run."

Makeda stopped laughing. She did not like the sound of that. "Meaning?"

"Meaning they want to put a bullet in each of you, take the nuyen we have, and go."

"You run with the kind of team that takes on wetwork?" She couldn't keep her distaste hidden.

Imre made a face. "No. I mean, we will if we have to, but no. Not generally."

"But shooting a couple of people in the back because of Beauty's dumb mistake is just fine?"

"LaFroideur." The correction was automatic. "You two get caught, and Tojo will crack. No doubts. We don't know about you. So, answer the fraggin' question. Do you actually have the codes? I'm trying to save your life here."

Makeda nodded. "Yes. As soon as I found them, I uploaded them to a very safe place. Then I destroyed the data chip disguised as a credstick. I'm the one who has what your team needs, and you won't get it if Tojo is hurt or killed."

Imre opened his mouth to speak. He stopped when she raised a single finger to his lips. "I'm not done. I'm going to help both of us. Give you the exact solution you need."

He gestured for her to continue.

"You want the codes. I want to get Tojo and me on my plane in Bern. I think your team escorting me and Tojo to the Bern airport is a suitable payment for a copy of the codes, don't you think? Also, we—me and Tojo—get our credsticks back."

"How do I know you aren't lying to me?"

Makeda locked eyes with him and knew she'd already won. Just like she hadn't wanted to kill him, he didn't want to kill her. He believed her and would believe her until she stabbed him in the back—something she did not plan on doing. At least, not yet.

"You don't. But, that's life in the shadows, Imre. You know that. You also know I helped you out of the train wreck. I didn't hurt B—LaFroideur—I'm sorry about her, though. I liked her when she wasn't tranqing, punching, or robbing me. Also, I didn't shoot you the multiple times I could have, and I'm not lying to you. I do have your codes. I know what they're worth."

Imre shoved his hands in his duster pockets. He was quiet for a long time as he scanned the horizon. At one point, he got that faraway look of being on his comms. Then he shrugged and focused on Makeda again. "A full copy of the codes in exchange for an escort to the Bern airport."

"We get our credsticks and gear back."

"And your gear back."

She put her hands on her hips. "And our credsticks."

Imre grimaced. "Yes, but not the one with 242,500 on it nuyen. The one with 100,000 nuyen on it, like I originally bargained for. Tojo gets his, too. I am a man of my word."

It was better than she expected. She'd been prepared to lose some of the nuyen. Makeda knew they must really need those codes, or have a hell of a lot of money on the line to make the deal. Her thought that the codes could be worth millions must be correct. Makeda made a show of thinking about his compromise for a count of twenty before she nodded. "Since I don't have to pay for a seat for you on the plane or get you an alt ID, deal."

He stuck out his hand. "Deal."

The two of them shook on it. Imre handed her two certified credsticks. Each displayed 100,000 nuyen on them. "We were going to Bern airport anyway. What's a couple more people?"

Makeda shrugged. "Then it all works out. I'll need a private, secure way to contact you. The real you. Not the 'Imre' you. You're the only one I'll give a copy of the codes to. Since I know what they're worth, I'm keeping a copy for my own use."

"Imre is me." Imre took his comms off private mode. "I'll need the same from you."

She shook her head. "I'm not opening myself up again. Not after the drek your hacker pulled."

"Like yours wouldn't have done the same thing." He shook his head, thought for a moment, then dug out his datapad. "Write it down."

Makeda gave him her secured contact information and paused as he wrote out his for her. She memorized it. "'Rabenhaupt'? What does that mean?"

Imre eyed her, looking for the joke.

She shook her head. "I don't know German. I know Spanish and Italian. When I'm in the civilized world, I use skillsofts or a translator app. Both are in short supply right now."

"Raven's head. It's like the head of a household." Imre shrugged.

"Ah. Right. I'll remember that. Shall we tell your team that we're working together now?"

"Technically, you two are our clients. You *are* paying us to escort you to the Bern airport after all. Thus, we are not working together."

"I—"

The rest of what Makeda had to say was lost to Richter's surprised, "What the hell?" and Gregor's furious roar.

FIFTEEN

Still bloody from Imre's garrote and Makeda's pistol shots, the mutant troll threw himself at Richter. Makeda saw his re-grown eye—as yellow as before but now ringed with gore—and she groped for a weapon she didn't have. Richter got a three-round burst off from his HK MP-5 TX before Gregor was on top of him, bowling him over.

Imre's entire team boiled out of the barn, weapons ready. No one fired as Gregor and Richter wrestled. It was too easy to hit the wrong troll.

Tojo hurried to Makeda's side. "Now's our chance." He grabbed her arm and pulled.

She pulled back. "Chance for?"

"To escape."

Makeda shook her head. "No need. I've just made a deal with Imre. They're going to escort us to the Bern airport."

Tojo looked at her as if she'd grown another head. "Have you lost your senses? You can't trust them."

"We can. Would you rather have them hunting us or protecting us?" She gestured to the heavily armed group.

"I don't want either. I just want to get away. They'll kill us."

Makeda shook her head, keeping her voice low and patient. This was not how she wanted to deal with her extraction clients. Next time, friendly or not, she swore she'd drug them until they got to the hand-off. "I've got what they want. They won't hurt me or you because of it."

He scowled. "We need to talk about that, too."

She watched the trolls punch each other. "No. We don't. You were right, once the codes left your hands, they were no longer your business."

"But you knew about the codes. You stole them from Beauty."

She grimaced as Richter took a hard punch to the face. "Only after you told me about them. It was an opportunity, and I took it."

"But—"

Makeda cut Tojo off with a sharp gesture. "*Enough*. This isn't a discussion. They're going to escort us to Bern, and that's that."

Tojo winced as if she'd slapped him. He whirled and stomped back into the barn. Makeda continued to watch the fight, wishing she had a weapon.

Richter threw Gregor off of him. Every member of Imre's team fired at almost the same time. The air filled with the echoes of gunfire that lasted a couple seconds after the shooting stopped. This time, after the mutant troll hit the dirt, Imre used his monofilament garrote to sever Gregor's head from his body. "Regenerate from that. I dare you."

Richter, bleeding from the nose and mouth, kicked his enemy's head away. "Boss, I need five to get patched up."

Imre nodded. "Fatima, on patrol."

The Arabic woman shifted her weapons to a more comfortable carrying stance. She headed towards the other side of the barn. As she passed, Makeda raised a hand to stop her. "Got an extra pistol for me?"

Fatima blinked at her. "What? You've got to be kidding. "

"I need a weapon. We're working together now. Better to have me working than not." Makeda pointed at Gregor's body. "That's a perfect example."

Fatima gave Imre a questioning look. Then shrugged at whatever he comm'd to her. "All right." She pulled a Colt America L36 from an inner sheath. "Can you use this?"

Makeda nodded, familiar with the weapon. "Yep."

"I'll give you the holster when I'm off patrol." Fatima shook her head. "You got nerves, woman."

"Nerves of steel and brains of tofu, my team tells me." Fatima didn't look back, but Makeda caught the edge of the woman's smile.

As she walked back into the barn to Tojo's side, Makeda checked to make sure that the light pistol was loaded. It was. Eleven bullets in the magazine. Tojo watched her, frowning. Makeda sighed and gestured to Imre's team. "It's not perfect, but I'd rather have this group of runners on my side. Wouldn't you?"

Tojo shrugged. "I see what you mean. I just don't like it." His face settled into discontent as he watched their new protectors.

Makeda shifted the pistol to her jacket then handed him his credstick. "You like it better now?"

Tojo smiled, his face lighting up with surprise and pleasure. "Yeah. I guess." He stuffed it into his pants pocket. "How...? Never mind. I don't want to know."

"Know what?" Imre asked as he walked up.

Tojo looked away. Makeda half-shrugged. "He doesn't want to know about the shadows. It's better that way. He's got a life in the light to return to."

Imre clapped Tojo on the shoulder. "You've got the right of it. We'll get you to the Bern airport. Makeda will get you to your new home."

Tojo nodded then moved away from them. He found a comfortable spot to sit and all but collapsed to the ground. Imre and Makeda watched him for a couple of seconds before glancing at each other. They quickly found other things to look at.

Makeda watched Pongolyn manipulate her commlink and curse at her booster. She climbed to the top of a boulder and lifted a collapsible pole into the air. Watching the hacker balance the device in one hand and the pole with the other was amusing. Pongolyn cursed aloud. Makeda caught the phrases, "...drek signal..." and "...stupid wireless world..." before she focused on the other two runners. Imre stared at them as well.

"How's your man?"

Richter was being patched up by Ollietronic. The troll's skin purpled in bruises on his face, neck, and biceps. Ollietronic had sewn up and bandaged the troll's neck. He worked on the claw marks across Richter's shoulder.

"He'll live. He's taken worse. Soon as we get to Bern, we'll get him healed." Imre shook his head. "We're lucky that's all that happened."

"Yeah. Vasti said Gregor had a hate on for other trolls." Imre looked like he wanted to ask questions, but he kept his mouth shut. They stood there in an uncomfortable silence until Makeda couldn't stand it. "So, now what?"

A large raindrop splatted to the ground next to them, followed by another and another. Imre muttered in German under his breath. "It looks like we stay put until the rain passes."

As he spoke, Pongolyn, Ollietronic, and Richter came inside the barn. A couple moments later, Fatima, moving at double time, reappeared and entered. Imre gestured for Makeda to go toward the unoccupied corner before he followed. She waited for him. "And after the rain?"

"We walk until we find a decent signal and call for a cab." He smiled at her. "Or until we find a major road. We've got a plane waiting for us at the airport."

Makeda wondered how big the Bern airport was if the city was, as Vasti said, only a "tarted-up jenny." She'd look it up when she got a signal. But only when she was sure Pongolyn was distracted. She didn't want another hacking attempt on her. "We've got the same."

It wasn't a complete lie. Still, she wanted him to know that she wasn't alone, that she had people waiting for her. Makeda watched his expression. Imre had a good poker face when he wanted it. She could tell he added the detail to his plans, but not much more.

They both settled to the ground, sitting cross-legged, at the same time. Makeda tilted her head. "Can I ask you a question?"

Imre smiled. "You just did."

Makeda rolled her eyes. "A bunch of questions?"

"Yeah."

"What did you think of me when you first saw me in the Party Train lounge?" She watched his face carefully, looking for reactions and clues. Now that she knew for sure that he was a shadowrunner, she wanted to know how much he thought like her—or didn't.

Imre tilted his head, a smile playing about his lips. "I thought, 'There's my perfect cover for getting on the train. She's so beautiful, no one will look at me twice.' It was true, too. Everyone watched you."

"And when the alarm went off?"

He didn't say anything for a couple of moments, just picked at the fabric of his duster. "You always wonder if you've been made on a run, but I didn't think it was me. It was the first time I wondered if you were who you said you were. An heiress who helps orphanages? Not really that believable."

Makeda nodded. "Based on a true story of an heiress from about five years ago." She leaned against the barn wall and listened to the rain come down in buckets. "But you weren't really scared about your cover? Was any of the casino story you told Tojo true?"

They both looked across the barn to where Tojo sat propped up against a support beam. He had his eyes closed and looked like he was asleep. Makeda was sure he wasn't.

"Yes. It was. In my much younger years. It's what prompted me to leave the life of a gilded cage for one made of shadows. It's easy to keep a SIN running when it was once real."

The answer came out quick and smooth. That made it suspicious. Makeda wasn't certain Imre told her the exact truth, but it was enough for now.

The mini-storm was short and fierce. It left the clean smell of rain and wet grass behind as the sun peeked out of the leftover clouds. Most of the mountain was still in shadow, but the afternoon was mild and pleasant. The group of them walked with an eager step, each of them looking forward to their separate destinations.

Richter scouted ahead. Fatima took the rearguard position. The rest walked together in a clump. Ollietronic and Pongolyn in front of Tojo. Makeda and Imre behind. This appeared to be the general travel order they did; street samurais in guard positions, hacker, fixer, and face in the middle.

Makeda took the time to watch the other team in action. Most of their communication was silent, comm chatter or hand signals she didn't understand but noticed. It was very much like her and her team on a run. A mixture of communication styles that kept everyone on the inside informed and everyone on the outside in the dark.

It was clear that Ollietronic and Pongolyn were a couple. They even looked a bit like each other despite their different races: pale skin, green eyes, brown hair. None of the rest of Imre's team were romantically involved with each other. Though all of them deferred to him. Imre ran the op from start to finish, with each of the rest fixed in their team roles.

"How long have you been running with this crew?" Makeda kept her voice low but not secretive.

"Long enough to know we're a good team." Imre kept his head on a swivel.

It was the same thing she'd done when she was escorting them. Now that the shoe was on the other foot, it was interesting to watch Imre take on the mantle of responsibility. "I understand that."

"You been in Europe long?"

Makeda recognized the heading-off of runner questions at the pass and shook her head. She didn't blame him. She wouldn't tell a client anything important about her team, either. "A few weeks. Had the right background for this one, and I wanted a vacation from... home." This, of course, was a complete lie. She'd spent the last couple of years in France and Belgium under various names.

This last year had been the hardest, after losing her lover and partner in Belgium. She grimaced and shoved thoughts of Zaria—that laughing, beautiful elf—away. She'd thought too much of the woman these past couple of days. The reminder of a paradise lost drained her of her curiosity about Imre and his team.

"How do you like it?"

"Other than the train wreck, running, screaming, and mutant trolls? Just fine." She gestured to the land. "Beautiful countryside I never really wanted to stroll through." *Especially not in fashion boots.* They'd been fine for a short hike, but now were shifting over into painful territory.

"Ah."

They lapsed into silence. Makeda forced herself out of her head. She refused to think about Zaria or the mission gone wrong or the elf's disappearance. Instead, she focused on the features around her. The dirt path that was more goat trail than road. Flowering fields. Random boulders. Small groups of trees. Green flashes in the sky.

Makeda blinked a couple of times and looked up. The clouds weren't any thicker, but the sun hid its face, and a chill had crept into the air. She stopped walking. At the same time, Imre and the rest of his team did, too. Tojo was the only one who stuttered to a stop a couple of moments after everyone else.

"Richter's spotted a house." Imre tilted his head. "It seems occupied." He lapsed into silence.

Makeda didn't respond. She stared hard at the sky and hill behind Fatima as the samurai caught up to them. Green flashes winked in and out of existence, and a green fog rolled out of the hills. "Maybe it's the city girl in me talking, but I'm really sure that fog isn't supposed to be green. Also, isn't the aurora borealis only at night?"

Imre and Fatima turned to see what Makeda was looking at. "Oh, frag me," Fatima muttered. "What's that?"

Makeda touched Imre's arm. "Mana storm? Is that what a mana storm looks like?" She zoomed in on it with her cybereyes. Things changed as the fog touched them. Foliage curled in on itself before opening up again, twisted and wrong. As far away as the fog was, it seemed to have weight and moved far too fast. She backed up on instinct. "The fog is changing things. I don't want that touching me."

"Whatever it is, we don't want it touching any of us. Move!" Imre didn't need to tell anyone twice. As one, they ran in the direction Richter had taken. Makeda stuck next to Tojo. If there was a house, it might be a safe place. She wasn't sure. A quick glance over her shoulder made her grab Tojo's arm and run faster. The fog seemed to chase them like a thing possessed. It would be on them in minutes.

As soon as Makeda crested the hill, she saw the house Richter found. It was a strange thing, twice the size of Vasti's cabin, and laid out like a long house. It had two chimneys—one in the middle and one at the end—a row of small windows with two of them lit, and the whole thing was covered in vines that looked like evenly spaced out ivy. The plants were too regular to be anything other than cultivated. Rain barrels sat below the two back corners of the roof.

Surrounding the house was a neat, groomed lawn about thirty meters in diameter. There was a wind turbine to the south and solar panels to the east. All of this was enclosed by a high, white picket fence about two meters tall. Those same evenly spaced vines covered the fence. A stone path traveled from the front door of the house to where Richter stood at a high archway in the fence.

Once he saw his team sprinting toward him and the fast-moving green fog beyond, he stepped through the arch to get to the house, only to have the vines come alive and wrap themselves about him. Makeda heard his curse from where she was. Guardian vines. What the hell were guardian vines doing out here in the middle of the alps?

Ollietronic got to Richter first with a knife out to free him. Pongolyn, Makeda, and Tojo sprinted past him into the yard, with Fatima and Imre stopping to help. There was no time for polite knocking. Pongolyn threw open the door. Makeda yanked her out of the way of an expected shotgun blast. Behind them, the group at the gate gave a collective sound of pain.

Inside the doorway stood the two oldest people Makeda had ever seen. The short man waved the rifle at her while the tiny woman readied another arcane blast. Makeda did the only thing she could do: She jumped on them.

The three of them crashed to the ground. Makeda yanked the shotgun from the old man and shouted, "Mana storm!" She slapped at the woman's hands as they began to glow again, then pointed out the door, "Mana storm!"

Pongolyn appeared in the doorway. "*Magie sturm. Wir werden alle sterben.*"

Her words and calm voice had an immediate effect on them. The woman struggled to her feet and shoved her way to the door. She looked out and waved a wrinkled hand at the vines. They stopped trying to kill everyone and returned to their place. "*Schnell rennen. Schnell!*"

As Makeda helped the little old man up, keeping the rifle in hand, Pongolyn yelled, "Run!" She moved out of the way as her team pounded up the stone walkway. She shifted the old woman out of the way as well. Once everyone was inside, the old woman untied the vines from either side of the doorway and let them hang free. She closed the door and turned back to the mob milling in her house.

Makeda stepped forward with her hands raised in a calming gesture. She smile what she hoped was a reassuring smile. Before she could say anything, though, Imre touched her shoulder and shook his head. "Let Ollie do his job."

He drew her away from the woman as Ollietronic stepped up and spoke in German and offered a hand to her. She dimpled at him as he bowed over her hand, then escorted her to her husband's side.

Imre herded everyone except Ollietronic and the old couple into the sitting room. Makeda acquiesced enough to stand in the wide doorway of the room and watched the trio sit in the kitchen. Imre stood next to her. "Ollie is very good at talking to everyone. He'll fix things."

Makeda nodded. The sitting room was a lovely throwback to an age where acquaintances were invited into the parlor and not the home. Roomy and pleasant with stylized cityscapes on the walls, it had plenty of places to sit with small tables next to the couch, loveseat, and overstuffed chairs. This was a room for temporary visitors.

Tojo took off his hiking spikes and put them in his shoulder bag. He leaned back against the softness of the chair and closed his eyes with a sigh. For a moment, Makeda envied him his innocence. The ability to relax in a stranger's home was a skill she'd lost a long time ago.

Raised voices in the kitchen drew her attention back to Ollietronic and the couple. Imre shifted next to her and smiled. "What is it?" she asked,

He tilted his head close to hers. "They're bickering about whose turn it was to feed the plants and who was supposed to keep up on when the mana storm was supposed to come. She, Nora, says that it was Nils turn. He is sure that she's right, but that she always looks after him. So he's not to blame for forgetting."

Ignoring the sudden pain of remembered arguments that pierced her heart, Makeda nodded. "So, we're all right?"

"Yes, I believe so. The Zumthors think we're a rescue party for people from the train. The fact that Tojo's already asleep is going to help with that." Imre glanced at the sleeping man and then returned his attention to the kitchen. "They're going to get a small reward for helping us evade the mana storm, and they forgive us for barging in like we did. The fact that Richter waited outside the yard for so long, waiting for us, convinced them we aren't brigands."

"Brigands?" Makeda smiled at the word. "Brigands," she repeated, letting it roll around in her mouth. "I haven't heard that word used in conversation ever."

Imre winked at her. "Loose translation." He straightened as the trio stood and Ollietronic led the old couple to the sitting room. Pongolyn woke Tojo as they entered.

"Ladies and gentlemen, may I introduce you to our hosts, Nora and Nils Zumthor." Ollietronic gestured to the old human couple. "Long time retirees from Celltec Bioengineering, they apologize for reacting so badly. It isn't everyday a heavily armed group bursts through their door."

There was a choir of greetings. Then Ollietronic went around the room, introducing everyone by name. Everyone stood and either shook hands or bowed as they were introduced.

"Celltec Bioengineering. That explains the guardian vines. Wonder what else they've got here." Makeda made a mental note not to touch anything growing in or around the house.

"Don't know, but I do know they are very old school. No Matrix connection except for a computer, and that only works when it's sunny. At least, that's what Nils said."

Makeda gave him a look. "No Matrix? How do they survive?"

"That has yet to be determined. Though they seem very happy here."

The mana storm lasted well into the night. Nils checked the glowing moss that edged the fence. As long as it glowed, there was magic out there, and it wasn't safe to leave. During that time, Nora cooked a simple dinner of sausages and potatoes for everyone and refused help of any kind—not with the cooking, serving, clearing, or cleaning. Aged or not, this was her home and she could manage it, *thankyouverymuch.*

It was a fine meal. Ollietronic kept a pleasant conversation going with Imre chiming in from time to time. Though Makeda got the impression a lot was being said over the comms. It made her miss her own team all the more. She needed to get in contact with them—especially since circumstances had changed so drastically.

After the meal, Nora showed the women the guest room and told them that the men could sleep in the parlor room. There was a certain grandmotherly quality in the way she wished them a good night and shut the door with a firm *click*.

They looked at each other with big grins that faded into silence. The guest room had a couch, a bed, two end tables, a dresser, and a closet stuffed with boxes.

Makeda sat on the couch. "I know where I'm sleeping. You two get the bed."

Fatima and Pongolyn looked at each other and nodded. Fatima took off the weapons she still had on her and placed them on the dresser. Pongolyn dropped her backpack next to the bed and pulled out her commlink and the booster. She gazed at Makeda for a long, frank moment as her hands set up augmented reality overlays... AROs...that only she could see, in an automatic fashion.

"I never did thank you for keeping me from being shot. Especially after me hacking your PAN."

Fatima looked up, surprised. She didn't say anything. She just listened.

Makeda shrugged. "We're on the same side. We weren't then. We are now. Circumstances change."

Pongolyn and Fatima exchanged a glance. The elf nodded. "Yes. Circumstances change, and thank you for keeping me from getting shot."

"You're welcome."

Silence descended again, broken up by Pongolyn's almost silent movements and Fatima's restless checking and rechecking of her guns. Fatima dropped to the floor and opened up a cleaning kit. She picked up the smallest of her weapons and examined it.

Makeda watched Fatima's automatic movement of stripping the pistol down to its parts and examining each one before cleaning it. "What happened out by the fence? I heard you all get hit with something."

"Stun spell. Hit us all at once. Reminds me of a concussive grenade. No shrapnel. All pain." Fatima set the Fichetti Security 600 to the side. "It weakened the vines a little. Gave the rest of us a headache."

Pongolyn jumped with a small whoop. "I did it. It's not much, but I've got a signal. And I got word to the rest that we'll be coming in tomorrow." She paused. "You want to contact your team? I'll give you a temp password to the booster. No funny business. Promise. You're paying us for protection. That means from us, too."

Fatima smiled, tight-lipped, into the pistol she was cleaning.

Makeda hesitated. She wanted to. She needed to. With the Zumthors willing to ferry them to Bern, the timeline was shifted. Either they needed a pick up tomorrow, or they needed to find a place to stay. Makeda had to get a message out to Galen and to Vasti. She eyed Pongolyn. Trust was in short supply. Still, she nodded. "Let me get a couple of messages ready."

She would get online just long enough to get the messages out, then shut everything down again. She typed out the quick message to Galen—*Situation changed. Will be in Bern tomorrow with an escort. I'm on the bike.* To Vasti, she wrote: *I owe you nuyen. I'll make good our agreement when I've got a stable connection.*

Makeda marveled at how tempestuous this run had been. Then again, a run could be like that. Stabbed in the back and running for your life from those you thought were friends to relying on the kindness of strangers to get you through to the other side.

Still, this run wasn't over until Tojo was handed off to his new corporate masters, whomever they were. There were still many kilometers and obstacles to go. Getting to Bern was just one more leg of the journey.

SIXTEEN

Nils may have been an eighty-year-old man, but he drove like a drag racer down the mountain goat trail. It was the one time having eight people crammed into an SUV worked. Makeda was thankful that none of them could move to be bounced around the vehicle. Except for Richter. The poor guy bounced his head against the roof every couple of seconds. He finally put his hand on his head to protect it, saying bruised knuckles were better than a cracked head.

This, and the fact that the Zumthors had been so kind and helpful, kept everyone from suggesting they steal the SUV from Nils. Ollietronic had spun a tale of forthcoming travel that had nothing to do with the Bern airport, which meant that when the authorities eventually caught up to Nils and Nora, they'd tell the story Ollie wanted them to tell.

Getting back to the wireless world was a relief Makeda couldn't express. Everyone seemed to feel it. Even Tojo, who had lapsed into a sullen silence she didn't want to understand, perked up. Makeda kept her headware in private mode and was able to get a message back from Galen that included all of the appropriate code words and the promise that the team was ready, waiting, and loaded for dragon.

Once Nils dropped them off, looking askance at the seedy part of town, Makeda and Imre stepped to the side and watched him drive away. The rest of the team stretched and worked the kinks out of their bodies. Tojo hovered nearby, scanning his datapad. Makeda scanned to see who had open PANs. No one in their group—which was what she wanted. Especially Tojo.

"Nice couple. Too old to be a danger when people come looking for us." Imre gave Richter and Ollietronic a head nod. "We'll rent or buy a van big enough for all of us."

"My hacker says me and Tojo need to be at the Bern airport at 1500 hours. No sooner. No later. Means we have about a five minute window to be there. I'm guessing whatever flight plan he's got is scheduled to leave at 1500, and it'll be a close thing. Either way, he's gone dark for the duration. I'm not sure why. I trust he knows what he's doing, and it's needed. There may be a sniffer out there looking for me. Probably is."

"We'll get you there on time. Safe and sound."

She glanced at him. "As soon as we're on the plane, I'll e-mail you your payment."

Imre nodded. "And then I'm going on an actual vacation."

"What's that?" Makeda laughed. "No such thing."

Tojo stepped up to them and touched Makeda's arm. "We're listed among the missing. They think we've been kidnapped."

Makeda and Imre gave each other a look. She took the datapad and scanned the news article. Fifty-nine people dead, one hundred and seventy-two injured. Twelve still in the hospital and not expected to make it. Six people still missing. She scanned the pictures of the six. It included both her and Tojo as well as the Saeder-Krupp executive she saw early on, a pair of elven siblings, and another American heir.

"How come you aren't listed here?" She frowned. "They seem pretty thorough."

Imre pointed to the American heir. "I put my Party Train band on him. He was dead. Head and face caved in."

"Isn't that going to throw suspicion for this whole thing on you?"

He shrugged. "Probably. But they'll be looking for a mint-haired casino worker."

She glanced at his mint mop. It had looked so good on the Party Train. It would still look good styled. Though, right now, it looked terrible and clashed with his dirty clothing. "It does stand out. But, they're not looking for it right now."

"Exactly."

Tojo reached over and swiped to the left. "There's more." He pointed to a paragraph near the end of the article. "I know of this guy. He's not in PR. He's in one of those divisions you just don't talk about."

Makeda read the paragraph aloud. "'*Ralph Petry, Saeder-Krupp PR representative, had this to say about the missing S-K personnel. "You must understand, Saeder-Krupp is a huge company with many subsidiaries. The two Saeder-Krupp employees had nothing to do with each other. We do not believe this was an attack on our company. That said, we are doing everything we can to find Tojo Isoshi and Aki Nakamura and bring them home." Mr. Petry would not state what resources the company was using to rescue their people.*'"

She looked down the street as she considered this. "Do you think the train attack was meant to capture Aki Nakamura?" There were people walking about. After the isolation of the mountains, this many people made her nervous. None of them were openly armed. Some walked like they were. It made her glad that she had her back to a wall and Fatima as obvious muscle.

The two men shrugged. "Maybe. I can have Pongolyn take a look around the Matrix for rumors." Imre frowned. "But really, it's none of our business."

Makeda nodded. "Point conceded. Just curious." But even though she conceded, she couldn't get the idea out of her head that Aki Nakamura's disappearance was somehow linked. She just didn't know how. She gave herself a mental shake. It was her lack of control again, looking to make patterns and conspiracies where there were none.

A beat-up van trundled toward them. Makeda stepped between Tojo and it, her hand in her jacket. It stopped a couple of meters away. Ollietronic opened the sliding door and jumped out.

Pongolyn said what they were all thinking. "*This* is our ride?"

Grinning, Ollietronic nodded. "No one would suspect it."

"That's because no one in their right mind would ride in it."

Richter clambered out of the driver's seat. "She's better than she seems. Besides, it's temporary, and it fits all of us. No one's going to look sideways at it except to sneer. That's what we wanted."

Pongolyn shrugged. "If you say so."

Makeda relaxed and checked the time. "Well, we have a couple of hours until we need to be there. Now what?"

"Food. I'm hungry." Richter looked at everyone as they blinked at him. "What? Look. Bern airport, or *Flughafen Bern* as it's called, is *tiny*. It's got all of one airstrip and parking for maybe four planes. We're gonna drive up to one end, they're gonna walk a hundred meters to their plane," he gestured to Tojo and Makeda, "then we're gonna wait five minutes while our plane taxis in. If Pongo gets on the comms with our guy, we can have them line the two planes up and take off two minutes later instead of ten. Okay?"

Everyone stared at him. Makeda wondered when he'd researched the Bern airport. She decided it would be one of those mysteries she'd never know. It also made her wish he was on her team.

"Okay. I'll comm our pilot." Pongolyn got that same faraway look she had when she was on the comms.

Richter scowled. "It's handled. Now, I'm gonna go find the Bern equivalent of a Stuffer Shack. Anyone want anything?"

It was as good of a plan as any. There was literally nothing Makeda could do to improve on it, especially with Galen in radio silence mode. He knew the other team was flying out from the same place. With Pongo's warning to their pilot, Saladin could line up the planes. She trusted him to do what needed doing.

Also, you ate when you could on a run, because you never knew when or where your next meal was coming from. So, food it was. "Shmoozies and a FantaZack. Or whatever they have that seems closest." Makeda glanced the question at Tojo. He shrugged. She nodded. "Times two, Richter. Thanks."

Makeda regretted her snack choice more and more as they drove toward the airport. Her stomach roiled and sloshed with every turn of the ramshackle van. She hunched deep within her armored jacket, grateful for its roominess and warmth. The van rattled like it was on its last legs, but Ollietronic and Richter assured everyone that it was stable enough to get them where they needed to go.

When they stopped at last, Makeda was second out of the van after Fatima. The street samurai scowled at her. "Next time, you wait until I give the all clear."

Bent over and breathing in slow, deep breaths, Makeda only thought the words, *"There won't be a next time. We're done here."* She nodded. "Sorry. Motion sick." Straightening, she looked around.

The Bern airport really was tiny. They were parked at the southeast end of the airstrip. There were small buildings between the official parking lot and where they stood. A single private plane sat, ready to go. As soon as they pulled up, it started its engines in pre-flight readiness.

Pongolyn and Ollietronic walked around the van. She had all her gear stowed in her backpack. "That's our plane." Pongolyn looked at Makeda. "Where's yours? Why are they late?" Ollietronic kept walking.

Makeda checked the time. 14:59. "They should be here." As she debated over whether or not to poke TechnoGalen for an ETA, two large SUVs arrived with a screech of tires. They stopped one hundred and twenty meters away. Men and women in Saeder-Krupp corpsec uniforms came tumbling out of the vehicles.

Ollietronic, halfway between the van and the plane, had no cover. He took off running toward the plane and was shot. He crumpled to the tarmac as everyone took cover.

Pongolyn pulled two pistols and fired. Her smartlink made sure she didn't miss. Two of the guards went down.

15:00.

Makeda grabbed Tojo and pulled him behind the van's back tires. They were next to Imre. He lay on the ground, firing at the enemy from beneath the van. Before she could say anything, her comms came alive.

"Coming in hot. Get to the chopper. Down in sixty seconds."

Makeda had never been so relieved. "Under fire. Corpsec. If you're armed for dragon, use it." All around her, weapons were fired. Pongolyn fired two more times, and two more of the corpsec guards went down, headshot. The beaten-up van would never drive again.

There was a pause. *"Acknowledged. Where are you?"*

"Grey van, south end."

"Make a run for us as soon as we get there."

Pongolyn holstered her weapons. She looked at Imre. He nodded to her before firing a rapid set of three-round bursts in covering fire. Pongolyn sprinted to Ollietronic. He was still moving, but blood was everywhere. She picked him up and kept going, running to the plane.

"Acknowledged. I'll have Tojo ready." Makeda looked at her client. He had his shoulder bag clutched to him and his eyes shut tight as he hunkered next to them. "The helicopter coming in is mine."

A large silver-and-black helicopter with no markings came in fast. The side door was open. Makeda could see HiddenPlath and Obscura tethered to keep them from taking a header out the door.

"Mana wall coming in." That was Obscura, her mage.

"Keep your head low." That was HiddenPlath, her street samurai.

She wanted to leap for joy. Her team was here. Makeda saw the Gatling gun seconds before its unmistakable sound split the air. Weapons fire from the Saeder-Krupp side of things paused as corpsec personnel dove for cover. A moment later, the SK rifles started up again, this time focused on the helicopter as it landed.

Imre rolled to his feet, dropping an empty magazine and ramming another in his pistol. "I'll escort you two, running interference." He raised his voice. "Fatima, Richter, evac!"

Makeda nodded. She grabbed Tojo and yanked him to his feet. He blinked at her with wild eyes filled with fear. She pointed at the helicopter landing near the plane. "When I say go, you run. You get to the chopper as fast as you can. Your life depends on it. Do you understand?"

He gazed at her with those fear-filled eyes and winced at the roar of the Gatling gun.

She shook him. "Do you understand? Tojo!"

"Run to the chopper." His voice was very calm. "Run when you tell me."

The helicopter touched down.

Obscura took a bullet to the head. The glowing wall between the helicopter and the Saeder-Krupp people disappeared.

Makeda sucked it a breath and watched her friend fall backward into darkness. She grabbed Tojo and turned him to face the helicopter. "Get ready."

Richter's back exploded. He stumbled but kept going.

Fatima backpedaled behind him, firing her HK 227-X until it ran out of bullets. She pulled the next weapon in her arsenal, an Ingram Smartgun XI.

HiddenPlath screamed as the meaty part of her thigh exploded, but she kept firing the Gatling gun.

"Run!" Makeda shoved Tojo forward. She followed, keeping her body between the enemy and her client. Imre did the same for her.

Out of the corner of her eye, she saw Fatima shove the troll up the short stair and into the plane.

Imre continued to lay down covering fire as Tojo scrambled aboard the helicopter. Makeda looked at the plane. Fatima was in the doorway. She waved the street samurai off and grabbed Imre. "Get in. You won't make it to the plane. Do it."

He nodded and shoved Makeda into the chopper, following suit. Galen, keeping an eye on things, shut the door and took off hard, sending the helicopter straight up into the air.

"I thought we weren't going to have an extra passenger." Galen sounded irritated.

"I don't know what he is. But he wouldn't have made it back to the plane." Makeda mentally shrugged. "We have an extra person. I need to figure out what to do with him."

"Think quick. I don't like an armed stranger in my helicopter."

"Stay calm."

Saladin, watching Makeda as he followed the conversation over the comms, slapped a patch on HiddenPlath's leg. The ork let out a half-gasp before relaxing. Saladin moved to the downed Japanese woman, checking her over just to be sure.

Makeda reached over and took Imre's Fichetti off him. She locked eyes with him as she did.

Imre didn't argue. He did furrow his brow. "Am I a prisoner?"

"No. Not yet, at least." Makeda shrugged. "Host's prerogative. You're a stranger in his vehicle. He's uncomfortable."

"Can't argue with that. May I become a client?" Imre moved his hand slowly up to his breast pocket. He tapped the credstick there. "Escape from a hostile country?" He gave her a half-smile.

Makeda returned it. "What's your life worth?"

Saladin covered Obscura's face with a tarp, then answered for him, "50,000 nuyen." His voice was flat with anger and grief.

That same grief slapped at Makeda, trying to overwhelm her. She forced it away. At least one of them had to stay calm, and it had to be her. Makeda looked between Saladin and HiddenPlath. The ork nodded, her lips pressed together in a thin white line. When she spoke, her voice was rough from the suppressed emotion. "I'm gonna need new 'ware after this."

"Concur," Galen said over the comms.

Imre looked at Saladin's face. "Agreed. 50,000. Right here. Right now. You get me to a safe place that isn't in the middle of nowhere. And if I can choose, I'd like Spain." He slid two fingers into his inner pocket and pulled out his credstick. He handed it to Makeda.

Saladin handed Makeda a credstick reader. She transferred the 50,000 nuyen. "Done. Welcome to being my client, Mr. Dahl."

"Please, I prefer Imre or Rabenhaupt."

Before she could respond, Galen's voice erupted over the comms again. *"Makeda what in the fragging hoop of a hoser are you doing wearing a Saeder-Krupp corpsec jacket? What is this, amateur hour, or are your hormones beating the drek out of your survival instinct?"*

SEVENTEEN

The team's reaction was immediate. HiddenPlath grabbed a pistol and held it at the ready. Saladin's head snapped to Makeda. "Where'd you get that?" He gestured to the jacket. At the same time, he subvocalized, "What's wrong with the jacket, Galen?"

"It's a Saeder-Krupp corpsec armored jacket."

"So?" Makeda spoke aloud, ignoring Imre's quizzical look. She pulled everything out of the jacket before she shucked it off.

The helicopter's side door slid open. HiddenPlath held onto her tether. "What the drek, Galen?"

"Throw it out. Now."

Makeda did as she was told, grabbing HiddenPlath's tether to keep from going out after it. Plath grabbed her wrist to keep her steady. As soon as Makeda dropped the jacket, watching it spin in the air, the helicopter's side door slid shut. She shifted back into a steadied stance before sitting down again. "Right. Now what's the big deal?"

"A lot of Saeder-Krupp corpsec jackets have trackers in them. Like the one on your bracelet. It's not well known, and it's a very narrow band."

"Well, that explains why they were there at the airport to meet us." Makeda scowled. "They knew where we were the whole time. At least, in theory."

Imre looked between Saladin and Makeda. "What does? My team was discreet. We didn't trip any alarms." He grimaced, then admitted, "Not that I know of. Don't lay this on my team."

Makeda shook her head and gestured to the side of the helicopter. "The jacket. Apparently Saeder-Krupp tracks their personnel."

"That's new." Imre frowned. "Why didn't they jump us up in the mountains?"

The pilot chair turned around, revealing it to be a wheelchair and the short Hawaiian man within. He was jacked into the chopper through the chair. "Two reasons. One, that costs money. You were headed toward them anyway. Why spend the resources? Two, there was no signal out there to get. You need to be close to that kind of tracker. Without wireless, drones are damn near useless for communication. They'd go out, find you, come back, report your position, but by then, you would have moved on."

Makeda smiled wide and got to her feet. She gave Galen a hug. "How'd you get here? I thought you were...," she glanced at Imre, "... at home."

"Not when you needed rescuing."

"My hero." She sobered. "Seriously though, how are we going to get out of here? Switzerland isn't the best at letting people in and out."

TechnoGalen shook his head. "Took care of it. At least in the short term. Got all the proper everything. Plus, we aren't in the chopper for long." He looked around the vehicle through his cybereyes. "But I'm gonna miss her."

"I don't want to know what all this cost, do I?"

"No. But you will. You've got to chip in."

Makeda had a sudden realization and looked around. "Where's Tojo?"

"You mean my sleeping co-pilot?" Galen pointed at the other chair.

Makeda craned her head to see. Tojo was curled up in the chair, hugging his shoulder bag. He wore headphones and a white patch on his neck. "What happened?"

Saladin gestured for Imre to move to one of the side seats and came forward. "I grabbed him as soon as he came in. Put him in my seat. He was freaking out. Didn't need him doing that. Besides, I'm sure he needed the sleep."

"And the headset?"

"I've got those turned off. It's mostly to muffle the sound. He'll sleep until we switch to a plane." Galen shrugged. "Did what we needed to."

Makeda nodded and looked back at the covered body. "How much time do we have?" This time, her grief would not be denied. She turned her head, blinking away the tears that sprang forth, unwanted but there nonetheless.

"Enough for you to send word and stuff." Galen patted her hand and turned back to the cockpit.

Saladin and HiddenPlath sat together. He checked on her wound and grimaced. She grimaced, too. The two of them put their heads together, speaking over a private comm.

Makeda knelt next to Obscura's body with her back to the rest. She let the tears come, silent messages of a painful good-bye. Then she smiled, helpless to do anything else as she thought of the dirty jokes Obscura would whisper to her from time to time. The woman was—*had been*—sharp. A good member of the team. She'd also wanted out of the shadows. That's partly what this run was for her—her last.

"In more ways than one," Makeda whispered. She pulled back the tarp and gazed at the small Japanese mage. A single shot to the head. It was the golden rule of a fight in the shadows: *Geek the mage first.* Makeda removed all jewelry, fetishes, and identification from Obscura's body. When there was nothing left but her clothing, Makeda covered Obscura up again and tied the tarp around her like a shroud.

"Galen, we got a plan for bodies?" Makeda didn't have one. She kept the question to a private channel. When you ran the shadows, you assumed you'd be victorious. To do otherwise was a fast death. You needed to believe you were immortal. The run may suck, but you would survive.

"I can ask when we get to where we're going. I also have instructions for what to do with her things."

"Thanks."

Makeda patted the tarp-wrapped body once and wiped her face. Then she returned to her seat next to Imre and sighed.

"How long did you run with her?" He kept his voice low and respectful.

"Long enough. She was a good one." Makeda leaned against the hard metal of the chopper wall. "She was my queen of No. No, you can't see us. No, you can't hear us. No, you can't shoot us. I'm going to miss her. She was a trustworthy team member, but..." Makeda sighed, "we weren't really close."

It was a lie, of course. The lie about her personal life was an automatic thing. Obscura had been a friend. They had gone shopping together and drinking together, and they had bled together. They hadn't been lovers, but they had been friends. That was something Makeda could admit to herself, even if she refused to admit it to Imre. Part of her wished Obscura had been a lover. Lovers were easier to leave behind than friends. Lovers always left. Real friends didn't. At least, not in her heart.

"Close in the shadows is dangerous." Imre leaned forward on his elbows and gazed at his hands. They were silent for a few long moments. Then he straightened up. "We have a transaction to finish, you and I. I got you to your ride."

"Ah. Yes." Makeda packaged up the elevator maintenance codes and encrypted them before she e-mailed the lot to his secured account, knowing Galen had their connection locked down tight. "You have mail. Passive acceptance only, please. Nothing out for the moment. Passphrase is #1Ghoul. Pound sign, number 1, capital G."

Imre gazed at his hands for a long time. "Got it. Thanks."

She deleted the copy of the codes she had in temporary storage, keeping the encrypted copy in her protected folder. "I'm keeping my copy. We'll be using them. For now we don't plan to sell them. Or, if we do, only one at a time."

"No use glutting the market."

"Or letting people know we have them." Makeda shifted toward him, reached out a hand, and raised his chin so their eyes met. She turned the gesture into a caress. "I gotta ask, who hired you to get the codes? I need to know if it's the same guy who hired me to do the extraction."

"Herr Schmidt. German. White male. Blond. Clean cut. Aryan wet dream, really." His lip wrinkled into a sneer.

"Sounds like him." Makeda nodded. It wasn't anything she hadn't already known. This was just for confirmation. Do your due diligence.

Imre glanced at Saladin and HiddenPlath with their heads together. "I wonder if he hired out a third job that ended up with the tracks blown."

"I don't know, but something's not right with this guy. You don't do two runs on the same target in the same location without telling the other team unless..." She shook her head. "I don't know. Unless you want it to go wrong."

"I want to know why he didn't just have you get the codes from Tojo. That would've been the smarter decision. Probably cheaper, too." Imre let his gaze drop to the tarp-wrapped body for a second. "Why two teams?"

"Don't know. I do know that after I get Tojo to his drop point, I'm washing my hands of this particular Johnson." Makeda looked out the front window of the helicopter as it started to dip. "Either way, you and I are even."

"I actually think I owe you one." Imre gave her a soft smile. "Not officially. I've paid dearly for this ride. But, in general. I think you've earned that much. I mean, I wouldn't have thought to stay in the helicopter. Doing so probably saved my team time. Maybe saved my life."

Makeda watched him out of the corner of her eye. "Thanks. Not sure I'm going to ever use it. I think I'll go home, take a break, and figure out what's next."

"Take a vacation? No such thing in the shadows." He smiled then shrugged. "As you will. You know how to get in contact with me."

The two of them lapsed into silence. A few minutes later, the helicopter landed in a grassy field next to a private landing strip. It was a well-maintained, paved airstrip in the middle of the boonies. It was also used a lot by the locals if the large plane garages lined up on either side of the smooth tarmac was any indication. The fact that it was a paved strip instead of dirt said that this was a serious set of flyers with a decent amount of money to spend.

Makeda suspected that this airstrip was used for a lot more than hobby flying. She transferred 10,000 nuyen to each of the surviving members of her team. She kept Obscura's share to see who the woman left behind. Galen would give her the details when they had a chance to grieve in private and settle Obscura's affairs properly.

As TechnoGalen motored down the ramp and out of the helicopter to the waiting dwarf, Makeda peeled the sleep patch from Tojo's neck and removed the headset. She tapped his face as she shoved the sleep patch into her pocket. "Wake up, *nemu-sōna hito.* We're switching to a plane. Wake up."

Tojo blinked his eyes open. "What happened?"

"You went to sleep. You got into the helicopter and checked out."

He sat up, looking around. His eyes hardened. "Did you drug me?"

"Nope." It was the truth. *She* hadn't drugged him. "Sometimes, when things are stressful, clients just shut down." Makeda shrugged, making it a casual gesture. She knew that trust was broken, and she wasn't going to get it back in a day. Then again, she was all he had. "It happens. Don't worry about it. You needed the sleep." She helped him out of the helicopter.

"You know, this has been different. And exciting. But, I kinda hate it. When will we get there?" Tojo's brave façade crumbled into something tired and worn.

Makeda patted his shoulder, thankful it'd taken this long for him to get to the "are we there yet" stage. This was why she liked to keep most extraction clients drugged to the gills until she handed them off to their new corporate masters. "Not long. A flight to Spain. A meeting with your final transport guy, and then you'll be there."

She had no idea if she was lying or not. That was the scheduled plan. Get to Málaga, make contact, drop Tojo off, and get paid. She had told him the truth as she knew it. Then again, plans had an unfortunate habit of dropping by the wayside when the shadows and corps were involved. Not that he needed to know that. Ignorance was bliss.

"Okay. That's good. Really good." Tojo looked up as Imre approached. "I'll be home soon," he told him. "I'll have some stories to tell my new friends."

"Yeah? Nice to hear." Imre turned to Makeda. "Can I comm out from here?"

She shook her head. "Best not. Wait until we're in Spain. I'd rather we be as far from here as we plan to get."

"All right. My message can wait." Imre eyed the two rows of plane garages. "I just wanted to make sure everyone made it out."

"I don't want to sound callous, but—" Makeda glanced down at her scuffed boots, "—that news can wait. If they didn't, they won't be looking for your call. If they did, happy news keeps."

Imre didn't say anything for a long moment. He stared at the airplane garages. It looked like he was counting them. "Point conceded. I wonder what it costs to live up here...wherever this is."

Makeda scanned the garages. Thirty in all, by her quick count. "More than I have for the moment. Maybe someday, but not right now."

TechnoGalen left the dwarf's side and beckoned Makeda over. She hunkered down to be on the same eye-level with him. "What's up?"

"My friend, ah, Herr Keller, said that he'll take care of the body. No charge. Though Plath bleeding all over the place is an extra cleaning charge."

Makeda sighed. "We've got the nuyen, and we're still going to come out in the black. Especially with the bulk of the payment coming when we get to Spain." She hoped she wasn't fooling herself with her optimism.

"He also asked me to take care of his jet. He pulled out the pilot seat to fit me and my chair. I think he's trying to sell her to me, and considers this a test drive." Galen dimpled at her, wrinkles creasing his tanned skin around his eyes. "I think he wants to buy something newer and shinier. Don't blame him. There's always something newer and shinier to buy."

"What you do with your nuyen is your own business. Mine is dealing with Herr Schmidt once we get to Spain."

"Let's hope we don't get the same welcome there that we got in Bern." Galen spun his wheelchair around and rolled to "Herr Keller."

"From your lips..." Makeda glanced at Imre and Tojo. She would be glad to see the back of Tojo. She smiled to herself. She'd always be glad to see Imre's backside—from an aesthetic point of view.

Her smile disappeared. She hoped their arrival in Málaga was as boring as boring could be. Then again, the most dangerous part of a run was the final hand-off. It was the last chance for betrayal, and more than one corporate Johnson had tried to take advantage of it. Herr Schmidt seemed to be that type. Makeda narrowed her eyes. She'd just have to make sure that didn't happen.

EIGHTEEN

"When we get to Málaga, I'm just dropping you off." Galen had a tired, boneless look to him as he leaned back in his wheelchair. He was jacked into the small jet, flying it without looking at the main instrument panel on a physical level. He focused on Makeda, intent on being heard. "I need to get home. Things have been weird on this run. Also, I know the new mage, MissTree, has a hacker lined up for you. That's what Plath told me."

"They won't be as good as you, but I understand. I don't blame you." Makeda stared out the cockpit window. "This one has backstab and double-cross written all over it." She took a breath. "I'll get paid—we'll get paid—when I drop Tojo off. Should be within a day of us getting to Spain. I'll wire you your share."

Galen didn't say anything for a long time. Makeda thought he looked like he'd fallen asleep. She knew that wasn't the case. Sometimes though, he moved inward and forgot there was a meat body conversation going on. If there was more to say, he'd comm it to her. She got up to return to the back of the plane when he grabbed her hand. "I got a bad feeling about this one. Maybe not drop him off?"

She raised an eyebrow. "And do what with him? He's not cut out for the shadows." Makeda shook her head. "I don't want to babysit him for the rest of my life. He's got a cushy corp job waiting for him. He can go back to being a happy, oblivious salaryman. He's looking forward to it."

"How do you know?"

"He told me." Makeda sighed. "He's had enough adventure for one lifetime."

Galen tapped her wrist. "You be real careful with the drop off. I don't trust this."

"Neither do I. But that's life in the shadows."

He squeezed her hand. "I'm serious."

"I'll be super careful. Promise." She squeezed his small hand. "You fly home safe. Ping me when you touch down. Yeah?"

"Yeah."

Makeda stretched as much as she could in the small plane. Pausing in the doorway between the cockpit and the cabin, she gazed at her charges. Imre looked like he was asleep, but he had his eyes cracked just enough to give himself away. Tojo was asleep again. A real one this time. Saladin bent to check on HiddenPlath's wound. She slapped his hand away from her leg without opening her eyes.

"Status?" Saladin asked over the comms.

HiddenPlath blinked a couple of times and turned her eyes to Makeda.

"As planned, though TechnoGalen is going back to Belgium after dropping us off in Spain. We'll have to find a different way home." She paused before asking, "Anyone want to join him?"

Saladin shook his head.

"You need me. I'm not as bad off as this worrywart thinks I am." HiddenPlath touched the wound in her thigh. *"MissTree will heal me as soon as we get there."*

Makeda glanced at Tojo. "Right. Then the plan sticks. We go to the haven MissTree set up, and I'll contact Herr Schmidt to get a drop off point."

She hadn't met the prospective new healer yet, but Makeda appreciated the language play in her name. She also appreciated the fact that HiddenPlath trusted the woman so much. Plath was shy around new people and gregarious with her team. You wouldn't think an ork could be shy, but you would be wrong. They had their quirks just like everyone else. It was why she'd been quiet for most of the trip. Tojo was nothing more than a package and Imre, well, he could be many things. Part of the team wasn't one of them.

"You gonna interview MissTree for the next job?" This came over the general team comms.

Plath really must like the healer. Makeda nodded. "Yes. No worries. As soon as Tojo is handed off, we can have dinner together."

"It's been a while," Saladin chimed in. *"All work and no play."*

"Awww. And I'm gonna miss it." TechnoGalen bounced a frowny face through the general comm.

"Nah." Makeda erased the frowny face and replaced it with a smiling one. "Just ride with me. You can be my roll-buddy."

"Har-har."

Imre beckoned to Makeda.

"Back on the clock." The group sobered as she headed over to Imre and sat. "What's up?"

"Got an ETA on when we'll land?" He didn't look her in the face. Instead, he watched his hands.

"Forty minutes. Five to taxi," Galen supplied.

"Forty-five, fifty minutes on the outside." Makeda tilted her head, watching him. "Why?"

Imre looked out the jet window. "I need to inform my team and get a status update. I still want to know if everyone made it."

Makeda had forgotten that Imre didn't know who was alive, dead, captured, or free on his team. He'd been a lot more patient than she would've been. She would've been climbing the walls. Though, she did hold the cards here. It paid for him to be patient, even if he was at his patience's end. "All right. Can you do an e-mail burst? Or do you need a sustained chat?"

"E-mail is fine. Nothing's come in, but I haven't forced the sync."

"I've got everything obfuscated, routed, and bouncing."

"Galen's got you covered. Just try to keep everything to a minimum. I think we're fine, but with this run, better safe than sorry."

"You sound like me to my team."

The two of them exchanged a knowing smirk. "Just because you're paranoid doesn't mean they're not out to get you. In this particular case, we both know they're out to get me. Maybe you. I'm not sure." She paused before she added, "I'd change my hair color if I were you. You stand out."

Imre flushed. "Top of the list. It worked great on the Party Train. Perfect camouflage. The only thing everyone's going to remember is the mint color of my hair, and nothing else."

More than that, you beautiful man. She didn't say what she thought. Best to leave that inside for now. "When you get an answer from your team, let me know. My thought is once the plane is down, we part ways. If I need to get you out of the *Aeropuerto de Málaga*, tell me."

"You won't. It's a smaller airport. Just tell your pilot to taxi to the southwest end. There are vehicle pull-ins near there."

"You tell him not to teach his grandmother to suck eggs."

Makeda hid her smile at Galen's annoyance by rubbing her mouth and subvocalized, "I'm fine with the southwest end if MissTree is."

"Already planned. Stupid meat body trying to tell the rigger what to do. It's not like I haven't done this before."

"He's helping." Makeda couldn't stop her smile. She turned her head to hide it and watched the front of the plane.

"Tell him knock it off. This isn't his team."

He had a point. Makeda glanced at Imre over her shoulder. "Galen has things in hand."

Imre nodded, a half-smile struggled to the surface. "I'm sure he does. No disrespect."

"I'm sure there's none taken."

"Says you." Despite his words, Galen sounded mollified.

"Hush." Makeda leaned back and closed her eyes.

Landing was smooth and on target. Makeda stretched and yawned, feeling rested and ready for what was next. She reached over and shook Tojo's knee to wake him, then ignored his momentary panic. "What? What? We're here?"

"We're in Spain. Wake up. We've got to move."

HiddenPlath and Saladin exited the plane first and then gave the all clear. Makeda gestured for Imre to disembark.

He paused at the stairs. "There's a limo coming. Please don't attack it." Turning, he took Makeda's hand in his. "I do owe you one. You may not think so, but I do. If you need anything, you contact me. You've got the details."

She squeezed his hand before letting go, her face guarded. "Maybe dinner or a run in the future. But not until after this one's done and a distant memory."

"Agreed. I'll see you sometime."

They stopped and watched the limo pull up next to MissTree's SUV. Saladin nodded to Fatima as she got out of the luxury vehicle. She waved Imre down. Makeda watched Imre disappear into the limo and leave before she beckoned Tojo to come forth.

"Your kind of guy?" Tojo tilted his head. He seemed curious and interested.

Makeda shrugged. "Sometimes."

"He seemed like a nice enough guy when he wasn't taking my money from me."

She shook her head. There was no way to respond to that without insulting the drek out of her client. "C'mon. Galen needs to get this plane home."

"Every minute you two chat is another nuyen into the radio tower's pocket."

Makeda didn't need to be told twice. She led Tojo down the stairs and over to her waiting team. Plath gestured to the small dark-haired woman in the driver's seat. "MissTree, this is Makeda."

The woman wore a sharp, red suit jacket, a white blouse, and a pair of jeans. She screamed corporate casual chic in smart glasses. She also had a couple of blue, swirled tattoos peeking out from her collar and her cuffs. "A pleasure. We should go before someone gets irritated." She spoke with a pleasant French accent.

Makeda nodded at the woman's words "Of course. Business later."

Everyone piled into the SUV. Makeda kept an eye on the roads and tensed at the chaotic driving. Tojo winced and closed his eyes. Makeda wondered if she should slap patch him again. After one near miss, she wanted to slap patch herself.

"You can relax. I can sense danger to the car. I'm following the normal pattern of local driving. No hidden enemies. If someone targets the car, I will know immediately." MissTree's voice was cheerful as she wove her way in and out of the heavy traffic.

<No one intends to crash.> Makeda sent this over her private chat to Saladin.

<Go boneless. It's what I'm doing. Better chance of survival.> Saladin's text message was filled with broken glass and an exaggerated amount of blood.

Makeda knew he was making fun of her. She made brief eye contact with MissTree in the rear-view mirror. "Thank you." She hoped things worked out with the mage. They were invaluable team members, but sometimes hard to work with. "I need a safe place to call Herr Schmidt."

HiddenPlath looked over her shoulder. "It's already set up. We have a private hotel. I gave MissTree the details on what we needed."

"We will be there in twenty minutes. You may make any calls you need."

"There's a good chance we'll have to immediately go out again." Makeda watched Plath as she spoke to MissTree. From the way the ork gazed at the French woman and the smile on her lips, there was a much better than even chance that Plath and MissTree were already an item. It made Makeda hope all the more that MissTree worked out. Such joys were few in their line of work.

"Also expected." MissTree glanced at HiddenPlath. "Though, I would ask that we fix all wounds before we meet with Herr Schmidt or whomever he sends. No good looking like you've already been run through the ringer."

Plath turned around and gave Makeda a look. It wasn't a threat. More protective and a warning. She wasn't sure that Plath realized she was doing it. Makeda noted it for future teasing. "How much time do you need?"

A message popped up in a private chat from Saladin. <Don't push her too hard.>

<Who? Plath or Tree?>

<Both. Rough day.>

<You'll have to tell me later.> Makeda nodded at Saladin.

"Depends on who's hurt. I'll need at least ten minutes for Sylvia. That thigh wound looks like hell." MissTree swerved around a truck parked in the street and blared her horn.

Saladin and Makeda exchanged grins. Sylvia, was it? "You'll have it," Makeda said, clutching the "Oh drek" bar. She refused to close her eyes. If she was going to die, she was going to do it knowing what was coming.

"Oh Plath......'I dreamed that you bewitched me into bed / And sung me moon-struck, kissed me quite insane.' Isn't that how it goes?" Saladin grinned wide.

HiddenPlath threw a glare at Saladin's private teasing. "Shut up."

"Yes. It is. 'I think I made you up inside my head.'" Saladin continued quoting "Mad Girl's Love Song" by Sylvia Plath—HiddenPlath's favorite poet.

Makeda smiled. It was good to be in a safe enough place to be able to joke about a teammate's love life. This was what she'd been missing the entire time she'd been cut off from her team. Her smile faded. Perhaps that's why she hadn't caught onto Imre until it was too late. She relied on her team to keep things light. She'd been too comfortable with him.

This was a personal flaw she would have to examine later. As Imre said, close in the shadows was dangerous.

The hotel was a square two-story building with a protected inner courtyard. MissTree parked in the back and led them through hallways covered with tiled mosaics filled with vibrant colors. No one peeked out of doorways as they passed by in a parade of non-local clothing, armament, and dried blood.

Makeda wondered if the set up included a bath and a fresh change of clothes. The ones she wore were stiff with sweat and dirt. Even Tojo had quite the scent about him. They'd all showered, but their clothing had not.

"How long do we have this place?" Makeda sent the private comm to HiddenPlath.

"We have the top floor for the next two days. Then we need to move again."

"All right. Tell MissTree she's got the time she needs to heal everyone. I want a shower and clean clothes. Or at least a quick dash through some water."

HiddenPlath dropped back to walk with her, leaving MissTree to lead the way. Saladin stuck next to Tojo. *"It may not fit exactly, but there's some clothes to wear and hot water. MissTree likes her comforts as much as you do."* Plath elbowed Makeda with a smile on her face. One tusk stuck out at a rakish angle.

Makeda looked down at herself. Mud-spattered boots, torn and dirty pants, borrowed linen blouse. God knew what her hair looked like. Probably sticking out in every direction. It's not like Vasti had hair gel for her to use. Fortunately for her, natural, kinky curls looked good in every direction. "She going to be able to deal with days in the field, with dirt and muck?"

Plath nodded, face going neutral. "Yes. Though, we don't usually end up with one of us trekking through the Swiss Alps."

"No kidding. Not something I want to do again."

MissTree stopped at the end of the hallway. One side overlooked the inner courtyard with a small fountain, some growing green plants, metal benches, and a blue tiled floor. The other side of the hallway had four doors.

She pointed to the closer doors. "We have these four rooms. The other four rooms on the other side of the top floor are empty and are paid to stay that way. Communal baths and washrooms are at either end of the hallway. Women here. Men down there."

She handed room keys to Makeda, Saladin, and HiddenPlath. "I had to guess at your sizes. Luckily, Sylvia gave me a good estimate. Here's a room key and I'll bring what I have for you."

The others disappeared into their rooms as Makeda eyed the old-fashioned metal key. A tag hung from it emblazoned with "9" on one side. It was the first door. She couldn't help but notice it was the same room number as the one she had on the train. She hoped like hell there wouldn't be a similar end to her stay here.

Tojo shifted from foot to foot, watching with an anxious eye.

Makeda suppressed a sigh. "C'mon." She beckoned him over.

She unlocked the door and took a quick look inside before she let Tojo in. It was a single, simple room without even a closet. A bed with a wooden chair for a night stand were against the far wall. A dresser and a mirror stood against the wall opposite the door. A small couch and a low table sat opposite the bed. Small, functional, and absolutely no place to hide.

Tojo walked in and looked around before sitting on the bed. "Now what?"

Makeda sat on the couch. "You're nervous. What's up?"

He shrugged.

"You sure?" She shifted as if to get up and go.

"I...I don't know. I just..." He gestured helplessly. "New people I don't know."

Ah. Imre's fake friendship and betrayal. "*I* know them. These are *my* people. You can trust them to do right by you." She wasn't sure on MissTree, yet. He didn't need to know that.

"You're sure?"

Tojo's eyes begged for something she would not give him—emotional comfort. This time, she stood and walked to the door. "I'm positive. Very positive. This is my team. You're safe. I promise. Everything is going to be fine." It was the best she would do.

Tojo nodded. "Okay." He bobbed his head in a bow. "Thank you."

"You're welcome. She opened the door and spoke to the group comm. "Saladin, you're on client watch. I need a shower. Hell, *he* needs a shower. Babysit him in there."

"You don't want to?"

"No. I want some alone time. I need to prep myself for the conversation with Herr Schmidt." That was an unspoken request to give her ten minutes alone.

All teasing left his voice. *"On my way."*

She remained in the doorway. "Now, I'm going to get cleaned up, and Saladin is going to protect you."

"Protect me? Aren't we safe here?" He furrowed his brow.

Makeda knew Tojo didn't want her to leave. She hoped he would get used to disappointment. "Think of Saladin as your escort. Or valet. You're very important to us. He'll get you set." As soon as Saladin reappeared, Makeda turned on her heel and escaped to the baths.

The communal bathroom was broken out into three areas: a changing room, showers, and a tub and sitting area. It had two shower stalls and a large tub that would take forever to fill. Makeda opted for the shower and promised herself a soak after all this was done. For now, the alone time was enough. The ability to hand over a client to one of her team and trust he would be taken care of was a relief after days of depending on only herself.

Getting spoiled by the wireless world.

Makeda acknowledged the thought. *Why not? I've paid my dues. I've been an experienced runner for a while now.*

Prime runners die in the shadows as easily as baby runners do. It just takes them longer.

She scowled and hated the ruthless survivor side of her. Her internal argument was headed off at the pass by the sound of the bath door opening. She turned the shower head toward the wall and grabbed the Colt from her pile of dirty clothes. Then she waited behind the shower curtain.

"Makeda?"

It was MissTree. Makeda didn't lower her pistol. "Yes?"

"I have clothes for you. Where do you want me to put them?"

"In the dressing area is fine." She tracked the other woman's movement through the baths. A pause in the dressing area. A pause in the shower area.

"One other thing. When you are ready, we can have that call. I have a hacker standing by. Come to room twelve."

"That's good. Thank you. I'll be there soon." Makeda listened for movement. MissTree stayed where she was. "Is there anything else?"

"Yes." MissTree hesitated. "How bad will this get?"

Makeda wanted to laugh. She didn't. "It could be a cake run, or it could be a nightmare. I don't see an in-between. Is there a reason you're asking?"

"Yes, but I will wait until you are out of your shower."

That was not what Makeda wanted to hear. When a mage said she had a reason for such a question, it probably wasn't a good one. "All right. Give me ten minutes."

Makeda listened to the mage leave. She sighed. So much for a relaxing shower.

NINETEEN

Makeda let everyone know that she was going to call Herr Schmidt and they should be ready to move at a moment's notice if it all went bad.

She tossed her dirty clothing into her room, then stopped. There was nothing of hers in the room except for her dirty clothes on the bed next to the backpack Vasti gave her. She opened the bag. Not much in it. An empty water bottle, a magazine for her Colt, an unopened MRE, and a half-empty package of Buzzbuzz caffeine chews. She had everything else important on her.

Taking a breath, she took stock and set herself: Tojo was still with Saladin and didn't need anything. Plath was resting in her room after being healed. MissTree was waiting for her in room twelve. Galen was on his way home. Obscura...Obscura didn't need anything anymore. Makeda looked at herself in the mirror as she refused to think more along that vein of thought.

It felt good to be in clean clothes, and MissTree did a decent job. Their outfits were almost identical, though the jacket was a burnt-orange color, not as corporate, and filled with pockets. Makeda made do with her boots. Dirty or not, they were still functional and fashionable enough to not stand out in the heat.

Makeda nodded to her reflection. She looked calm, cool, and collected. Perfect for a call with Herr Schmidt. It was time.

She knocked on room twelve. MissTree opened the door and let her in. The hotel room was exactly the same as the one Makeda had been assigned, though it had more hardware. An actual old-time computer, attached to some peripherals Makeda couldn't identify, sat on the low table along with a headset and extra batteries.

"The public grid is nice, but not secure at all." MissTree gestured for Makeda to sit on the floor. "So we use our own." As soon as Makeda was comfortable, MissTree set up a curved rack behind her and hung a red brocade curtain. It made it look like Makeda was in a tent. "We also don't want anyone to know where we are."

Makeda nodded. "Smart."

"Not my first run." The mage half-smiled at her. "But we can talk about that later."

Makeda kept her face neutral. Inside, she was pleased at the precautions and the way MissTree used every interaction as an interview for joining the team. It made Makeda wonder what the mage was like when she was relaxed. That was a question for HiddenPlath. "Yes. But, before we do this call, there is something you want to tell me?"

MissTree slowed her movements. "I have...a couple of my spirit friends sense danger about all this. Forthcoming danger."

"More than normal?"

"More than normal. They don't usually natter at me. But something bad is going to happen, and soon. I think I should be there on the drop. Just in case."

Makeda *hmm*ed in a non-committal manner. "Let me think about it." She watched the mage, gauging her reaction. But MissTree seemed calm; her message had been given. It was back to business.

"Everything is set up. I'll ping my friend."

"Your friend?"

MissTree gave her a polite smile. "My hacker friend. They wish to remain anonymous."

Makeda narrowed her eyes. "Can they be discreet?"

"I'd bet my life on it."

"Good. I guess you are coming to the drop." Makeda understood MissTree's hesitance to give her the hacker's name. Trust was earned in the shadows, and you didn't just give out a name without someone's permission. Still, she didn't like not knowing who was running the wires behind the scene.

The two women locked eyes for a long moment before MissTree nodded. "Ready to connect?"

Makeda nodded. She pulled up the comm program and pinged Herr Schmidt with: *One fish, two fish.* She watched the cursor blink, settling into a cool, professional mode. When then the response came back: *I don't like blue,* Makeda accepted the incoming call.

Herr Schmidt appeared in all his blue-eyed, blond-haired glory. With his impeccable suit and cleft chin, Makeda thought Imre was right. The man really was the Aryan wet dream.

He smiled a killing smile. "*Frau Makeda, Wie geht es Ihnen?*"

"You know I don't speak German, Herr Schmidt." This was a lie. Makeda had taken the time to download a skillsoft package of Romance languages while she was in the shower. But it was better to be underestimated.

He made an attempt at an apologetic expression. "Ah. Let me begin again. Hello, Frau Makeda. I trust you traveled well?"

Makeda nodded. "I'm in Málaga and ready to drop off your package. I need the address."

Herr Schmidt leaned back. "There's some talk on the news of the train wreck. You are missing. So is my package. There are search parties out looking for you both."

"You didn't happen to have anything to do with the train wreck, did you? I know you had a lot of work happening during the party."

His eyes hardened. "We all have work to do. First, I need—as you say—proof of life. The Captain will be paying you upon delivery. I need to know my package is alive."

"One moment." Makeda turned from the screen and covered her mouth as she subvocalized. "Saladin, bring Tojo here. Tell him not to say anything and not to knock over the backdrop. He's just to wave to Herr Schmidt."

"Acknowledged."

Makeda turned back to the laptop. "He's coming."

The two of them stared at each other through the screen. Someone off to the side spoke in German. Text appeared to the side of Herr Schmidt's face. Makeda kept her surprise concealed.

The signal is obfuscated. I can't tell if it's coming from Spain or not.

Herr Schmidt nodded to his left, pursing his lips.

"All is well?" Makeda leaned forward.

"Yes. Yes. A man's work is never done."

MissTree opened the door at the knock. Saladin and Tojo stood there. Tojo looked much more relaxed now that he was cleaned up and had rested. His hair was combed, and he wore a loose blue tunic and matching pants. Saladin gestured Tojo inside and remained in the doorway.

Tojo gave the backdrop curtain a look, then shrugged. He knelt next to the low table and leaned in so he could see Herr Schmidt and be seen. The blond man nodded to Tojo. *"Kon'nichiwa, Isoshi-san. Daijōbudesuka?"*

Tojo nodded and bowed. *"Hai, Schmidt-sama."* He glanced at Makeda. She nodded. *"Ie ni suru junbi ga dekimashita."*

"Sugu ni."

As they spoke, the English translation appeared on the screen:
Hello Isoshi-san. Are you OK?
Yes, Schmidt-sama. Ready to be home.
Soon.

Tojo gave Makeda a questioning look. She returned it with a bland, pleasant smile. "That will be all, Tojo." He bowed to her and backed up. Saladin was there to escort him back to the hotel room.

"Enough proof of life for you? Your package is safe, sound, and secure."

"Yes. I'm sending you the time and place of the drop. Captain Harrak will pay you the remainder of your fee upon delivery. Do not be late."

"We won't be. Thank you."

As soon as the file finished uploading, Herr Schmidt cut the connection without a good-bye.

Makeda leaned back as MissTree removed the backdrop. "I like your hacker. The translations helped."

"I didn't realize the conversation would be in multiple languages. As soon as you said you didn't speak German, I had my friend translate everything that wasn't English." MissTree shrugged. "I figured you wouldn't mind."

"Nope." Makeda looked at the delivered file for the information on the drop. An hour from now. Not much time. "Málaga Marina. What do you know about this location?"

MissTree shook her head. "Not too much. It's not far from here and in the better end of town. Rich tourists. I know a lot of discreet business happens there. I know there are some good vantage points where you can watch the piers if you have the right equipment. I've not done business there myself. I know some who have." She smiled. "I've heard that no one ever *sees* anything that happens there."

"An hour isn't much time." Makeda considered. "Right. You and HiddenPlath will provide cover for me and Tojo. Saladin will operate." She tapped her lip. "I'll talk to Saladin about the specifics. He'll loop you into the internal comms."

MissTree nodded. "As you wish."

The drop point was a pier on the far end of the Málaga Marina. While there was no gate guard, there were cameras everywhere. Not surprising, considering the number of sail boats and speedboats moored to the piers. Makeda and Tojo walked side by side down the boardwalk.

"Are you sure this is going to be all right?" Tojo craned his head around, looking at the parking lot, then the boats, then back again.

Makeda adjusted the sunglasses she'd borrowed from MissTree. "Yes." She couldn't fault him for his nervousness. He didn't have her team in his head with him. Saladin operated the group, keeping track of everyone and an eye on the law enforcement in the area. As they walked, HiddenPlath and MissTree kept watch from different parts of the marina. Both were armed with scoped rifles.

Tojo hung back. "Why aren't you going with me?"

"I've already explained this." Makeda linked her arm within his. "Because I'm not going to be your live-in bodyguard at your cushy new job. You won't need me." She pulled him when he resisted. "Look, I understand you're nervous. Fear keeps you alive. If you're afraid, you're still living. Now, c'mon. The ship is waiting for you."

Tojo relented and walked alongside her again, clutching her arm in a sweaty hand.

Ahead, at the end of the boardwalk, a gruff man in all-weather gear and a cap waited next to the small gate onto one of the floating piers. On the other side of the gate, a younger dusky-skinned man in an identical sailor's unofficial uniform waited. They talked and smoked, watching the pair of them approach.

The older man stubbed his cigarette out and walked toward them. He met them a few meters from the gate. "Why would a man like to starve better?" he asked without preamble.

Makeda didn't hesitate with her answer even though the strength of the cigarette smell made her want to cough or gag...or both. "Better to enjoy his feast in heaven." She didn't understand the call and refrain. The phrases made no sense to her. It was probably a local saying that didn't translate well into English.

He nodded to her then turned a gruff gaze on Tojo. "I'm Captain Harrak. This is my passenger?"

To his credit, Tojo stood his ground. He gave the Captain a haughty look.

Makeda nodded. "Yes. This is Tojo Isoshi. He is your passenger once I have full payment." She ignored the slumping of Tojo's shoulders and the almost wounded look he gave her as he realized that he really was just part of a transaction to her. Nothing more.

Harrak patted his various pockets until he found the one he wanted. He pointed to Tojo and made a "stop" motion with his hand before he beckoned Makeda to come with him toward the gate. She extricated her arm from Tojo's hand and followed, also gesturing for Tojo to stay put.

Once they were out of earshot, Harrak showed Makeda the certified credstick. 110,000 nuyen glowed at her. She tilted her head. It was 10,000 nuyen too much. The Captain grinned, one gold canine gleaming. "Herr Schmidt is happy with your speed."

Makeda accepted the credstick, making it disappear into her pocket. "Pass on my gratitude. He's all yours." She turned to walk away.

He grabbed her forearm, halting her. "You need to escort him to the boat personally. He is yours until he is on the boat. Then he is mine. These are Herr Schmidt's orders."

Makeda gave him a look at the unexpected command. All of her alarm bells sounded at once. "All right." As she returned to Tojo, she subvocalized, "Heads up everyone. If something's gonna happen, this is it."

She squared her shoulders and pasted a lying smile to her face. "All is well. Time to go." Linking arms with Tojo once more, she led him to Captain Harrak.

The gruff man eyed Tojo with suspicion. "Do you get seasick?"

Tojo shook his head.

Makeda thought he was going to get sick right then and there. She squeezed his arm. He gave her a wan smile.

"In case you do." Harrak handed Tojo a small package of over-the-counter anti-nausea medicine. "Tastes like berries."

"Thank you." Tojo gave him a small bow. Then he shoved the package into his shoulder bag.

The trio of them walked to the small pier gate. It wasn't more than a clear door with a punch code. You could get around it if you had a bit of agility and luck. Captain Harrak punched in the numbers 8-4-8-6 and opened the door for them. He gestured to the younger man. "Follow Eduardo."

The walk down the pier was one of the longest Makeda had ever taken. There was no cover that wasn't in the water or breaking into someone else's boat. The whole pier swayed with their collective stride. Only the large boat at the end of the pier and Captain Harrak's clomping steps behind them kept her from spiraling into complete paranoia.

Over and over, she listened to Saladin, HiddenPlath and MissTree clear the areas around the quartet. No one watching. No one aiming. No one loitering. Just the four of them on a late afternoon in the middle of the week. It was as expected. Except MissTree's spirit friends had said different.

"Here we are. This is the *Ciervo Saltando*. The *Leaping Buck*." Captain Harrak hooked his thumbs into his pockets. "She is mine." His smile peeked out from his beard as he puffed his chest with pride. For a moment, the old captain gazed up on the boat in silence, giving a heaviness to the exchange.

"'*And know that it was meant to be sailed upon*,'" Makeda quoted. Captain Harrak grinned at her. "Well, Captain, my ward is now yours."

"*Si*." He gestured to their fourth. "Eduardo."

No other command was needed. The younger sailor took Tojo by the elbow and guided him to the boat, pointing at the ladder to reach out to and climb.

Tojo paused before he got on the boat. "Good-bye, Makeda."

"Happy sailing." Makeda did not wave good-bye to him. They were not friends. He was a job and nothing more. Fully paid and job done, she nodded to Harrak. "Captain."

"Señora." He turned to watch Eduardo and Tojo get on the boat.

Makeda walked away. She did not look back or to the sides. She kept her head high. The entire walk back up the pier, Makeda felt watched. Even the hair on the nape of her neck stood on end. "Anything?" she murmured under her breath.

"*Nothing here*," Saladin confirmed. "*Still all clear.*"

"MissTree? What about your little friends?" Makeda stopped at the clear door, grateful for its small amount of cover.

"Still antsy."

That was not the answer Makeda wanted to hear.

"Stay sharp, Makeda. Walk back to the parking lot and to the car. Don't deviate, no matter what."

"Acknowledged." Makeda breathed a calming breath as she pushed through the door, stepping from the pier back onto the boardwalk. It felt good to be on solid ground again. She counted her steps as she walked.

As runs went, she'd been on worse ones, but not by much. At least she hadn't been shot or stabbed on this one. Even if she did have to hike through the Alps and be attacked by corpsec. They'd gotten out, and Tojo was on his way to his new home—wherever that was. She shook her head at the folly of not knowing who you'd be working for when you agreed to run away from the corp you were working with. Tojo had not asked the right questions.

Then again, wasn't that what shadowrunners did when they worked with a Johnson? They often didn't know who they actually worked for or the corporation the Johnson represented. The irony of the realization made her smile as it flitted through her head.

She continued to count.

Plath's voice broke through as Makeda reached step eighty. *"The Ciervo Saltando has pulled away from the pier."*

When MissTree's little red Honda came into view, she relaxed. Perhaps everything was going to be fine after all and the mage's spirits were wrong. Makeda could almost taste that celebratory drink....

At step ninety-two, HiddenPlath spoke again. *"Uh, why are Harrak and the other sailor leaving the boat?"*

TWENTY

Makeda stutter-stepped. Only Saladin's sharp, *"Makeda, keep going!"* kept her from looking back. Flicking her eyes around, looking for enemies, Makeda saw nothing unusual. Still, her skin crawled with the paranoid, intuitive knowledge that she was in someone's crosshairs.

"Plath, status?" Saladin remained calm, continuing to operate.

"The Ciervo Saltando *is still motoring out of the harbor and into Málaga Bay. The other two have been met by a small speedboat. No name or number."*

"Keep track of both."

"Acknowledged."

Makeda hit the parking lot, walking fast. She adjusted her sunglasses and flicked through the range of her cybereyes, looking for hidden people. Thermal was almost useless in the heat, but it still worked. No one around the small car she'd used to get here. No one at all in the parking lot. Part of her thought it was unusual. Part of her stated she wasn't a sailor, didn't know the area, and had no idea what kind of movement happened in the marina on a weekday, late afternoon.

"The Ciervo Saltando *is in the bay now, moving south. I–frag!"*

The explosion was loud despite the distance between them. Makeda flinched a little and looked towards the sound. She slowed her steps, confused. "What was that? Was that the *Ciervo Saltando*?"

"Yes. And sinking fast."

"Drek—"

Saladin's voice broke in and pushed her forward. *"Keep going, Makeda. Get in the car and drive. Debrief later. Pick up MissTree as previously discussed."*

The operator was God during a run unless the runner had information the operator didn't. Right now, Makeda had no information. She did as she was told. It was better than dealing with the train wreck of thoughts in her head. She'd done everything right. Yet, the *Ciervo Saltando* was sunk, and the package was dead.

"Makeda, acknowledge."

She blinked. "Acknowledged. Picking up MissTree as planned."

Already, she could hear the loud sirens of the local police in the distance, coming nearer. They would have her on camera, walking Tojo to the boat, and the boat exploding. They wouldn't have Captain Harrak and Eduardo getting off the boat and speeding away. No cameras at sea. Not that she knew. There might be. That might save her.

Makeda looked into the car before she unlocked it and got in. It was an automatic action. With her hands on the steering wheel, she didn't see anything in front of her for a moment. Flashes of the plan whipped through her brain as she tried to figure out where she went wrong. She shook her head. Later. She would figure it out later. Makeda started the car and drove it out of the marina. She refused to look at the cameras she passed as she went.

"Frag. The package is dead. Tojo..." She didn't realize she'd spoken aloud until Saladin answered her in that calm, just-buying-groceries-totally-in-control voice.

"We will discuss that when we are all in a secure location. MissTree, status."

"I will be at the drop off point in five."

"Good. HiddenPlath?"

"Harrak and speedboat are headed southwest. Losing sight of them."

"Right. Wrap it up. Everyone back to home base."

Makeda stopped listening and focused on the road. Málaga's traffic was chaotic at best and lethal at worst. Fast speeds and rotundas made for dangerous driving conditions. The only benefit to such traffic was the fact that no one could tell if you were trying to speed away from a crime or not. *Everyone* drove like they were.

She saw MissTree as she zipped out of a roundabout and down a side street. Makeda stopped the little Honda next to the mage and got out of the car. MissTree cocked her head to the side, then hurried around to the driver's side while the cars behind them blared their horns before whipping past.

The two women rode in silence. MissTree drove as Makeda examined the new problem from all angles. She had done what Herr Schmidt wanted. She had delivered the package to the person and place of his choice. His man paid her and mentioned Herr Schmidt. In Spain, Mr. Johnson usually went by the surname Fernandez. Thus, it was the same Johnson. His man then left the boat, knowing it was doomed. Logic said this was all part of Herr Schmidt's plan.

"Then why the proof of life?" It was a rhetorical question. Not one she expected an answer to.

MissTree answered it anyway. "To see if he had to destroy his boat or not." A moment later, she added, "Resource management. Pah. *Germans.*" This last was a curse. "They need their asses kicked every hundred years, or they get uppity. They are overdue."

Makeda studied MissTree's profile. "I need to contact Herr Schmidt again."

"It will be double with what just happened."

"Can you negotiate it down?"

She shook her head. "No. Everyone's going to be snooping comm traffic, looking for the cause of the explosion and the reason. Explosions, even ones that do no damage, are news. I'm not sure my friend will even accept the job."

"All right. Pay it. I've got to talk to Schmidt. I need to know if he thinks I failed or what. But first, we need to stop at a store. I need to get a few things."

MissTree did not ask questions. She nodded and whipped the car to the right, cutting off another car, earning its wrath with the blaring of its horn. "I know where to go."

By the time the two women returned to the hotel, Saladin had it on lockdown. The front desk was closed for the day, and HiddenPlath stood sentry in the hallway with an Uzi III in one hand and a Colt M23 assault rifle hanging next to the other.

"Took you long enough." Saladin was armed with Ares Predator pistols.

HiddenPlath and MissTree exchanged a long look that spoke volumes before the mage disappeared into her room to set up another call to Herr Schmidt.

Makeda watched this without comment, figuring the two women were talking on a private channel. "I know. Needed some things. What can you tell me?"

"Right now, the explosion is a huge mystery, and no one knows anything." Saladin walked with her to her hotel room. "No police statement, yet."

Makeda opened the door, Colt in hand, expecting someone to be within. It was as she'd left it—dirty clothes and bag on the bed. "Right. I'm going to call Schmidt back. I need to know what he's thinking. He paid us, and the package is dead."

"Not going to be good for our rep as clean extraction specialists."

"I know. That's why I need to know what he's thinking. Is he pissed?" She paused. "Is this what he planned?" She shook her head. "I don't know." Makeda focused on Saladin. "Keep an eye on things. Figure out if we need to move tonight rather than tomorrow."

Saladin nodded. "Will do." He put a hand on her shoulder. "It will work out. It may suck, but we'll make it work out in our favor."

Makeda patted his hand. "I know. I'm just pissed. What did I miss?"

"I'm not sure you missed anything."

She didn't respond. Saladin left her in her room. Makeda shook her head. "Clearly, I missed something." For a moment, she wondered if Imre was involved. She shook her head again. That didn't make sense. He was out of the picture.

Unless he'd waited until he had the elevator codes to complete the second part of his job: kill Tojo, the one who had furnished the codes to begin with.

The thought twisted Makeda's stomach in knots.

This time, when they called Herr Schmidt, Makeda sat cross-legged against the cool stone wall of the hotel room. It was beige and featureless, but gave the impression that she was calling from a different place than last time. The low table and its equipment had been moved to accommodate this.

"Payment received." MissTree nodded. "Ready when you are."

Makeda pulled up the comm program and pinged Herr Schmidt with: *I draw in fresh sustenance.*

After a full minute, forever in Matrix time, the response came back with: *Goethe was the better poet.* Makeda accepted the incoming call.

Herr Schmidt appeared. He still wore the impeccable suit from before, but his tie was missing and he seemed to be in good spirits. "Frau Makeda. I trust you are well?"

"I am not. Your man's boat exploded without him on it."

"Ah. That. Well, these things happen." He tilted his head. "You got paid, yes?"

This was not what Makeda had expected. She'd expected him ticked off, not in a good mood. She nodded. "Yes."

"Then there is no problem."

She leaned towards the laptop camera. "You knew this was going to happen?" He stared at her; a frown crept into his expression. "Herr Schmidt, when I took on this contract, I was specific that I would not be party to any wetwork."

He tilted his head as if contemplating a mysterious stain on the table. "You were not. You were paid to deliver the man. You delivered him. You were paid. You left. The job was done. The boat blew up." He shook his head. "I do not understand your problem."

"My problem is the fact that it looks like I failed to complete my run. Or it looks like I, one," she held up a finger, "specifically delivered him to die. Or two," she held up a second finger, "failed to stop the sabotage of your boat."

The blond man scoffed. "That is, as you say, a personal problem. You and I, we have no problems. You did the job I paid you to do."

Makeda pressed back against the wall, feeling the cool stone. "What actually happened? Why pay so much money to deliver an engineer to a doomed boat?"

He glanced to the side and nodded. "When I hired you, the corporation that had engaged me had every intention of bringing Herr Isoshi onboard. Then I got a better offer." He shrugged. "Some corporations would rather see their assets burned than let them go."

Makeda refused to consider the implications of *that* right now. "So you changed the deal. You have no idea what you've done to me and my team. You should've given us the option of dropping him off somewhere for Saeder-Krupp to pick up."

"I did not change the deal." Herr Schmidt scowled. "I do *not* understand you people and your insistence on making everything about you. *We—*" he gestured to both of them, "—completed our transaction. What happened at any time afterward doesn't matter."

Makeda took a deep breath, pushing away the insult and the man's inability to understand the possible damage he'd done to her team's reputation as clean and safe extraction specialists. She also ignored the fact that this was too close to what happened to Imre's team when they lost the codes to her and took Tojo's money back. Tojo had been correct. He'd given them the codes, he deserved his payment even if Imre's team had lost them.

This was different. This was about her team's reputation and the contract they'd agreed to. "It does matter. I—"

Herr Schmidt disappeared, and she was left staring at her surprised reflection in the laptop screen. She looked up. "What happened?"

"He was tracing the call. He almost got through." MissTree worked fast, unplugging every piece of equipment from every other piece of equipment.

"Drek." Makeda helped, pulling at the cords she could reach. "Almost?"

The mage nodded. "Almost. My friend said he had to drop everything in Germany."

"No wonder he was willing to argue with me. Trying to get the trace." Makeda scowled. "This isn't going to go well for any of us." She hesitated. "If it isn't obvious, I want you on the team. You've reacted and adapted well. You have resources. The question is, do you still want in now that it looks like Herr Schmidt might be gunning for us?"

MissTree gave her a small, feral smile. "Someone's always gunning for you in the shadows. This isn't the first time. It won't be the last. I'm still in."

"All right. Welcome aboard." Makeda turned on her internal comms. "Saladin, HiddenPlath, please come to room twelve. TechnoGalen, consider this the bat signal, you need to monitor this."

It took a moment for Galen to respond to the alarmed keywords. He showed up at the same time as Saladin and Plath did. Both were openly armed, carrying their pistols and Uzi, respectively. Plath moved in to help MissTree pack the electronic equipment into two small cases. Saladin closed the door and leaned against it, in guard mode.

"*I'm here,*" TechnoGalen said. "*How bad is it?*"

"Patch MissTree in as part of the team. We'll skip the dinner interview for now." Makeda shook her head. "I don't know how bad it is. But here's the sitch as I see it. We got hired to do a willing extraction. There were some bumps in the run, but we got the package to the boat. The boat then exploded on our employer's orders. Schmidt doesn't care what this does to our rep as a reliable extraction team. To the outside, we're going to look incompetent at best or like backstabbers at worst. None of it is going to turn into future runs for a while."

Makeda gestured to MissTree. "Her hacker friend said Schmidt tried to locate us twice. That means he may be looking to tie up loose ends."

"Why? What loose ends?" HiddenPlath shook her head, confused.

"The fact that there are runners out here who know that Herr Schmidt is willing to back out on an agreed-upon extraction for more money." MissTree snapped the first case closed with more force than needed.

Saladin nodded. "That'll get around. Any other client he wants extracted is going to think twice. Plus, local runners will know that he changes the deal in mid-run."

"There's one other thing." Makeda threw herself to the small couch. It creaked under the force of her momentum. "I made a mistake. I let him know that I knew about at least one other run he'd commissioned against Tojo."

"Imre's team?" Saladin rubbed his chin.

"I didn't name Imre. Just mentioned multiple runs. Could've been Imre's job. Or maybe Schmidt had something to do with the explosion. Either way, he knows I know about at least one of them."

The comms came alive with Galen's voice, thoughtful and worried. "*What if this whole fraggin' thing was to get the elevator codes and then muddy the waters with multiple runs? To make it seem like it was only an extraction. Not a paydata run. Easier to get the codes from the engineer than to break into Krupp Specialist Engineering. Then kill the engineer before anyone realized this was about the codes and not the man. That way no one would know the codes were taken to begin with. No one would suspect, and Saeder-Krupp wouldn't know they needed to change them.*"

"Oh, frag." Makeda put her face in her hands.

"Elevator codes?" MissTree looked around the room.

Makeda waved a hand without looking at her. "One of those things you don't need to know the details of right now. Suffice it to say, paydata worth millions in the right hands."

"Either way, we qualify as loose ends." Saladin pushed himself from the door. "We need to get out and lay low for a couple of months."

Makeda was glad that neither Saladin nor Plath called her out about the elevator codes. She hadn't told them about that yet and she'd have to do so as soon as she had a quiet moment...but not in front of MissTree. "Yeah. And that's my main point here. Tomorrow, everyone disperses. Tonight, if you really want to. Separate ways. We can't move as a group. Meet back in Belgium in the next week or so. Take your time. Make sure you're safe." Makeda looked up at MissTree. "Plath'll give you the address and pass phrases to our meeting place in Belgium so you aren't shot on sight."

"*Merci.*" MissTree snapped the second case closed and set it next to the first.

"*I'm already home. What do you want me to do?*"

"Keep your head down, Galen. Monitor and report. But don't do anything to get them looking at you."

"*Okay. I can do that. I'll put the home guard on watch duty, too.*"

With that, there was nothing else to do except pay everyone and make plans to run and hide.

TWENTY-ONE

Saladin stopped Makeda as they left MissTree's room. "Can we talk?" He glanced at the cracked door behind them where HiddenPlath and MissTree were making plans. "In private?"

Makeda's heart dropped. He was going to go his own way, too. She steeled herself and nodded. "I need your help anyway." She led him to her hotel room as she set all her internal comms to private mode. She cleared the small room before entering and closing the door behind him.

Saladin leaned against the door. "You know they're going to go together, right?"

Makeda refused to ask what he wanted. If he was going to leave her on her own, she wouldn't give him the opening. "Plath and MissTree? Yeah. I gave them their instructions. How they fulfill them is their business. You know that's my management style." She dug into her earlier purchases and handed him a pair of scissors and a hair pick.

Saladin raised an eyebrow and asked, "What cut?"

"I was going to go with as 'short as possible' when I was going to cut it myself. But you're here and you're better at this than me—at least when cutting my own hair." Makeda put down a towel from the communal bath in front of the dresser mirror and moved the wooden chair to the middle of it. "So, very short and cute."

"You know that's not going to be enough to stop people from recognizing you." He picked out her curly hair with slow, careful strokes until it was like he needed it to be. Then he began to cut.

"I know. That's what the hair dye is for. I'll go for something more permanent when I'm in a safer place and home territory."

Saladin smiled at her in the mirror. "I suppose you want me to apply it for you, too."

"Yep." She watched him work, sighing at the loss of her beautiful, natural curls. It took forever to grow her hair out. He seemed content to do this for her. Heart beating faster and impatient curiosity won out over her desire to be stoic about all things. "So, what did you really want to talk to me about? It wasn't to tattle on Plath and MissTree."

"I know you've got Rabenhaupt's contact info. You gonna tell him about Herr Schmidt?"

It took a moment for Makeda to realize he was talking about Imre. That was what he wanted? She considered the idea. She wanted to. One runner to another. But she didn't owe him anything. Then again, Schmidt was an ass. "Maybe. I don't know. I don't know if he was the one to blow up the boat or not. What do you think?"

"I think Herr Schmidt did that on his own." Saladin concentrated on turning her curls into a cute pixie cut. "When it comes to Johnsons and runners, I'd trust the runner first. If it were me, I'd drop Rabenhaupt a warning to watch his back. If all Schmidt wants is the codes, he might use the pickup as an opportunity to screw over another runner."

Makeda eyed him. "Galen told you."

"About the codes and what they're worth? Yeah. When the run went bad."

"Saved me for the codes?"

"That and more." He yanked the conversation back to his original thread. "Warning Rabenhaupt could help us get the bastard back."

Saladin had a point. She trusted Imre more than Schmidt. Makeda considered what she'd say in an e-mail as her longer hair disappeared. Between this, the fire-engine-red hair dye, and the hair gel she'd bought, it should be just enough to change her appearance to give her those few seconds she needed. "All right. I'll give him a warning."

If Schmidt killed Imre after he got the codes, she would be the only other person to know he had them in the first place. Makeda sighed. This was going bad. Really bad. Better to let the other runner know that the Johnson was not on the level. Tojo had been right. Shadowrunners had a code of sorts. Trust the runner over the corps.

While Saladin finished her haircut, she sent a message to Imre's account: *Schmidt hinky. Careful with your goods. Watch your back.* It was the best she could think of on short notice. She did not receive a reply.

An hour later, Makeda dried her hair as Saladin scanned the headlines. Wet, her hair was the color of drying blood. Dry, it had a cherry pop that suited her tight, natural curls. Just as she was about to suggest dinner, Saladin said, "Oh, hell," and Galen *bing*ed an alarm.

Makeda grabbed the Colt and had it at the ready as she looked for the danger.

"On the news." Saladin pointed at his datapad.

"Bat signal: Streaming news to everyone."

This was Galen's only warning before the Spanish news report popped into Makeda's comm, automatically translated into English.

It was an aerial shot of Makeda walking with Tojo, pulling him along down the pier. Under the video, the words "Brussels2Rome Party Train kidnap victims murdered" scrolled. The screen split in two with the footage of Makeda handing Tojo over and walking back up the pier as the older news anchor, a human man with graying temples spoke.

"Here we see the suspected terrorist Martina 'Makeda' Aldon handing off drugged and reluctant Saeder-Krupp engineer Tojo Isoshi moments after the Saeder-Krupp executive, Aki Nakamura, was forced onto the same boat. Minutes later, you see the boat crew abandon the vessel and the Ciervo Saltando *explode. At the same time, you see that Makeda barely reacts to the explosion and the murder of the two innocent people."*

The split screen shifted to show the Ciervo Saltando *explode and Makeda hesitate a moment before continuing on to her little red Honda.*

The news anchor reappeared. "Again, if you are just tuning in, four of the six missing Brussels2Rome Party Train passengers have been seen. Unfortunately, two of them—Tojo Isoshi and Aki Nakamura—have been murdered by Martina Aldon, who goes by the moniker, Makeda. The fourth passenger, Imre Dahl, a VIP specialist for the Hanover Casino, was last seen in Makeda's presence in Switzerland. It is unknown at this time if he is a victim or a co-conspirator with this known terrorist."

Images of Imre with mint-colored hair and Makeda with her longer, natural curls appeared on the screen with their names emblazoned underneath and a commcode to use if they are seen.

The news anchor continued speaking. "If you see either of these two people, please contact the number on the screen. It is important that Mr. Dahl is found and Ms. Aldon is captured before she can hurt anyone else."

The feed snapped off. It left Makeda blinking and stunned. She shook the surprise away, shifting into survival mode. "Is there feed of the executive?"

"Yes. Hold on." Galen sent it to her.

Makeda watched the struggling, crying Japanese man pulled down the pier and forced onto the *Ciervo Saltando*. "How long was this before me and Tojo arrived?"

"Clock says fifteen minutes. But that could be faked."

"I never saw the man. The whole thing could be faked. Or, they really did murder both Tojo and Aki." Makeda thought fast, considering her options. She comm'd the group. *"Right, everyone in my room ASAP."*

Saladin opened the door and watched for HiddenPlath and MissTree. They arrived in a hurry. Plath looked annoyed. MissTree looked concerned.

"Why would they do this?" Makeda asked this as a rhetorical question then answered herself. "To lock us down. Or lock me down. Galen, did they get anyone else on camera?"

"Not yet. But they might trace you to the pickup with MissTree."

"That's what I'm thinking." She looked at the mage. "You need to lock down anything that could point to you. Change your look. I assume this hotel isn't under your name?"

MissTree shook her head. "It's not. I've been ready to leave for days. There shouldn't be anything for them to grab onto."

Galen broke in. *"By the way, 'Martina Aldon' suddenly exists. From Denver. Terrible grades. A lot of B&E busts. No pictures from when you were younger, but a decent fake profile."*

"Drek. So this was planned from the beginning?"

"Don't know. I could make a profile like this in an hour and seed it in thirty."

HiddenPlath took this in. "What do you need us to do?"

Makeda looked at Saladin and dropped into private comm. "I think we stick to the plan. We run right now, since it's still all over the news. Some gun bunny is going to try to be a hero."

Saladin clasped his hands and rubbed the pads of his thumbs together. *"I want to run now, but I think you're right. Send Plath and MissTree on?"*

Makeda gave him a nod and turned to the women. "I want the two of you to go as soon as you can. Leave behind whatever you don't need."

"I hate running." HiddenPlath glanced at MissTree. "But it's the right thing to do."

"I'm ready. I can call a friend to get a ride out to—"

"No." Makeda held up a hand to interrupt the mage. "Don't plan in front of me. Just do it, and I'll see you in Belgium in a week or so. Do what you need to do to survive."

HiddenPlath took MissTree's hand and led her from the room. The last thing Makeda heard was Plath saying, "—so she can't be tortured into revealing where you are."

Makeda turned to Saladin and opened her mouth to give him the same instruction.

He mimicked her "stop" gesture. "Don't. I'm sticking with you. You're going to need me. They'll be looking for you to travel alone or with another woman. They won't look for you to travel with an Arabic man. You need me as cover and to watch your back."

Makeda's heart filled with his words. She was relieved she didn't have to go alone. She could and would if she had to, but it was better to have a trusted companion to guard her blind spots. "Thank you."

"What? No argument?" A smile played about his lips. Though, the question was a serious one.

She was quiet, trying to capture what she felt in words. "You're my best friend, Saladin. You helped me more than anyone after Zaria." She stopped then, not wanting to think about her still missing, probably dead lover.

"And you're mine. It's more than what happened in Fleming. I've got your back, Makeda."

It'd been almost a year now. Makeda frowned. Almost a year and still nothing. It was time to accept the truth and move on, out of Belgium. Tears sprang forth and threatened to spill over. She dashed them away and repeated, "You're my best friend."

Saladin walked over and bumped his shoulder into hers. "None of that. No tears. We're still in crisis mode. Time enough for a breakdown later, as you like to say. Now, we have to figure out where to get you a *burqa*."

Makeda cocked her head. "Why a *burqa*?"

"What better way to hide than to play into the stereotype of the Arabic man and his hidden, silent, dutiful wife? Emphasis on silent." He grinned, pushing back the mournful mood that followed every thought of Zaria.

She faked a smile. "Hate to admit it, but it might work." Makeda pulled herself together. "Right. A *burqa*. That won't be hard to—"

"Enemies!"

They both heard MissTree's shout in the hallway at the same time HiddenPlath comm'd *"Incoming."*

Makeda opened the hotel door as Saladin pulled his pair of Ares Predator pistols, both of them smartlinked. MissTree was halfway down the hallway with HiddenPlath at the end, already exchanging weapons fire around the corner and down the stairs.

"Go!" Plath danced back from a couple of shots and grabbed one of the shooters, pulling him into sight. Black-clad, armored, ear wire, and armed to the teeth. No symbols, corporate or otherwise.

The two of them shoved each other, punching and kicking. HiddenPlath used her enemy like a shield, keeping the other shooters off her. He punched her twice, knocking her against the railing and following up with a rush. The ork twisted and used her attacker's momentum to throw him to the courtyard below.

Makeda ran to MissTree. "C'mon!"

HiddenPlath backed up, but couldn't dodge the hail of gunfire that filled her with bullets. She stuttered and jerked as automatic weapons fire pierced armor and ruined flesh. Three black-clad human men came into sight as the ork crumpled to the ground.

"NO!" MissTree's shout came at the first volley of bullets from both sides with the women in the middle—two three-round bursts and two aimed shots from Saladin. At the same time, MissTree threw a manaball at the trio.

Makeda yelped as two of the bullets grazed her hip. MissTree stumbled into her, bleeding from the leg and stomach. Makeda yanked her back toward Saladin. Behind them, the three enemies became two as Saladin focused two more shots on the lead man, destroying his face.

"Move it!" Saladin gestured for the stairs.

Makeda almost dropped MissTree as a porpoise manifested in midair and swam into the mage. The two women scrambled for the stairs as Saladin gave them cover fire. Halfway down the stairs, healed, MissTree regained her feet and stood. She turned to watch the top of the stairs. The porpoise swam around her.

Makeda grabbed MissTree's arm. "She's dead. If she's not dead, she's going to go out the front or hide."

MissTree shook Makeda off. "I know. Let me do my *damn* job."

Makeda let go, her Colt aimed at the top of the stairs as Saladin cleared the way.

As soon as the two attackers reached the corner and took cover, peeking around the wall, MissTree pointed and whispered, "*Echo, brûlez-les.*" Then she ran past Makeda, following Saladin to the back parking lot. Makeda continued to aim.

The dolphin swam to the top of the stairs and waited for the two men to look around the corner. It splashed itself over them as they did. Both of them caught fire. Everything the spiritual water touched flamed.

Makeda fired three shots. One of the men fell, still burning. She sprinted for the exit, jumping down the last two stairs. She stumbled, her right hip screaming its pain. Saladin pulled her from the building and pointed her at the SUV. Makeda half-stumbled, half-ran for the vehicle.

Saladin fired four more shots. Makeda turned. The last black-clad attacker, still burning, was on him, a sword in hand. The augmented man moved fast, slicing at Saladin's arms. Saladin dropped both empty guns and pulled a pair of long knives. The two men were a whirling dervish of flashing blades, clashing metal, and blood.

Makeda aimed and aimed again. She fired as Saladin stabbed a knife hilt-deep into the man's throat. She followed this up with a bullet to the head.

MissTree, already in the SUV, honked the horn and leaned out the window. "*Dépêche-toi!*" Makeda ran for shotgun and Saladin for the side door. As they got into the vehicle, MissTree turned. "I'm going to drive to—"

The rest of MissTree's words were lost as her left shoulder disappeared in an explosion of flesh, bone, and blood.

TWENTY-TWO

MissTree's eyes blinked wide with shock. She didn't have time to scream. Saladin pulled the mage into the back of the SUV as another shot came through the window. Makeda crawled to the driver's side and slammed on the gas. Blind, she turned the wheel hard to the right, putting the rear of the vehicle in the shooter's path before she climbed into the driver's seat and narrowly avoided the corner of the building.

Two more bullets slammed into the driver's side. Makeda's enhanced reflexes saved her from the first as it hit where her shoulder and neck had been, but not the second. Hot, searing pain stabbed deep into her left thigh. She jerked the wheel to the right again, speeding onto the road. Ignoring traffic, she forced the other cars to swerve to avoid her. Horns blared. People gestured.

Makeda bled a steady, throbbing stream. "Galen! Bat signal! Galen, call them off. Make something else happen. Set off fireworks in Málaga. Do something!" Makeda didn't care if she sounded panicked. She *was* panicked and hurt in body and soul. HiddenPlath was dead or captured. MissTree might be dead. Both she and Saladin were bleeding.

"Makeda, calm down."

"Don't tell me to calm down! Plath is dead. Everyone else injured! Get them off us!"

"There are no calls out for you." Galen kept his voice low and modulated. *"Relax. Just relax. There's a couple of emergency calls to your hotel but that's it. What happened?"*

"We just got hit by an assassination team."

"Police don't assassinate. They capture and question. Let me see if there's something in the data havens."

"First, get me a route to the safest part of town. Send it to my eyes." She was driving blind. She had no idea what parts of the city were good to run to and which should be avoided. Everywhere she turned, there were more cars with angry drivers.

"Done. Sent."

The map appeared in her left eye and overlaid the actual street. There were three color-coded routes with arrows pointing the way. Makeda picked the green one. She liked green. "Got it." Checking the rearview mirror, no one followed. She couldn't decide if this was good or bad.

Behind her, MissTree gave a small cry of pain. Makeda glanced over her shoulder. "How is she?"

Saladin hunkered next to the mage, supporting her and keeping her from sliding around. "Her spirit has her. I'm watching her heal. I think she's going to be okay. Focus on driving."

"I'll head to a Stuffer-Plus. It'll be open. We can clean up and regroup." Makeda grit her teeth and breathed in small, shallow breaths, trying not to move her left leg. The less panic ruled her actions, the more her leg hurt. The pain grew with every movement. It took most of her concentration to drive and not throw up.

Three klicks and five turns later, Makeda drove them into the almost empty parking lot of the Stuffer-Plus. She headed to the darkest corner of the lot. It wasn't that dark, but it was enough.

MissTree gasped and cried out as Makeda parked the SUV and turned off the engine. *"Non, Echo! S'il vous plaît, Echo, ne me quitte pas!"*

Makeda looked back to see MissTree reaching for the porpoise spirit as it swam away and disappeared. She and Saladin exchanged a worried look as the mage, now fully healed, burst into tears. "Saladin... is there a medkit in here? I've been shot."

He gave her a startled look that morphed into his neutral we're-going-to-talk-about-this-later face. "I think so." He rummaged around, looking under the seats and in the wheel wells.

MissTree pulled herself into the passenger seat. "Let me see." She hiccupped, tears still rolling down her face.

"Are—are you all right?" Makeda didn't know what to make of the mage and her tears.

She nodded. "Fully healed. But Echo said he wanted to go find his friends. It was his last promised service." She rubbed the heels of her palms against her wet cheeks. "He's been with me for a long time."

"I'm so sorry. Will...Echo...return?" Makeda bit back a curse when MissTree reached across her lap and grabbed her wounded left leg. She gripped the steering wheel tight to keep from smacking the mage.

"I don't know. Maybe. I never forced him. He agreed to the binding. He's a friend. All my spirits are friends." Her hands glowed as MissTree spoke in a soft, heartbroken voice.

Makeda relaxed as the stabbing, searing pain receded into a dull, thudding ache. "Oh, thank you. That's better." Even her right hip stopped hurting. She shifted the jeans fabric and saw a new scar on her leg. It faded as she watched. The ache turned into the memory of pain and the soreness of a newly mended muscle.

MissTree moved to the back of the SUV to where Saladin sat, watching out the windows, looking for signs of pursuers. "What about you?"

"Mine's mostly cosmetic." He raised an arm to show bleeding skin with chrome underneath. "Probably best for me to stick to conventional medicine." He pointed to the medkit.

She nodded and dug into it, getting out everything she needed to patch him up.

Galen reappeared on comms. *"Good news: no one hired a shadowrunner team to take you out. Bad news: either it was a merc unit or corpsec. No way of telling, and no one is talking. Even the emergency calls to the police have been muted. Someone big called them off."*

"Any word on HiddenPlath?"

"No. Either she's dead or she's hidden deep. I'm not getting anything to or from her on the comms."

Makeda nodded, not looking at MissTree. "I need a clean, secure e-mail account. One I can burn after tonight."

Thirty seconds ticked by. *"Done."* Galen sent her the details.

"Right. I'm going to take a long shot here. I'm going to e-mail Imre. If he was involved, we're screwed. If not, he'll help us."

"Why not use MissTree's contacts?"

Makeda gazed at the mage as she answered Galen. "Because they knew I'd be with her, not anyone else. You don't send four with one in the nest to take out four enemies. You send four to take out two. So, they know about her and will be watching her contacts. They didn't know about Saladin or HiddenPlath. That's why we're still talking."

MissTree nodded, agreeing.

"So ka. Let me know if there's anything else I can do."

"We will."

Makeda considered the e-mail for a couple of minutes as her team cleaned themselves up as best they could, wiping the blood from their faces and adjusting their clothing to cover the stains. It didn't help that they looked like they'd been hanging out in an abattoir. That gave her an idea.

She typed: *Dollface - Calling in that favor. Me and my friends went dancing in a blood-rave. Need to clean up. Love, your #1 Ghoul*

The e-mail sent, all she and her team could do was wait. Contacting Imre was a risk. She didn't know where he stood. Sometimes, you had to take a blind leap of faith from one shadow to another and trust that there would be a ledge in the dark to catch you. He had not responded to her original message about Schmidt.

Makeda wondered if he would respond to her at all.

TWENTY-THREE

They waited in the Stuffer-Plus parking lot with their lights off and everyone in the back of the SUV. Makeda had made an attempt at cleaning up the driver's seat. She'd only succeeded in smearing the blood—hers and MissTree's—around until it made her want to throw up. She conceded to the failure.

Outside the sky had deepened from orange into dark blue. It was fast becoming night. The traffic lightened, making their parked vehicle all the more obvious.

Six minutes later, her internal comms binged that she had an e-mail from Imre's address. Now was the time to see if his "I owe you one" actually meant anything.

Makeda read his answer: *Meet me at Bar Moraga at the Plaza de los Blanes. Come now.* She pulled the bar's page up and got the address. "It's not that far. Twenty minutes."

MissTree, still despondent, shrugged. "Never been there."

Saladin shook his head. "You know as much as I do."

"It's a plan. Better than none." Makeda sent the message: *3 of us. Black SUV. You'll know it when you see it.* "Right, current resources? Saladin?"

"Two knives, one pistol with eight bullets. Nuyen. Some corp scrip. Fake SIN. And half a medkit." He held it up. "Not much."

Makeda nodded. "MissTree?"

The mage blinked at her a couple of times. "Some magic, but not much without passing out." She patted her body. "Nuyen. Smart glasses. That's it. Everything else is back at the hotel. I told my friend we were running. I'm pretty sure any devices I left behind are slag now."

Makeda checked her Colt out of habit. She already knew she had four bullets left and no more magazines. Credsticks in her pocket. Clothes on her back. She'd been in worse situations, but not by much. "Saladin, go buy shirts for me and MissTree. Something that will hide blood." She looked at her pants. Not much she could to about it.

"Long skirt for me, maybe? Towels to cover the front seats so we're not sitting in semi-dried blood."

Saladin stretched forward and looked at the damage. "Easier for me to cut the pants legs off and make shorts."

"Shorts and boots. What a combination."

He shrugged. "It'll look good. I've seen the style around town."

"Leave a knife. I'll do it while you're getting the towels and shirts."

Ten minutes later, with Saladin driving, all three of them were in tacky tourist shirts, looking almost respectable and mundane. Makeda hoped that Bar Moraga was the type to take in tourists as well as locals.

The front of it looked normal enough. Not too nice or too seedy. They found a parking spot in the middle. As Saladin turned off the SUV, Makeda reached a hand out and touched his elbow.

"I want to go in alone. I need to. I know Imre. He knows me. If it's a trap, I want you two to go. No fighting." She poked his elbow again at the storm clouds brewing in his frown. "No fighting. Listen in. It may be noisy. I don't know. If I tell anyone that I'm 'all by my lonesome,' you run. Got it?" She quoted the warning phrase with finger quotes in the air. "'All by my lonesome.'"

"We got it." MissTree had the calm, cool look of a woman who had just lost everything and decided to deal with it later. "We'll go. I'll make him go."

Makeda knew the look well. She'd seen it enough times in the mirror. "*Merci.*" She ignored the flat glare Saladin gave them both.

As did MissTree. "*De rien.*"

Makeda didn't know what Saladin would actually do if she sent the order to run. That wasn't her concern right now as she slid the side door open, half expecting to be shot as she did so. When the death blow failed to show, she put on a slow swagger, giving her hips an enticing roll, and walked into the bar.

Its inside matched its outside. Just enough kitsch to please a tourist, but not enough to irritate the locals. The bar had five stools, three of them occupied. Small tables with chairs were dotted around a jukebox. About half the tables were filled. Most of the people at the tables had a mixture of cyberware, and most were human. A good third of the bar watched her with open curiosity.

At the jukebox, a slender man with short dark hair stood in jeans and a gray form-hugging shirt with his back to her. She didn't recognize the hair color, but she recognized the shape. She smiled at his back.

A tall Spanish man with obvious cyberarms gestured wide. "*Bonita! Si la belleza fuera delito, yo te hubiera dado cadena perpetua.*"

The jukebox came to life with the song, *#1 Ghoul*. Imre turned and smiled at her. He was such a beautiful man. Makeda glanced at the man beside her. "I deserve to be in prison for a lot more than my beauty."

She left him there, clutching his chest, declaring to the world his heart was broken. He returned to the bar with his buddies laughing at him and clapping him on the back. Makeda kept half an ear out in that direction, just in case. Most rejected men dealt with it well enough. Some took the rejection as an invitation to attack.

Imre opened his arms for a hug. Makeda slid into them, letting him hold her for a brief moment. He pressed his lips to her neck, just below the ear. "I like the new color. Red suits you."

"Same to you. I like your hair longer, but the black works so much better." She pulled back. "We got trouble. Not just me. I think you, too."

Imre kept his smile, but his eyes hardened. Swaying his body to the music, he held her hands and leaned forward. "C'mon. I've got a place we can talk. Really talk."

"My team is with me." Makeda tapped her temple before she slid her arm around his waist. Imre draped his arm over her shoulders as if they'd been friends and lovers for ages. The two of them walked to the "*Employees Only*" door. The sudden quiet of the soundproofed hallway told her all she needed to know about the bar. Nothing was ever what it seemed.

He led her to a room with an unmarked door. It was an office. The desk was mostly cleared, with some knick-knacks on it and a small trid player. The walls were covered in photos of people who'd come through the bar—some of them famous, some not. A dented metal filing cabinet sat in one corner. A single, scruffy chair sat in front of the desk. Nothing sat behind it.

She gestured to the room. "Yours?"

Imre shook his head. "A friend's. I'm just passing through. What's the situation?"

"Immediate, two injured, one dead."

"I'm sorry."

"Me, too.

Makeda pressed her lips together and looked away, debating. She focused in on a black-and-white picture of a Spanish elven woman in a white dress. It was signed. She couldn't read the signature. She turned and locked eyes with him. "I gotta ask. Did you blow up Tojo's boat?"

Imre blinked. Whatever he thought she was going to ask him, that wasn't it. "Blow up Tojo's boat?" His confusion cleared. "Ah. The explosion." He shook his head. "No. My deal was to get the codes and nothing more. I didn't have anything to do with the exploding boat. It's a drek thing to have happen. I was rooting for him to make it to his new home. To leave all this behind."

If Imre was acting, he was doing a bang-up job of it. "Okay. I needed to know." She paused. "Your team? Everyone get out?"

Imre looked toward the door they'd come through. "No. Richter was too far gone. Pongolyn and Ollietronic disappeared off the map. They dropped Fatima off in one of our places, then faded. I want to say they're fine, but they're not answering messages. I know Ollie was shot, hurt bad. Could be that Pongo took him some place very safe. Fatima made her way here. She's with me."

"We saw her pick you up from the airport. I hope Pongolyn and Ollietronic are safe." Makeda sat on the edge of the desk. "Have you given your paydata to Herr Schmidt?"

Imre hesitated. "No. We need to meet. That was part of the original deal."

She nodded. "Let me float a theory. This came from my hacker. How much are those codes worth in the shadows now?"

"A lot. Hundreds of thousands. Probably more."

Makeda noted that. It might be a very good way to make money if she needed it. "How much if everyone associated with them were dead...and Saeder-Krupp, Thyssen-Krupp, Krupp Specialist Engineering had no idea they were taken, and no visible way they could've been taken?"

Imre shook his head. "I don't understand."

"Tojo is dead. I'm wanted for kidnapping, murder, and probably causing the train wreck at this point. The only known person to have the codes is you. Not that Herr Schmidt is going to tell anyone. If he gets them and you die, they were never taken in the first place. Rumor of them never even hits the shadows. Now, how much are they worth to a corporation that isn't Saeder-Krupp?" She watched the light of understanding blossom into a glint of anger.

"Millions in corporate espionage alone. Maybe more." He sat on the edge of the desk next to her and frowned. "You mean, all of this was to steal the paydata and cover it up with multiple runs, then kill everyone involved?" He shook his head. "Too complicated. Even for a Johnson like Herr Schmidt."

Makeda shrugged. "Maybe. Maybe not. Corporate espionage is a very profitable business. Easier to steal from an employee than break into a corp. Also, I had nothing to do with the Saeder-Krupp executive, Nakamura. Haven't even heard a whisper involving him in the shadows, and he's as dead as Tojo."

"That's a hell of a waste of resources to hide the real run within multiple runs."

She leaned back on her hands, feeling all her muscles complain. "Here's another question for you: when's the last time a Johnson insisted on an in-person meet for paydata that could be packaged, encrypted, and couriered or, hell, e-mailed through the Matrix?"

Imre grimaced. "I know. I didn't like it when I made the deal."

"Are you still going to meet with a person who not only set me up but also sent a wetwork team after me?"

He stood and listened to his comms. "Speaking of which, we need to get your people out of that SUV. It just popped up on the radar as stolen. I'll send Fatima out."

Makeda stood close to him, watching his lips. "Cameras?"

"Mysteriously went out right after I got a particular e-mail."

"Great, I'm going to get blamed for that. Wish I was as talented and powerful as they're making me out to be." Makeda stood and faced him. "Ah well. Saladin, did you get that? Fatima's coming out."

"Got it. I see her."

Imre watched her speak and didn't move.

"They're ready for her." Makeda drank in his handsome face. *Damn, I want to kiss him again.*

As soon as the thought crossed her mind, Makeda threw caution to the wind and did exactly that. Imre was already reaching for her as their mouths met.

They explored each others' lips until Imre pulled back and glanced up as he spoke. "Take the Rover. We'll be there in a moment." He gave Makeda an apologetic shrug. "Gotta get moving. Get you and your people safe and figure out what to do with Herr Schmidt."

Makeda let the shiver of pleasure run through her before she shook it off. "I know. Did you catch the part of the broadcast where he set you up as either another one of my victims or my co-conspirator?"

His face stilled into something neutral and flat. "Yeah. I did."

"He's going to kill you at the meet... Unless we kill him first."

"I know."

"I want to be there. I owe him for HiddenPlath and Obscura."

Imre nodded. "I know."

"And for Tojo." Makeda didn't mean she wanted to revenge Tojo. She wanted vengeance for her damaged reputation. A small part of her also wanted revenge for the salaryman. Like Imre, she'd been rooting for the naïve fool.

"I know."

"That's not an answer on whether or not you're going to kill Herr Schmidt. Or let me help you kill him."

Imre bared his teeth in the parody of a smile. "I know."

She returned it to him. "What else do you know?"

"I know we need to get moving. Now."

Five minutes later, Imre, Fatima, Kraken—the tall Spanish man with the cyberarms from the bar—Makeda, MissTree, and Saladin were in the Rover, a modified Renault-Fiat Eurovan. All of them had lightly armored jackets on in varying degrees of repair. It was what Imre's team had on hand, and it was better than nothing.

Kraken drove. MissTree rode shotgun while Fatima worked on Saladin's sliced synth skin, repairing it and making it appear normal. Makeda and Imre sat in the back and talked. She handed him her credstick with its dwindling resources and refused to wince as he pulled half of what was left from it.

"This will get the three of you out of Spain. It's a good thing you contacted me both times. Your first warning let me push Herr Schmidt off. The second came as we were figuring out what to do with Herr Schmidt's implied threat."

"Where are we headed?"

"Same place I am and have always been headed: Rabat, Morocco."

Morocco. People who thought of Africa as some third-world backwater were wrong, but never so wrong as they were about Morocco. Anyone who'd been to Morocco could tell you it was as modern as Seattle. It also had the added benefit of being a safe haven to mercenary units since the Alliance for Allah and the Federation of Islam States tussled for control of the region.

It had been a long time since she'd been to Morocco. Last time, she'd only passed through Casablanca. She'd never been to Morocco's capital city of Rabat.

"Are you going to kill Herr Schmidt? Let me kill him? Or help me do it?" Makeda watched Fatima and Saladin as they repaired his arm. "I noticed you still didn't answer me."

Imre followed her gaze. "You're used to running your own team."

"Meaning?"

"I'm not part of your team. The way I do things is different than you. Also, I wanted to talk to my team first. Killing a Johnson is serious business. There will be consequences."

She narrowed her eyes and crossed her arms. "Any Johnson who pulls the drek this one has doesn't deserve to live."

"I agree. But if we do this, we do it my way." Imre sat back, watching her out of the corner of his eye.

Makeda wanted to shout him down. Her people were dead and hurt. Her team's reputation was in tatters. But none of that mattered. When it came down to it, Imre was the one with the resources, the local knowledge, and the means of getting Herr Schmidt into killing range. She had come to him and asked him for help. This was not an operation she could control.

"I'm listening." She uncrossed her arms and watched the moonlight on the water as they drove down the edge of the coast. As they passed by gated palatial homes of the ultra-rich, she figured they were going to a privately moored boat and would motor across the bay into Morocco, sidestepping customs and all other authority.

Good thing, too. She had no non-terrorist SIN or passport. She curled her lip, just thinking about what Herr Schmidt had pulled.

"First, there's nothing guaranteeing that he'll come to Morocco. If he doesn't, I'm going to have to figure out what to do with the codes."

"I know some people..."

Imre nodded. "I'm sure you do. If we need to sell the codes on our own, we'll call them. Second, if he agrees to come and he is planning on killing me, I'm in charge. It's my team. My plan. You work with me."

Makeda glanced at him and nodded. "Operative word: *with*." She returned her gaze to the water.

"Correct. No assumptions. We spell it out." He raised his voice for the whole van to hear. "And no one else is required to be in on this. We pull this off, and there will be consequences. Bad ones."

"I will kill everyone I can responsible for Sylvia's...HiddenPlath's... death."

Makeda heard MissTree's flat, angry voice over the comms, but from the way Kraken's head snapped to the mage, she spoke aloud.

"I got your back. No one should have to deal with a dirty Johnson." Saladin didn't look up. Neither did Fatima, but her sudden smile matched the one on Makeda's face.

"My team is in. And, yes, I agree, there's only one leader. I'll work *with* you." She poked his arm. "But I won't be ordered about without knowing the reason why."

Imre nodded. "Agreed. My team has also agreed. Our eye in the sky is Bobishere2. Once we get to where we're going, you'll be linked into the team comms. Then we'll see if Herr Schmidt is ready to play ball."

They turned down the gated driveway of a huge house on the water, and the gate swung open without challenge. The ornate, elegant decorations on the grounds and house gave it an elven feel. There were no lights on in the home, and no people around at all. Makeda side-eyed Imre. He didn't look at the house. He only had eyes for the back where they were headed.

"Who lives here?" she asked.

"A friend." The answer and his flat tone cut off all follow-up questions.

Makeda gave a mental shrug. Imre was not one to talk about his past or his connections. At least, not yet. She studied the home. It was beautiful. Old architecture. The way he didn't look at it in more than an automatic glance said that he was familiar with the place. Very familiar. She made note of it for a future investigation. She'd always cyber-stalked friends, interesting people, and other runners for amusement. It was amazing the things you could find out, especially on unsecured sites.

They turned the corner and revealed the private dock. Its sixteen-meter yacht pulled Makeda's attention from the house. The boat was sleek and huge. Tinted windows, plenty of space fore and aft, and even a canopy on top. *Reina Verda* was emblazoned on its side in green.

"The *Green Queen*. Wow. What kind of boat is it?"

"A Fairweather Phantom. She's a nice yacht. I like her. It'll take about three hours to get to where we're going."

Makeda glanced at the soft smile on his face. She realized the *Reina Verda* was his boat. If not his, he was possessive of it. That meant there was a really good chance that the house belonged to him, too. Either he was a prime runner, or he was slumming from his very rich family. Maybe a bit of both. Then again, why would a German man have a Spanish villa? Maybe it belonged to his wife?

Makeda shook her head. She was letting her imagination run wild. There were many reasons to love a boat—the love of sailing was only one.

Giving the house one last look as she got out of the van, she turned toward the yacht. It was what was going to get her to relative safety.

Assuming they weren't blown out of the water on the way to Morocco.

TWENTY-FOUR

Ten minutes into the voyage, Kraken called from above deck, "*Policía*." Imre nodded to Fatima and walked up the stairs, closing the lower deck behind him. An eyeball-searing light pinned the *Reina Verda* in the water as Kraken cut the engine to an idle.

Fatima herded Makeda, MissTree, and Saladin past the living/dining area into the back bedroom and closed the door after shushing them. The bedroom was small but luxurious, with enough seating for all of them and a dedicated bed space in the forward aft, hidden behind the couch with a small curtain.

At the sound of boots on the upper deck, Saladin pointed at Makeda and made shooing motions for her to hide. The boots stomped down the boat and to the stairs. The lower-deck door opened with a soft thump. Saladin beckoned MissTree to him. He put an arm around her waist, murmured, "Hide your face in the crook of my neck if they open the door."

MissTree slid her arms about him in a warm hug. She tilted her head, listening to the movement outside the bedroom door. Her fingers twitched with readiness as she watched Saladin's face. He gestured at Makeda with his chin and mouthed the words, "Move it."

Makeda climbed over the couch, through the curtain, to the far back of the bed, and hunkered down. If there was shooting, she'd have no place to go. She hated having Saladin and MissTree up front, but they were the ones who would survive best if there was a fight. She peeked out at her teammates through the small slit in the curtain, her Colt at her side. She still had four bullets. She would make them count.

The rapid-fire Spanish sounded pleasant enough. Makeda caught a couple of words—*dropped, found, no, yes, insist*—but it was too muffled and fast for her to catch more of the conversation. There was a pause. Laughter. Then the boots stomped their way to the front of the boat and off. The blinding light disappeared from the windows, leaving the bedroom in total darkness, with all of them blinking away amorphous afterimages.

Light returned in the form of glow-in-the-dark strips around the windows, the aisle, and the door. MissTree sat on the couch. A moment later, she announced, "No astral presences."

The *Reina Verda* started up again. Saladin waited by the door as Makeda poked her head out of the bedroom area. Someone knocked twice before slowly sliding the pocket door back.

It was Imre, with a commlink in hand. "All is well."

Makeda clambered out of the bed and settled in on the couch. "What happened?" She put the pistol to the side.

"The usual. Patrol came by to look at things. I found the credstick the officer dropped when he jumped over. He insisted it wasn't his. I insisted it wasn't mine. I forced it on him, asking him to take care of it since I *never* deal with certified credsticks. That I'd rather drop it into the ocean. He agreed it needed to be dealt with. He was an officer, and someone must be missing the credstick." Imre blinked in an exaggeration of innocence and shrugged.

Makeda grinned at him. "I'm sure."

MissTree stood with an abrupt jerk of her body. "I want to be close to the water." She wormed her way by Saladin and Imre to disappear on deck.

Saladin glanced between Imre and Makeda. "I should make sure she's fine. She's been depressed. You understand." He didn't wait for an answer and closed the door after himself.

Makeda and Imre watched him go and then grinned at each other. "Was it something I said?" he asked.

"Not in so many words, no." Makeda felt her stomach tumble with butterflies as she glanced between Imre and the rest of the luxurious room. She knew what she wanted to do. She didn't know what he wanted. All that foreplay on the run through the Alps could've been acting. The silence stretched out. "Alone at last. So, what now?"

That broke them out of their not-staring-at-each-other moment. "Now, I call Herr Schmidt and set up the meet." Imre made himself comfortable on the couch next to her. "You listen in." He handed her an earpiece and put one in as well.

"I shouldn't need this. Not if I'm going to monitor through my 'link."

He shrugged. "Have it just in case. I'm a double- and triple-plan kind of guy. My backup plans have backup plans."

"I understand that." Makeda gazed at the laptop. "He's going to try to find you. His hacker is good."

"Why do you think we're doing this on the water? Bobishere2 is good, too. Maybe she can get a lock on him and see where he is now."

Makeda raised an eyebrow. "She?"

"What?"

Makeda shrugged, rubbing the back of her hand. "Bob. I just thought...I guess it could be short for Bobbie or Barbara."

"Doesn't matter. Bobishere2 identifies as female and elvish. Thus, I treat her as such. That's all I need." He opened a shared ARO for the call. "As for Schmidt, if he insists on a meet, I'm going to make him meet us in Rabat. I've got people there. I'm pretty sure he doesn't. Or, at least, he can't hire that many in such a short amount of time."

"What do you want me to do?" Makeda put the earpiece in but didn't turn it on.

"Listen. Watch the feed. Advise silently. I said I'd work with you." He cocked his head. "This is just so we can be on the same page. You'll know everything that's said. Plus, you might see something I don't."

"I can do that." She shared a private message ARO with him. *<Testing.>*

Imre nodded. "Got it. Ready?"

<Ready. I won't talk. Just type here.>

Makeda relaxed on the couch and closed her eyes. In the shared ARO, the connection process started.

She watched Imre access the call program then type: *<Its fleece was white as snow.>* They waited in silence for Herr Schmidt to get back to them.

Just as Makeda was about to suggest they try another time, Herr Schmidt responded: *<Grilled lamb goes well with loganberries.>*

Imre accepted the call. From the slightly disheveled look of him, they'd woken Herr Schmidt up. His hair was combed, and he had on the corporate executive's uniform of a button-up shirt, vest, and jacket. But he also had circles under his eyes and a puffiness indicative of sleep. Makeda bet he was in his underwear beneath the waist and wondered if he wore boxers or briefs. He seemed like a tighty-whitie kind of guy.

"Good evening, Herr Schmidt. I hope I didn't wake you. I didn't think it was that late."

Makeda checked the time. Just before midnight.

"No, Rabenhaupt. I was reading. You missed your last call time. What happened?"

Both men spoke in German. Makeda's language linguasoft program translated the words as they spoke.

Imre tilted his head. "I got named on a news report as either a victim or a terrorist co-conspirator. I needed to take some precautions. Do you know what that is all about?"

"Just covering for you." Herr Schmidt glanced to the left before giving a calculated shrug.

<Liar.>

"You didn't need to do that."

Herr Schmidt smiled. "Oh, but I did. I received several reports that you were seen in the company of the terrorist, Makeda. I had to do something."

Makeda wanted to punch his teeth in for him. Instead, she typed. *<He shouldn't have turned me into a terrorist. Or murdered Tojo.>*

Imre kept his eyes locked to the ARO, not reacting physically to her anger. "She wasn't a terrorist until that news report."

The blond man spread his hands. "Things are what they are. Do you have my codes?"

Imre nodded. "Yes. But, as things are too hot in Málaga for me, I need to change the meeting place."

Herr Schmidt's scowl was immediate and fierce. "I do not like these sorts of changes." The words were clipped, irritated.

"I don't care. You're the one who made things hot. Now you need to deal with it. We're going to meet in Rabat, Morocco. There's a nice little international airport there. I'll call you in six hours and tell you where the actual meet is." Imre's voice was cool and professional.

Schmidt took a visible, calming breath and nodded. "Rabat? Why there?" Instead of angry, the words were smooth, oiled.

Makeda watched Herr Schmidt with an experienced eye. He nodded again and made a small gesture with the index finger of his left hand. If she hadn't been looking for the clues he was communicating to someone other than Imre, she would've missed it. All of them had been directed to the left, as he had before when he had his hacker come after her.

<He's stalling. He's trying to find you. Wrap it up. His hacker is good.>

"Because you'll have thirty minutes from the time I call you to make it to the meet. If you don't arrive, I'll assume you aren't interested, and I'll open the paydata up to the highest bidder. Privately, of course." Imre gave him an insincere smile.

"There is no need for threats, Herr Rabenhaupt. I will be there. I was merely curious as to why Rabat and not Casablanca."

Imre shook his head. "Because this isn't a romantic movie."

Herr Schmidt glanced up to his left and nodded.

<He's talking to his hacker.>

Herr Schmidt's voice took on a purr. "Speaking of romantic movies, how is Frau Makeda?"

"Dead. Assassination squad, as I heard it." Imre frowned at the screen. "Why do you ask?"

He clicked his tongue. "I don't think so. I think she's very much alive and with you now."

A firewall warning popped up as someone tried to hack into her headware—her cybereyes, specifically. Everything went red, and then black. TechnoGalen's counter-intrusion measures when into full swing. Her PAN shut down and locked up.

Makeda opened her eyes, but the blackness remained.

"You have an active imagination."

She stilled, not wanting to alarm Imre and have him give away her presence. She reached up to the earpiece and turned it on. Biting the inside of her cheek to keep the panic at her sudden blindness at bay, she listened and took slow breaths through her nose. The pain helped focus her as she tasted blood.

"...shall see," Herr Schmidt said. *"In the meantime, I will await your call for our meeting in five hours and fifty-seven minutes."*

"See you in Rabat." She heard Imre close the laptop. "Makeda, are you all right?"

"I'm not in pain. No. But, we might have a problem." She blinked again and again. "I might be blind. My cybereyes were attacked." She heard him put his commlink to the side.

He shifted next to her. "Bob says the attack didn't actually get through. It just traveled down the same connection she used to let you monitor the call."

Galen would never have let something like this happen. He would've burned the other hacker to bits. This is amateur-hour stuff. Makeda kept those thoughts to herself. No use insulting Imre's hacker. "That sounds like it got through to me." She waved a hand in front of her face. "Looks like it, too."

Shoving the marauding thoughts of being blind for the rest of the trip to the side, Makeda ran through her headware start-up process, keeping it in safe mode. "If I'm lucky, Galen was just a bit over zealous on his counter-intrusion shutdown procedures. If that's the case, we're going to have to revisit it. Going blind in a firefight would be a death sentence."

"This hasn't happened before?" Imre got up and paced in the small room.

"No. No one has gone after my cybereyes before. They look natural. I paid a lot of nuyen to make them like that. Make it look like a cosmetic touch with the gold, but nothing more. Hopefully, I can get them to restart. It may take a bit."

He didn't respond to this. Makeda got the impression that he was talking with Bobishere2. She couldn't tell if he was scolding or comforting her. Maybe a little from column A and a little from column B.

Seconds ticked by like hours. Makeda knew that time was passing as normal in the grand scheme of things, but it felt like forever. Either the reboot would work, and she would be fine. Or it wouldn't, and they would need to find someone who could fix whatever was wrong with her headware. Until then, she was Schrödinger's blind woman.

While she was waiting, Imre returned to her side. He sat on the couch and said nothing, just trying to be a comforting presence. It worked in a distracted sort of way. It made her want to jump him right then and there.

"Do you have pheromones?" The question came out harsher than she'd meant it to.

Imre twitched next to her. "Yes. I'm sorry. They're automatic if I don't think about them." There was a long pause. He took a breath. "I have a question for you."

"It's not like I'm doing anything else at the moment."

His voice took on a teasing quality. "What did you think of me when you first saw me in the Party Train lounge?"

She smiled. She couldn't help herself. It was a question she'd asked him earlier. She knew he was trying to distract her. It worked, as she thought about seeing him across the crowded room. "I thought you were the most beautiful man I'd ever seen. I wondered why you were watching me in a room full of beautiful people."

"Because you were the most striking woman there." He whispered this, his breath tickling her ear.

Her soft smile hardened into something a little more cynical. "I also thought you'd be the perfect arm candy to take with me onto the train."

"Great minds think alike. Also, I got a good look at your face earlier. I was able to get your name and look it up. That's how I knew about Queen of Saba, Queen of Sheba."

Makeda patted his leg. "Here I thought you were well read."

"Nope." He covered her hand with his. "I just wanted you to tell me your name so I could trot out the line...and not call you by name before you told me."

"You mean like when I—" Makeda stopped in mid-sentence as light appeared in the darkness. She wanted to cry when a screen popped into view and lines of text scrolled by, rebooting her eyes in safe mode. When the world reappeared, she slumped against Imre, relief making her weak. "Oh thank God."

"Makeda?" Imre craned his head to look down at her. "You all right?"

"I am now." Makeda looked up at those beautiful dark eyes and seized the moment. She kissed him, hard. He returned the kiss with the same urgency. When he pulled away, she murmured, "No. Stay with me."

"I just need to lock the door and tell everyone to stay topside." He gave her another searing kiss, then got up and pressed a button next to the door. While he was there, he took off his shirt, revealing his lanky, muscled, and scarred body.

Letting her eyes roam the roadmap of his skin, she realized what had been bothering her about him the entire time they'd been together. He was built wrong to be human. Too slender. Slightly too elongated. "Oh, you're—"

"Human," he interrupted, his voice hard and distant. "I was born human. I *am* human."

"I was going to say 'handsome.'"

It was a lie. They both knew it.

The one thing Makeda never would have guessed in a million years was that Imre was a human poser. Either he'd goblinized and he was older than she thought he was—over forty at a minimum, which would explain a lot—or he was born elven, and felt like he'd been born in the wrong body. He'd had work done to make him look human. Cheek implants and ears fixed.

Either way, he was still Imre, and she had business of the sexy kind with him. She beckoned him to her. "C'mere, lover."

Imre hesitated, then accepted the lie as truth and tossed his shirt at her. "You come here."

Makeda stood and took two steps to him. "If I have my way, we'll both be cumming."

He laughed, took her into his arms again, and kissed her over and over, murmuring, "Your wish is my command."

She shimmied out of the tacky tourist shirt and pressed her skin to his as his hands fumbled with the clasp of her bra. "I've wanted you since I first saw you."

"You and me both," he whispered. "More than arm candy distraction."

"Much, much more."

Then the talking was done. The two of them lost themselves in the slick skin and throbbing flesh of each other for a brief time on the rolling waves of the Mediterranean Sea.

Later, tangled up in the sheets, happy and satisfied, she walked her fingers up his pale arm. "Why Rabat?"

He blinked sleepy eyes at her. "I have people there. Resources, too. Plus, a place no one will care about if it gets shot up. No one but me, that is. Less trouble with the local mercs and authorities. It's one of my home territories. I am known. I am comfortable there."

"You really are an international man of mystery. Holdings in Germany, Spain, Morocco. In all my time in Europe, I never heard of the shadowrunner Rabenhaupt."

He rolled her over and kissed her. "I did that on purpose. Those who need to find me, can. If everyone knew who I was and how to get to me, I would've been dead long before now. I'm known for my discretion—no matter what you hire me to do."

"Smart." She rolled him over and pinned him to the side of the boat. "How much more time do we have?"

He gave her a slow smile. "Enough."

"For round two?"

"If you wish." He leaned up and nibbled her neck.

She slid her hand down to cup his ass. "I do."
"My command."

TWENTY-FIVE

There was nothing like satisfying sex before a dangerous run. It reminded you of what you could come back to. It also worked some of the mental kinks out. Makeda ignored Saladin's good-natured eyebrow waggling as they left the boat. She rolled her eyes at his comm'd teasing questions on their drive to Rabat, but said nothing.

She and Imre continued to share mingled hands and mingled glances at every opportunity.

Makeda considered what it would be like for the two of them to work together as a team moving forward. She didn't know how that would work. Right now, he was the man in charge, but he was correct: she was used to running her own team. With the two of them used to being in charge, the question was: Could they work together? She supposed they could, if they could come to an agreement on who would be in charge for each kind of run. Maybe she would lead extractions, and he could take charge on paydata runs.

One thing was certain, he'd be fun to keep around. She would never be bored.

Imre's team took turns driving the hours-long trip to Rabat. They were the ones who knew where they were going. All of them knew they were going into a fight with a dirty Johnson who wanted them dead to keep his convoluted plans secret. Sleep was caught in catnaps. Later, it would be substituted with stims to keep the team as alert as possible.

Rabat, the capital city of Morocco, was a mixture of old and new. Shiny, tall buildings stood next to dusty tent markets. Modern train stations ran on time next to the main highways. With a little elevation, outside the city center, there were swathes of rural land where dunes competed with walled palaces and fought a land war against the farmers. Outside the city was a bit more lawless and wild. Inside, it was a modern city with a fantastic metro grid and memories of its past dotted through alleyways and alongside the industrial districts.

Stopping at a two-story stone building with a cracked façade, Imre parked in front. "We're here. With three minutes to spare." He didn't bother to get out of the van, a twin to the one left behind in Spain. He gestured for his commlink. Fatima gave it to him and got out of the vehicle. She gestured for everyone to follow.

The building was dark. The word "*AVATARS*" glowed on the left side of it in the morning light. Makeda looked down the left side of the building and saw a set of stairs and a closed metal door.

"That's the dance club. It's downstairs. The main bar is upstairs." Fatima unlocked the double doors and pulled them open.

Larger than the Bar Moraga, it could've been its older brother. Nondescript with some kitsch, the bar had eight stools. Twelve small tables dotted the room around a jukebox. There were clear signs for the restrooms and a door marked "*Private*." In truth, there was nothing to recommend it other than as a place to drink. Makeda eyed the bottles behind the bar. Nothing looked top-shelf.

"Who comes here?" Makeda noted that while the place was worn, it was clean.

Fatima shrugged. "Locals. People with a need. Quieter than some places. Noisier than others."

Imre walked in. He now wore his red, sleeveless duster from the train. It'd been cleaned, but looked like it'd seen better days. "Clock's ticking. Meet officially in thirty. My bet is that they'll be here in ten. Fatima on the door. Saladin in here with me and Kraken. Makeda, you're in the corner and aiming. MissTree, you'll be in the private room, on healing duty, watching through the peephole. Bob has eyes in the sky. Any questions?"

As Imre spoke, Kraken handed out injectors. When Makeda gave him a quizzical look, he grinned. "My special combat helper. This side is a stimulant. One injection will keep you going. This side numbs the drek out of you. Careful with it. Too much, and you'll lose all feeling in that limb."

Makeda nodded and took the injector.

MissTree stood with balled fists on her hips. "I want to hurt him. I owe him."

"Be that as it may, you're on heal duty. If it looks like he might be winning, send in a spirit to eat his face. But we're counting on you to keep us up and alive. Got it?" Imre glanced at Makeda. The request was clear: *Control your people.*

Makeda touched MissTree's arm. "It's important that you keep us alive. Hurt him if you can, but *we* are your top priority. It's what Plath—Sylvia—would've done."

MissTree scowled. She didn't say anything more, though she refused to take Kraken's injector. Invoking HiddenPlath's name was dirty pool. Makeda didn't care. There was a job to be done, and they were the ones in the crosshairs.

Imre gestured with his head for Makeda to talk with him. He led her to the corner where he planned to have her. "Will she stay on task?"

They both looked over to see Kraken taking MissTree through the door marked "*Private.*"

"Probably." Makeda gestured to her intended spot. "What am I aiming with, and won't it be a bit obvious?"

Imre tapped on the wall twice. A small DJ setup slid out of the obfuscated panel. It had a table and chair with the corner of the wall acting as a barrier. "Obvious, yes, but less obvious than before. When he says something, I'll tell him you're an observer. And you will be. We're going to record the meeting through you and through other cameras we have around here."

She narrowed her eyes. "Why?"

He shrugged. "Blackmail or proof, I suppose. Let's see what comes of the meet. But you need to let Bob back in."

Makeda frowned, looking at the small wooden wall she would "observe" from behind. "The last time I did that, I went blind."

"You got better. Now that we know he knows about you and is gunning for you, we'll be a lot more protective." Imre glanced upward. "Won't we, Bobishere2?"

"*Yes. I'm sorry. I didn't watch my back channel. I will now. Promise. Your brain is safe with me.*" Bob sounded contrite and determined. "*We really need this.*"

Makeda didn't want to do it. Part of her wanted to call TechnoGalen in, but she'd agreed that Imre was in charge here. Also, keeping him out of the limelight was the best way to keep him safe. He'd probably yell at her when she told him about this, but if she survived, she'd take the scolding.

"All right." Makeda waited for the request, then let Bobishere2 into her eyes with limited permissions. "What if he just hands over the nuyen, and you hand over the codes, and he walks away?"

"Do you really think that'll happen?" Imre frowned. "This won't work if he does."

Makeda shrugged. "I don't think he's going to try to murder you straight out. The codes are too important. I do think all bets are off once he has the codes."

Imre mimicked her shrug. "We'll play it by ear. If he doesn't try to murder me, I'll think of something else to clear our names."

"Reckless man."

He grinned at her. "Yep. Reckless and impulsive walk hand-in-hand in the shadows."

The two of them turned as Fatima approached. She offered Makeda an Ares Predator VI heavy pistol. "I figure this will work well with that Colt you carry."

"You mean the pistol I stole from Imre?" Makeda accepted the weapon and checked it. Full magazine. Smooth mechanism.

"You've kept it with you. I figured you liked it." Imre touched his own weapons: pistols, garrote, and sword. "Besides, you earned it, and I have more." He looked to the air. "Bob? Give a comm check."

"You got it, Boss. Everyone comm in."

One by one they all comm'd in the check.

"Places everyone. They'll show anytime. Dark comms unless absolutely necessary."

Fifteen minutes later, Bobishere2 broke the silence. *"We've got movement. Two trucks. Looks like one Afzalat and one not. The Afzalat truck is taking the back road. I think they're backup. They've got five, and their lieutenant, LongJack, is with them. I can also see Matchstick. He's their local demolitions guy. The other truck parked right behind your van."*

Makeda sat in the DJ spot with the Predator at the ready. She wished she had TechnoGalen in her head. The waiting made her antsy. Galen knew it and would keep up a running stream of chatter, on and off topic, to keep her focused.

"Schmidt and five bogies are out of the truck. Headed for the door."

The double doors opened, and Herr Schmidt stood there, flanked by his bodyguards. All of them armed and armored with the exception of the Johnson himself. But, as every runner knew, looks were deceiving.

Schmidt nodded to Fatima before looking at the rest of the room. "I understand I'm early. I didn't know what the traffic would be like in Morocco. Surprisingly smooth. Civilized, even."

He addressed his comments in English to Imre, who sat at a table in the middle of the room with Saladin and Kraken on either side of him. Without invitation, Herr Schmidt strode in, leaving two of his men at the door with Fatima. Two walked with him, one shifted toward Makeda.

"Ah. No. Stay away from her." Imre's voice was a whip crack of command.

Schmidt sat at the table with Imre. He gestured the guard to the other side of the room with his head. "My apologies. I didn't know she was there."

They both smiled knives in the back at the lie.

Imre kept his eyes locked to the blond man. "She's none of your concern. We're here to do business, you and I. Yes?"

"Yes. You have my..." Schmidt searched for the word he wanted. He settled on, "...files?"

Imre nodded. "Yes. You have the nuyen?"

Schmidt pulled a matte-black certified credstick with ivory bands from his pocket. "Yes."

Imre pulled a datachip from his pocket. By tacit agreement, they handed each other the items at the same time. Imre looked at the credstick display and nodded. The credstick disappeared into his pocket.

Schmidt did the same with the datachip. "I trust this has my files, and I won't be disappointed later?" He tapped his breast pocket.

"Yes. We're done?"

"Yes. I believe we are." He put his hands on the table as if to push himself up.

Imre held up a finger. "What about you setting me up to look like a possible terrorist?"

Herr Schmidt paused, his muscles still tense from the aborted motion.

Makeda scowled. Now that Imre had handed over the codes, he had no leverage. Nothing to convince Herr Schmidt to do anything to stop what he'd already started. What was he doing? What did he expect Schmidt to do now?

"Ah. That. It will be cleared up soon." Schmidt stood and turned as if to go. He looked at Makeda. "Though, now that you bring it up, one more thing. I want Makeda." He turned back to the table and sat down across from Imre once more.

Oh hell no. Makeda shifted from the ready position to a firing one, putting Schmidt in her sights. All of Schmidt's bodyguards straightened and tensed.

Bob's voice sounded over the comms. *"Unknown drone in the air."*

Imre stood in a slow motion, pulling his worn duster back to reveal his sword, his implied threat clear: He would fight to protect her. He private-comm'd Makeda. <*Stay chill. This is what we need.*> It was text in their shared chat window. He expected this.

He said aloud, "You can't have her. That was not part of this deal."

Schmidt glanced at Imre before he gave Makeda a contemptuous sneer. "Oh, I don't want to keep her. I want you to kill her."

"You already set her up to look like a terrorist."

Schmidt pursed his lips. "And won't you be the hero, killing such a wanted criminal?"

"No. Get out." Imre shook his head. "Our dealings are done."

"Drone incoming, and it's got something strapped to it." Bob sounded a bit more alarmed. *"Gonna get control of it."*

Schmidt pulled another certified credstick from his pocket. This one had platinum bands. "You don't understand. I'm going to pay you for the service. You will be a hero, and 200,000 nuyen richer."

"I don't murder people in cold blood."

"But you *do* kill people." Schmidt waved the credstick and looked around. "The price for me to clear your name is for *someone* in this room to take this contract and make sure she's dead."

"Frag you." Makeda cocked the Predator. "You've got your files. You set me up for your fall. Get out."

"Yes, well, I..."

"Incoming!"

Bob's shout was the only warning they had before the world exploded in sound, heat, and flying debris.

Makeda blinked her eyes open, her ears still ringing from the explosion. Half of the front wall of the building was crumpled in on itself. Fatima was already in a firefight with one of Schmidt's goons. Makeda sat up, pushing rock off her. Still at the table in the center of the room, Imre stood with his sword drawn. He was covered with rock dust. Herr Schmidt stood in a fluid motion despite the debris that had hit him in the back—a telltale sign of augmentation. Makeda fired three times, hitting Schmidt in the chest. All three shots *ting*ed like bullets hitting iron.

Unphased, Schmidt moved with augmented speed toward her. At the same time, he pulled on his belt buckle. In the blink of an eye, he had a sword in his hand. *"Manchmal muss man die Drecksarbeit eben selber machen."* The smug bastard spoke in German. *Sometimes, you must do the dirty work yourself.* An anticipatory smile filled his face.

A memory sword, Makeda thought in wonder. Then her own enhanced reflexes were keeping him from cutting her in two.

Imre moved into the fight, blocking Schmidt's sword with his own. While the two blades flashed almost faster than Makeda could see, she backpedaled out of the way, firing and missing. When she hit, the room heard the telltale metallic crash of the bullet ricocheting again.

The more Makeda dodged out of the way, the more Schmidt closed in on her with Imre working to keep him at bay. She threw chairs and tables at Schmidt in-between shots. He batted them out of the way.

Around them, Saladin, Fatima, and Kraken fought Schmidt's bodyguards in a hail of bullets, blades, and returned fire. One of them screamed as an octopus manifested and attached itself to the man's face.

Makeda got partial cover behind the corner of the bar and focused her aim. Schmidt saw her do so and charged. He took two more shots to the upper chest—both ricocheting—before he brought his sword down, removing her firing hand at the forearm, finger still pulling the trigger. Makeda screamed as blood spurted from her severed limb.

Still, Schmidt didn't back off. She kicked him, hard, in the knee. It was like kicking a wooden post. He sliced her leg above the knee almost clean through. Makeda fell back as Imre bowled Schmidt—who seemed more like machine than man—over.

Makeda, bleeding more than she ever had in her life, was trapped behind the bar with Imre and Schmidt attacking each other. A wave of dizziness and nausea washed over her. She was going to pass out. She couldn't let that happen. She fumbled one-handed for the injector Kraken gave her, then realized that it wouldn't keep her alive. Not with the amount of blood she was losing.

With the two men right there, Makeda snarled and made a decision. Flipping the injector over, she wound up the painkiller as far as it would go. Then she dragged herself into the sword fight. Without a word or pithy quip, she reared up and stabbed Schmidt in the lower back, driving it as deep as she could. If she was going to die, she was going to take him with her.

Schmidt gave a yell and back-fisted her in the face, breaking her nose. Makeda let the darkness take her where it would. It was all she could do.

TWENTY-SIX

Makeda woke slow. When she realized she was alive, awake, and in a bed, her adrenaline kicked in. She sat up, groping for a weapon she didn't have. She turned on her comms as she looked around the unfamiliar—but also all too familiar—hospital room. "Galen? Saladin?"

"Here. You're safe. Stand down. Widgets do wobble."

TechnoGalen. She blinked a couple of times, focusing on his words and the passphrase. It was good to hear his voice, though this waking up from unconsciousness was getting old. "You sure?"

"I'm sure. Promise."

Makeda relaxed a tiny bit. She looked at her right arm. It was wrapped up. It felt like she could feel her fingertips, but she couldn't tell if the arm was hers or not. She grimaced at the memory of Schmidt severing her hand from her body. She had to know—was that her hand, her fingertips, she felt?

"Where am I?"

"Safe." He paused as she mentally threw a digital rubber duck at him. *"Fine. You're in the main Rabat hospital, in a private room under the best medical care we can afford. No, you are not under arrest, though we do have a rotating watch on your room. I've let everyone know you're awake."*

Makeda considered this. The hospital room was nice and cleaner than some she'd been in. There were no bars on the windows. She thought about doing a news search, then decided she'd rather know if she was whole or not. She picked at the bandage around her forearm, trying to get the medical tape to peel up.

Imre and Saladin came in as she struggled with the bandage. She looked at Saladin. "Give me a knife."

Imre made a "stop" gesture. "Hey, leave that alone. You paid a lot for that."

"I did?" Makeda looked at Saladin.

"Herr Schmidt did." He took a seat on the far side of the room and pulled out a datapad, leaving Imre at her side as he pointedly did not give her the knife she'd demanded.

She felt her leg where it had almost been severed. It was bandaged, too. "Mine or cyber?"

"Yours. Cyber limbs would've been cheaper, but he refused." Imre threw Saladin an inscrutable look.

She gave a sigh of relief. "That's because he knows me. I've already given up so much of myself for my reflexes. I need my own flesh." Makeda looked Imre in the eye. "To feel right. To feel like me. I know you understand."

He nodded. "I do."

Silence descended. Makeda broke it after a count of thirty. She hated being the least knowledgeable person in the room. She hated having to drag the information out of people just as much. "So, you survived."

"Yes. You helped."

"What happened?"

"I'll have Bob show you. She caught it all with the spy drones I had her put around the place." He tilted his head. "Bob?"

"I'm here. Makeda, will you let me send you the feed?"

Saladin looked up as Bobishere2 comm'd. Makeda glanced at him. He gave her a thumbs up.

"Yes." Makeda closed her eyes, accepting the connection to Bobishere2. The feed started at the point where Imre held up a finger and asked, "What about you setting me up to look like a possible terrorist?" From the footage, it is clear that Herr Schmidt was in charge and had set her and Imre up to take the blame for the train wreck and the murder of the Saeder-Krupp employees. It would be enough to clear her name—if she could get the right people to look at it.

Also, it was terrible to watch herself be maimed. Almost as bad as having it done to her. Makeda focused in on what happened next. It was so quick, she almost missed it.

Makeda popped up from behind the bar to stab Schmidt in the back with Kraken's injector. He back-fisted her in the face, and she disappeared from sight. Schmidt groped for the injector that had already fallen from his back and blocked another sword strike from Imre.

Schmidt tottered away from the bar, his legs awkward. He punched Imre, pushing him back and shouted, "Schnell!" But all of his men were engaged or down. Imre shoulder-slammed Schmidt, knocking him back. At the same time, a knife appeared in Schmidt's hand, slashing open Imre's neck. Imre stumbled back, grasping at his throat.

Schmidt followed this with a lunge, but his body refused to do as he commanded. Instead of piercing Imre, he lurched to the side, sword flailing. Imre slashed twice, slicing open Schmidt's stomach on the upswing and decapitating him on the downswing. For a moment, the world froze, then Herr Schmidt toppled to the floor.

The feed cut off. "Wow." Makeda opened her eyes and looked at Imre's throat. It looked fine and unmarred.

Imre nodded. "Yeah. After that, it was just mop up duty, and MissTree saving your life and mine. But that was the important bit. The one that should help us both."

"Yeah. So, now what? Who do we call?"

"I've been working on it. I convinced a local fixer to get me—us—a meeting with a highly placed government official here in Rabat. Convenient that it's the capital of the country."

Makeda furrowed her brow. "Working on it? How long have I been out?"

Saladin answered instead of Imre. "Five days. On my recommendation. You needed the rest and the healing. You couldn't do anything from your bed while your limbs reattached themselves." He stood up and walked over. "We woke you as soon as Imre had news."

She eyed him. "Just because you have a point doesn't mean I'm not mad at you."

He nodded. "As expected. I did for you what you did for me back in Fleming."

Makeda opened then closed her mouth. She glanced at his cyber arms and nodded. "*Touché*."

"In any case," Imre interrupted, "think of a new name. If all goes well, we'll both have new SINs and clean slates by the end of tomorrow."

"If it doesn't?"

Imre hesitated, his face going neutral. "We'll be in custody or dead."

Makeda felt human again. Dressed like a visiting dilettante in slacks, a loose silk top, and fashionable hat, she rode with Imre in a taxi. She pinged Imre over a private comm. "When is the meet?"

"In about ten minutes."

She gave him a startled look. "I'm not armed or armored."

"Neither am I." He glanced at her. *"I wasn't kidding. If this doesn't work out, we're in custody or dead. Unarmed ups our survival rate."*

"What in God's name makes you think that?"

"I'm pretty sure the person we're meeting finds it more valuable to capture us as live terrorists than dead ones."

She poked his leg. "We talked about this. No secrets."

Imre looked up. "Thank you." He made a quick transfer to pay the driver, with a generous tip on top. *"You were unconscious. Please, trust me. I do know what I'm doing."*

Trust was a hard thing in the shadows. Harder than surviving. Either you lived or you died once. You could be stabbed in the back a thousand times and still come back for more. Trust the wrong person, and you could learn that there were worse things than being dead.

They stared at each other for a moment, gold eyes meeting dark-brown ones. Yes, Imre had lied to her, just as she'd lied to him. But they'd fought for each other, protected each other, and saved each other. He'd earned a bit of real trust. That's what he was going to get. She would meet with this person unarmed and unarmored, knowing it could go very, very bad.

Makeda nodded. "All right."

They both got out of the taxi and looked at the ruin of Avatars. It was going to take a lot to rebuild it. Makeda shook her head. "I trust you, but I don't want you to surprise me like this again. Please. What did you tell Saladin and Fatima?"

"That they could meet us here in two hours. If we were here, all would be well. If we weren't, they'd be free to plan our escape from government hands." He led her around the side to Avatars and unlocked the metal door.

"Government, not corporate?" Makeda followed him in as he flipped on the lights. Avatars went from the antechamber into a low ceiling booth-and-table area across from a window bar. In the other half of the room stood the dance floor and DJ booth with a much higher ceiling and lights.

"Morocco is far more government-run than corporate-owned. There are private corp areas, but unlike a lot of countries, the government still has the power. It's why mercenary companies thrive here."

Looking around, Makeda found the restrooms, a dance nook, and a game room that had its own window bar. All of it had dust and fallen-over debris from Bob driving the drone into the enemy truck while wrestling it away from the other hacker. Also, there were cracks in the walls that would need to be repaired.

"So, our contact is government."

"Yes. I thought I mentioned that when I said new names and new SINs."

Makeda thought back. She nodded. "You did. I just didn't understand the implications of it."

The door to Avatars opened, and people entered the antechamber then stopped. "Rabenhaupt?" The voice was female and British.

"I am here."

"You are unarmed?"

Makeda walked to Imre's side on the dance floor. There was cover, but she still felt naked without weapons or armor. Imre raised his hands and turned in a circle. Makeda followed suit. "We are."

"Good. Wait one moment. There is something you need to see."

A man in Moroccan business wear—white trousers and an embroidered tunic—walked out from the antechamber and wove his way through the tables to hand Imre a datapad. On it, a raven-haired elven woman sat in a concrete room.

"Arcade?" Imre's eyes went wide. "What are you doing?"

"What I have to, to save you and your friend. I, and Mademoiselle Beaumont, wanted you to understand the situation and where I am if anything went wrong with your meet. This is what I had to agree to for you to meet with her."

The camera pulled back, revealing that Arcade was bound to a metal chair at her waist and legs with chains. Her hands were behind her back. Armed men stood on either side of her.

"You didn't have to..."

"But I did, little brother. Now you understand the magnitude of the situation; the risk we are all taking." She glanced at the guard on her left and nodded. He moved forward and put a black bag—a mage restraint—over Arcade's head and cinched it tight. The datapad screen went black. The aide took it back from Imre's unresisting hands and turned on his heel.

Imre flushed a hectic red. "You didn't have to do that! We came here in good faith."

Makeda put a hand on his arm. "All will be well." She understood what he was feeling. If one of hers had willingly put themselves in that position for her, she'd be having kittens. "Calm." She repeated herself in his head, "Calm, Imre."

"Ah, but I did, Rabenhaupt. Especially after the video you sent me." The woman, Mademoiselle Beaumont, walked around the corner. She was a beautiful Arabic woman with russet-brown skin and long, braided hair. She wore a red embroidered caftan, belted at the waist, and carried a leather portfolio. She chose a table, dusted off the chair, and sat. Her aide stood behind her.

<Imre. On the clock. Get it together.> Makeda added a bell *bing* to her text message.

He shook his head and nodded to her, then took a breath before joining the government woman at the table. Makeda sat next to him. "All right. Arcade will be murdered if all does not go well. Duly noted."

Mademoiselle Beaumont gazed at him. "It was necessary. You will understand soon. We will get to that in a moment." She turned her gaze to Makeda. "With the funds provided, I was able to do the following: You have your new SIN. Rune Red has lived in Rabat, Morocco for the last two years without incident. She has not left the country since she arrived. She is a citizen in good standing. She has no plans on leaving in the near future."

Makeda heard the implied command—and the implied threat. She would not be allowed to leave Rabat...or maybe it was Morocco... in the "near future." Who knew how long that would be? She had not planned to stay in Rabat, but it seemed she had no choice in the matter.

As Mademoiselle Beaumont spoke, she opened an ARO and displayed a number of documents. "This is every single legal document you need. I'll transfer copies to you. You are well set in Morocco. No one will question you. If they do, I will know immediately, and will be able to intervene."

"Thank you." Makeda's heart sank as the files transferred. She could hear the "but" from a kilometer away.

"However, as for Martina 'Makeda' Aldon, I cannot do anything for her right now except refuse extradition. Too many important and wealthy people lost their lives, or someone they loved, to that train wreck." The Arabic woman's face took on a parody of concern. "It's best to have Rune Red continue to stay here in Rabat, living a comfortable, productive life. I would like to see her as an asset to the community."

Makeda worked to keep the scowl off her face as she nodded, accepting her fate. "What about that video of Herr Schmidt setting me up?"

"Ah." Mademoiselle Beaumont tapped a manicured nail to the plastic tabletop. "It is inconvenient for me to reveal that to the public right now. Inconvenient for me, for Herr Schmidt's company, and even for Saeder-Krupp." She shook her head. "Their approval rating is quite high with their public concern for their murdered employees."

She patted Makeda's hand twice. "Corporations have long memories, but they also have short attention spans. No. Now is not the time. Perhaps in a year or so. Then, we can make you a hero. It will be more believable that we'd spent the time proving Herr Schmidt was behind the attack than to accept the information from those who work outside the law. You understand."

All Makeda could do was nod. She kept her anger in check. One of them had to stay calm. Perhaps it wouldn't be so bad after all. She'd get to find out what it was like to do local runs with Imre. She glanced at the man. He had his neutral expression locked in place.

Mademoiselle Beaumont turned to Imre. "In the meantime, we have a problem."

Imre didn't say anything. He gestured for her to go on. Makeda could tell he was fortifying himself for the worst.

"We have video of you, Rabenhaupt, murdering Herr Schmidt. Your Johnson. It doesn't matter that he attacked first. That isn't clear enough on the video. If I allow you to remain in Morocco, it will put all my corporate and government friends, enemies, and associates on edge. I cannot allow that." She shook her head. "You are exiled from Morocco. You have twelve hours to put your affairs in order."

Makeda was proud of herself for not reacting to the news. She needed to remain calm for Imre in this case. Later, she'd consider what it meant for her.

Imre's poker face did not crack, though Makeda saw him squeeze his fists so tight his knuckles turned white. "I suppose there is no chance to talk you out of your decision?" His voice was light and unconcerned.

The government woman gave him a bland look and didn't dignify the question with even a headshake.

"I thought not. Thank you for the twelve hours." Under the table, Imre opened his fists and pressed the palms of his hands to his thighs. He nodded to her.

Mademoiselle Beaumont made a show of checking her old-fashioned wristwatch. Makeda wondered if she'd put it on today just for this. "I don't care how you leave. But if you are not gone by midnight, I will have you captured, locked up, and blamed for everything that happened. Then there will be a very public trial." She glanced at Makeda. "Miss Red may even be called upon to testify against you."

Imre nodded. "I understand. I will be gone by midnight." His voice was mild, but Makeda saw him clench his hands under the table again before he forced them open, letting the tension drain from his arms. "Do you know how long I'm to be exiled?"

She shook her head. "At least a year. More likely, two. As I said, corporations have long memories."

"I see. Well then, if there's nothing else, I have some arrangements to make." Imre stood.

Mademoiselle Beaumont stood. "I'll give your love to Arcade. I think she'll be pleased at how the meeting went. It's good that her trust in you is not misplaced."

Imre nodded. He stayed where he was as Mademoiselle Beaumont and her aide left.

Makeda remained where she was as well. "Would she have really shot your sister?"

"No." Imre shook his head then paused. "Well, if I had shot her, yes. Her people would've killed Arcade. But she and Arcade are best friends. It was all a show. Mademoiselle Beaumont had to have something on record to show she took precautions when dealing with me to kick me out of the country."

"Why?"

"To show all the other Johnsons in the region that I could be dealt with. That I *was* dealt with in a decisive manner."

A light dawned. "Ah, Mademoiselle Beaumont wasn't her real name."

"No." He pushed his chair under the table with careful, controlled movements.

Makeda wanted to do something to comfort him but could not think of a single thing to say. "What is it?"

"You'll have to earn that from her."

"I'm used to Sidi Ahmed for the Johnson name in this area. I didn't know about Beaumont."

Imre smiled at her. "I guess you'll have to get used to it. I need to go do some things. You stay here. Meet with Fatima and Saladin?"

Makeda nodded, knowing he wanted to make preparations of the secret kind without her hanging around. She needed to think as well.

"I'll be back soon." He leaned down to kiss her. It was long and lingering and already full of good-bye.

TWENTY-SEVEN

Makeda waited until Imre was gone to look through the documents. It was all good. She'd have TechnoGalen give it a once over, just in case. She put the documents away and rested her chin on her clasped hands. Being stuck in Morocco was not something she'd considered. In truth, she could still leave. But that would allow Saeder-Krupp, and whomever Herr Schmidt worked for, to come after her. She was protected in Morocco, thanks to Mademoiselle Beaumont.

Protected, yes. But without the infrastructure and support system she had set up in Belgium. Then again, she'd been thinking about leaving Belgium anyway. Makeda nodded to herself. "Right. Let's figure out how to do this and what my resources will be going forward."

She toggled her comms. "TechnoGalen, are you there?"

Makeda snooped through the back of the bar while she waited for Galen to get back to her. No bag, but there was synthohol. She made herself a drink. Whiskey. Neat. She threw back two fingers, grimaced, then drank a third.

"I'm here. What's the word?"

"I need to confab with you, Saladin, and, ah, MissTree. Ping me when you've got everyone online." She'd almost said, "Obscura" and "HiddenPlath," too. But stopped herself in time. Now that the panicking was over and planning had begun, grief crept in on thorny feet.

Back in the antechamber, Makeda ducked behind the coat check. Bingo. Multiple forgotten and lost bags. She chose a shoulder bag, looked through it, and tossed out everything that wasn't of value. She added her commlink. Having the weight on her shoulder felt better. Almost as good as having a credstick stuck in her bra.

"Online."

"Right. We...I...no, we, have a situation." She returned to the table she'd sat at with Imre and Mademoiselle Beaumont. "Short version: I am stuck—whatever the opposite of exiled is—here in Morocco for at least a year. My resources are limited. I'm going to need some of my stuff from Belgium sent over once..." She paused then rushed on. "Once I figure out where in Morocco 'here' is. I don't expect you to stay with me. In fact, if you can leave, it's probably best for you to do so. The sooner, the better."

Silence reigned.

MissTree was first to break it. *"I will be on the first plane home. Good luck, Makeda."*

"You, too." Makeda couldn't blame the mage. She'd be out of here in a heartbeat if she'd lost everything MissTree had lost.

"She's disconnected." Galen paused. *"I'm going to stay here, but you can always call me. You know that, right?"*

"I do. I'll miss having you in my head on a regular basis."

"Hey now, just because I'm not there physically doesn't mean we're parting ways. The Matrix is everywhere. I can hack from here just as well as there."

"I know." Makeda waited for Saladin to chime in. When he didn't, she prompted him. "Saladin?"

"I'm on my way. About five minutes out."

"What do you mean?"

"Avatars. I'll be there in five."

Makeda pressed her lips together. Whatever he was going to say to her he wanted to say in person. He was always like that. Whatever he wanted could be good or bad. She hoped he'd stay, but the man had his own life. "Right. That's all I wanted. I'll ping when I have more information."

Starting over wasn't so bad. She'd wring some contact information out of Imre before he left. Then she'd do what she always did: survive.

Makeda grabbed the bottle of whiskey and two glasses—the one she'd drunk out of and one for Saladin—then sat at the table and waited. She poured the faux whiskey into both glasses but did not drink. Instead, she held her glass, rolling it back and forth in her hands, warming it in a way synthohol didn't need to be.

As soon as Saladin entered, she held up her glass. "Are we going to toast to a merry meeting or a merry parting?"

Saladin walked over and picked up his glass. "How about new beginnings?"

They clinked glasses and drank.

Saladin sat across from her. "How many have you had?"

"Enough." Makeda slid the bottle to him. "You staying or going?"

He wrinkled his nose at her. "Staying. You need someone to watch your back when you aren't in bed with Imre."

She smiled at him with a gratitude she didn't know how to express with words. "Imre's been exiled. He's got until midnight to get out of Morocco or a world of hurt is going to come down on his head—and probably mine, too."

Saladin eyed her. "When were you going to mention that?"

Makeda toyed with her glass. "Once everyone had made their decision or he was gone. Didn't want anyone feeling sorry for me."

Saladin shook his head. "I'm here. At least for now. I'll arrange for our stuff to get here."

"Why do you stay? With me, I mean." She peered at him. She knew what her answer would be if the shoe were on the other foot: Implicit trust is the most valuable thing you can have in the shadows, and she trusted him to guard her back.

"You're the sister I never had. You've saved my life multiple times. Besides, what else would I do with myself? You're the brain. I'm the brawn. You listen to my advice. A good friend is worth all the nuyen in the world." He grinned, white teeth against his dusky skin. "Besides, I'm bored with Belgium. Morocco promises to be interesting."

"Thanks. I'm glad you're staying. At least for a bit." Makeda put her glass down and clasped his hand. "Just so you know, we have almost no money, no place to stay, and no local contacts. We're starting all over again."

"You make it sound so inviting."

"Why else would I be sitting in a half-destroyed building instead of in a café, having a good cup of Turkish coffee and a pastry?" She patted the purloined shoulder bag. "At least I have Rune Red, and she's a citizen in good standing."

"Rune, is it?" Saladin tilted his head, considering. "Appropriate. I like it. It's a name I can support."

An hour later, when Imre returned, he had Fatima with him. He called them to come to the top of the building. After they navigated their way through the rubble in the front, he led them through the back hallway to his office door. He touched Makeda, stroking her chin. "We've got business to discuss, you and I."

Saladin and Fatima exchanged a look. "We'll be out front," Fatima said. The two of them disappeared together.

Makeda shivered and smiled. "What kind of business?"

Imre unlocked the office door and led her inside. He didn't say anything until he sat behind his desk, an old wooden thing with the scars and nicks of years gone by. "The club-owning business."

Makeda sat across from him and glanced around, taking in the bare walls and scant knick-knacks of a rarely used room. This part of the building seemed to have fared better than the front. "Avatars?"

"Or whatever you want to call it." He shrugged and opened up an ARO full of text. "Obviously, I can't take care of it anymore. You own it. I get fifty percent of the profit for the next ten years."

"If you've noticed, the building is missing a front wall, and I have no money to fix it. I don't have much of anything set up in Rabat."

He gestured to the ARO. "That's all in here. I'm leaving you rebuilding money. That's why the profit sharing."

Makeda read the contract and shook her head. "I'm your manager for five years and then become owner? No. If I do this, I'm the owner from the get-go. And you get five percent of the profit."

"If that's the case, then the rebuild fund is a loan. Forty percent of the profit."

"I'm doing you a favor. You have to leave. Who else can you sell it to? Who else can you trust to take care of it enough for you to profit from it when you're gone? Ten percent."

"I'm giving you a new start. A new place to make your own. A location people already know. Thirty percent."

Makeda eyed him. From the look on his face, he'd already given up this building as a loss and was just going through the motions of the bargain and the deal. "Twenty percent of the profit for five years, plus repayment of the build loan...*and* you give me a list of contacts that you'll vouch for and vouch me to. In the shadows and the light."

"Twenty-five percent." Imre smiled at her and held out his hand.

"Twenty percent. And I'll give you a ride to the airport." She grabbed his hand to shake.

"With my car." He laughed and shook with her. "Deal." Imre made the changes in the ARO. "So eager to see me leave?"

Makeda stopped smiling. "No. That's the worst part of this."

"No, the worst part is that I let you bargain me down from ten years to five and I didn't even notice." He tilted his head. "It'll be fine. I've been exiled before. It's not like we're saying good-bye forever."

He slid the new contract to her. "Besides, Kraken is coming with me. Same with Bobishere2. I'll try to find out if Pongolyn and Ollietronic are dead or alive as well. See if they want to meet up again now that the heat is off."

"Not Fatima?"

"No. She's going to keep an eye on my interest in this place for me. Besides, I think she's got something going with Saladin."

Makeda raised an eyebrow. "Really? That sneaky guy. Good for them. It's about time he chose someone for himself."

"You treat her well. She's loyal and good."

"I will. If she chooses to work with me. I'm not going to make that assumption. She could beat me up."

"You and me both."

Makeda doubted that. Then she read through the contract in silence. When she was satisfied everything was in order, she signed it, remembering to sign as Rune Red.

Imre glanced over it, barely looking at her electronic signature. "I guess that's it."

"Yes. Now what?"

"Now, I leave you to your gilded prison, while I go into exile."

"You make it sound like so much fun." Makeda threw off the morose mood that threatened and grinned wide. "It's going to be. Here's to new beginnings." She got up and leaned over the desk to kiss him. He accepted the kiss, reaching out a hand to cup her cheek. Makeda gazed at him with a sly smile. "How much time do we have before you leave?"

"Enough, if you wish."

"I wish."

Imre stood and opened his arms. "My command."

As she slid into his embrace, they both knew this would be their real good-bye, said more with their bodies than their words.

Makeda got out of the car and walked around to the trunk as Imre pulled a small suitcase from it. The busy Rabat International Airport buzzed all around them. "Thank you for everything you've done."

He put the suitcase on the ground. "Thank you for not shooting me in the Swiss Alps."

"It was a close thing."

"I know." Imre gave her a hug then searched her eyes. "Why Rune?"

Makeda smiled a Mona Lisa smile. "We all come from somewhere."

"That's not really an answer."

"I know. Now you'll have something to ask me when you return." She cupped his cheek with the palm of her hand. "Someday."

"I will see you again." Imre leaned in close. They kissed long and slow. "You taste like nostalgia," he murmured to her lips.

"So do you."

A smile lit up his handsome face. He picked up his bag and tilted an imaginary hat to her. Then he turned and walked into the airport. Makeda watched until he disappeared into the crowd. Dry-eyed, she got into the car and gestured for Saladin to drive.

"Not going to wait?"

"No. No need." It was always easier to say good-bye to lovers than friends. This time was no exception.

He pulled out into traffic. "Now what?"

Makeda watched the Rabat traffic go by. "Now, it's time for me to design *Rune's Avatar Café*. If I'm going to be stuck in Morocco like Rick in Casablanca, I might as well make the most of it."

BONUS STORY: RUNE'S AVATAR CAFÉ (FIVE YEARS LATER…)

AUTHOR'S NOTE

The short story, "Rune's Avatar Café," was written long before the novel, *Makeda Red*. John Helfers asked me to write a *Shadowrun* story for the *World of Shadows* anthology (Catalyst Game Labs, 2015) and stipulated that it needed to be set in a currently unused area of the world. We wanted to broaden *Shadowrun*'s horizons in a visceral, fictional way. I agreed.

Casablanca is a classic movie not easily forgotten. Morocco is a law unto itself, even in this day and age. I couldn't see that changing in the 6th World. I decided I wanted to create a direct homage to the movie with this short story. As you will read (or reread) you will see that it is more of a love story to the movie and its concepts than an homage.

Years later, I was still so enamored of the main character, Rune— my Rick equivalent—that I jumped at the chance to tell her back story. Thus, *Makeda Red* was born. This is where that story was conceived.

RUNE'S AVATAR CAFÉ

Rune remotely watched the beautiful blonde dwarf down shot after shot of her best sake. She shook her head, knowing Eva was just waiting for her.

She threw a silent message over the Café's internal comm channel to Saladin. He was the 'Sasha' on duty at the bar tonight. His AR form looked exactly like Sasha from the classic 2-D movie *Casablanca*. She didn't want to ask, but she did anyway: >*How long has she been here?*

Saladin glanced from Eva towards Rune's back office. >*About two hours. Looks like you hooked another one, Red.*

She didn't respond to the implied leer. Rune sighed, then smoothed her white jacket and lifted her chin. "Better get this over with." Strolling out of her office towards the far end of the bar, Rune knew she cut an impressive figure; spotless white linen against black skin, high cheekbones, and short, curly hair the color of fresh blood offset by tawny gold eyes. She came by her name—and her reputation—honestly.

Halfway down, Rune stopped and picked up the stack of papers and envelopes—an affectation to go along with the Café's theme. As she leafed through the various notes, invitations, and requests, she felt Eva glaring daggers into her back, then sensed the lovely dwarf abandon her drink to stalk toward her.

Saladin followed at a discreet distance; far enough away to pretend privacy, but close enough to be on hand as needed.

Eva stopped within touching distance behind her. "Where were you last night?"

"That was so long ago, I don't remember." Rune paused at a note informing her that LongJack, one of the local mercs, would be in this evening to see her.

"Will I see you tonight?"

She ignored the note of desperation in Eva's voice. "I never make plans that far ahead."

"Slot it, Rune. Why do I even bother?"

"I don't know." Rune paused at a reservation for one Renart Sud and frowned. Suddenly, she didn't have time to let her latest paramour down easy. "Sasha, call Eva a cab. It's time for her to go home."

"But...no!" The dwarf's startled denial was cut off by Saladin gripping her the arm.

"You know I love you, Eva, but Miss Red pays me. Time to go." Despite his slender frame, Saladin was far stronger than he looked, and Eva could do nothing but move along with the bartender.

Rune stared at the reservation: *Renart Sud and guest for the penthouse suite.* No end date mentioned. She wondered why such an infamous trid personality would be in Rabat and wondered if he was the reason LongJack wanted a word with her. She grimaced. Sometimes, Rune's Avatar Café was a little too much like its thematic twin. But what else could you expect in a country in the middle of a tug of war between the Federation of Islamic States and the Alliance For Allah?

Shrugging, Rune returned to her office and made preparations for the evening that included a heightened awareness and the looming presence of security.

The warm evening called for an elegant gown of antique white. Rune knew wearing the armored Amina was overkill. *A lady can never be too careful,* she thought as she selected a thin strand of pearls. *Besides, I look divine in this dress.* She took the time to make sure every part of her appearance was perfectly arranged. Between LongJack and Renart, it was going to be an interesting evening. Best to have all her weapons in place.

The Café was abuzz with activity as she entered the main room. Rune paused to survey her domain. In meat space, it was a pleasant, old-fashioned dinner club. She smiled at the almost full tables. Shifting her vision to AR showed the same room in black and white. Everyone who hadn't been wearing era appropriate clothing in the real world now wore something that wouldn't clash with the image she'd built her establishment on.

A splash of color and light briefly appeared as guests entered the "Members Only" gambling section through heavy velvet curtains. Gambling needed the luxury of color. It wetted the appetite for all of the pleasures available to those who could afford it.

Fatima's sotto voice came over the comm link. *"Miss Red? Captain Belali is here to see you."*

Rune glanced at the main floor again. Fatima was on 'Sam' duty tonight, playing piano to the guests at their whim. There, next to her, was a short, balding, Arabic man with a round face and a benign smile. That smile told Rune all she needed to know. "Seat him at my table."

She watched Fatima escort Rabat's Chief of Police to her table, but didn't hurry over. Instead, she sauntered through the diners, stopping at each table for a quick pleasantry. Paying customers trumped whatever Belali wanted.

The captain stood as she approached, and held out his hands to her. "Rune, you look splendid as always. Have a drink with me?"

She took his hands briefly, then sat. "You know I don't drink on the job. But, please, don't let that stop you. My treat, of course."

"Taéngelé, then." Belali sat back and continued to smile at her.

Rune quirked a half-smile at him. "What do you want, Captain?"

"Please, call me Hamza. I've told you a thousand times." He tilted his head towards her. "We could have a much less formal arrangement, lovely lady." Lifting up the glass of Taéngelé as it arrived, he toasted her. "Something far more...intimate."

"You know I like my women blonde and my men lanky. You, dear Hamza, are neither." Her smile was gone. "And this is a conversation we have had before. It's unlike you to revisit such."

Belali drank deep of the Tir Tairngire mead. "Well, speaking of lanky and blonde, I hear that you will have a special guest tonight and his lady friend. I believe that he is lanky and she is blonde..." He let the implications hang in the air between them.

"I'm not sure what you're talking about." Rune mentally swore in a silent burst of English, Arabic, and Sperethiel.

"Oh, come now. You don't think I know that Renart is here in Rabat, and has a reservation to stay in your lovely establishment? It is said that he is traveling with a lovely blonde elf. She's been at his side from Nigeria to Turkey to France and, most recently, Spain."

Rune watched him watch her as he took another long gulp of his drink. She shrugged. "I'm aware that I have a VIP coming in who has rented the penthouse indefinitely. If it's, as you say, Renart, then I will treat him like every single one of my VIP guests. This place is safe." She paused before adding, "I am up-to-date on my payments."

"Yes, yes. Of course you are, and I'd expect nothing less for such a well-connected woman as yourself." He tapped his fingers on the table in a light pattern that matched Fatima's playing. "But you would, in deference to our longstanding relationship, let me know as soon as he leaves?"

Forcing herself to relax into a less guarded position, Rune nodded and plastered a polite smile on her face. "Of course. If that is your wish." She held up her finger. "But, remember, his reservation is ongoing." She started to say more, but her comm link chimed that Renart had arrived. "And you must forgive me, but my VIP guests are here. I must greet them." Rune stood. "Please, enjoy your time here. The Baccarat tables are open tonight."

She turned her back on him as he toasted her again. Rune glided through the now crowded room with the smooth ease of long practice. Pausing by a pillar, she took in Renart Sud and his lady friend.

He was a tall, dusky-skinned elf, handsome in an arresting way. His mixed blood heritage gave him the complexion of his Arabic father with the light blue eyes of his French mother. Rune could see why he was the bad boy of the trid reporting world. Impeccably dressed, he spoke with a casual charm that caught everyone at the front desk. *Lanky, indeed.*

The woman traveling with him was covered from head to toe in an elaborately embroidered abaya and niqab of teal linen and gold thread. It covered every part of her except for her eyes. From this distance, all Rune could see was the heavy makeup that made the woman's light-colored eyes pop. There was no way to tell if she was blonde, but if she was as attractive as the elf next to her, it was safer for her to travel covered. Morocco did a brisk business in the slave trade. An exotic blonde would garner far more attention than she wanted.

Rune strode up to the front counter, breaking Walid out of his trance at whatever Renart had been saying. "Excuse me, Mr. Sud. May I introduce you to Miss Rune Red, the owner of Rune's Avatar Café and so much more?"

Renart turned his charm on her as he smiled, holding out a hand. "So pleased to finally meet you. I've heard so much about you, Miss Red."

"All lies, I assure you," she said with a laugh.

He sobered. "I sincerely hope not." Then the charm was back. He gestured to the veiled woman. "This is Elodie, my wife. We've had a very long trip."

Now that Rune could see her more clearly, she knew those eyes—knew them to the bottom of her soul. Shaken, Rune nodded with automatic politeness in the other woman's direction. She turned her attention back to Renart. "Well, a long trip requires a comfortable room, and you've booked the penthouse. Let me see you there personally." She nodded to the valet, already carrying two bags. "Shall I send for the rest of your things?"

"We're traveling light. That's it." Renart's voice was sober again.

"Ah. Then if you will follow me, please." Rune led the way to the lift as she spoke. "Rune's Avatar Café has all that you need. The penthouse is on the 6th floor. It has every amenity available. If there's something you need that we don't have, we will go get it for you. The main floor is a dinner club, with a gambling establishment in the back. The second floor has the spa. The basement floors are for those who are less enamored with the historical feel of the Café. Below us is Avatars, our underground dance club and bar. As a VIP guest, you have access to all parts of the Café, of course."

Rune knew she was rambling as they rode the elevator, specifically not looking at Renart's wife. It was the only way to get her shocked nerves under control.

As the elevator doors opened, she gestured to the double doors across the hallway. "Here we are. If you wish, I will show you how to set the security for the room so that only authorized people may enter."

The valet entered the suite's parlor after Renart and his wife. The parlor was adorned in rich brocades and silks of red and yellow, and accented in a deep blue. Three leather chairs sat around a low table of real mahogany wood. A matching leather couch sat opposite them. The accompanying end tables were made of filigreed wood that depicted dancing women. Every vase and painting was an antique. The far sitting room wall was a floor-to-ceiling window with a balcony overlooking Rabat. Even the Persian accent rugs that led down the small hallway were of the highest quality. Through the short hallway, open doors revealed the opulence of the other two rooms. One doorway opened to the washroom, gleaming with gold, green, and blue. The other doorway revealed the large bedroom in blue and gold with small red accents.

Renart glanced down the small hallway and into the two open doors. He nodded to his wife before moving to look out the windows. Elodie disappeared into the washroom. Rune frowned as Renart's posture took on the stiffness of an act. She smoothed her face over into a mask and tilted her head at the valet

One look at Rune's face, and the valet set the luggage down, then disappeared without waiting for his tip. Renart glanced at the security features around the suite and the security panel in the main sitting area before turning to Rune and giving her his full attention. "I'm familiar with this setup. I think I can manage."

Rune noticed his smiled seemed strained now that they were out of the public eye. "If there is anything you need, please don't hesitate to call." She stepped back towards the exit, thinking Renart was more tired than he let on, while trying to convince herself that Elodie couldn't be who she thought she was.

He shifted from one foot to the other. "Yes, well. Elodie told me much about you. Perhaps, the two of you could catch up with one another?"

Rune frowned and cocked her head to one side, not understanding. Movement at the bathroom door caught her eye. There, standing with the light haloing her blonde hair, stood the most beautiful elven woman she'd ever seen—and a lost piece of Rune's past.

"Zaria," Rune whispered in a prayer of hope and disbelief.

"Hello, Makeda."

Rune sat behind her desk, glaring at nothing. "You stupid slitch. How could you run like that?" She put her head in her hands. She knew exactly how and why Zaria had done what she did. The shock was designed to knock her off her game and to make her at least listen to what she and her husband had to say. *Her husband!* That woman could always get to her. Rune's cheeks flushed hot as the brief conversation looped itself through her memory.

"We need your help."

"I'm sure the kitchen will have everything you need."

"Makeda..."

"I have an appointment. Excuse me."

Then she'd ran for the back hallway stairs, not bothering to wait for the lift. To wait would've been a mistake. It would've meant more talk, more embarrassment, more of everything she didn't want. At least she'd found her composure by the time she'd had to walk through the main floor with a smile chiseled into her face.

Saladin knew something was wrong, though. He'd waited five minutes before knocking on her office door and offering her a glass of real whiskey. He paused long enough for her to tell him that she was unavailable tonight except for her established meeting with LongJack.

The whiskey sat untouched in front of her. Just the smell of it was enough to bring back the memories of Belgium and a run gone wrong...

...Makeda set the injured elf mage on the ground. The culvert wasn't a very good hiding place, but it was large enough and dry. It would have to do.

She touched Zaria's face. "Zar, wake up. You've got to heal yourself. Please..."

It had taken hours for Zaria to wake from her fatigue and injuries. That was the first time she'd kissed Makeda. An unwilling smile graced Rune's lips as she touched them in memory. From there, it had been weeks of running, hiding, loving. Rune closed her eyes, letting the memories cascade over her.

...Mingled hands and glances in the shadows of the Norbertine Abbey...

...Bodies entwined in the hayloft of an abandoned barn...

...A fleeting kiss before the two of them ran for their lives...

...The first night spent in a bed together in the Chateau de Mons...

Her comm link came to life. Saladin sounded frustrated. *"I'm sorry, Red. I've got an elf here who insists she needs to see you now. That you know her."*

Rune growled at him. "Send her away. I don't want to talk to her."

"I've tried. She's sworn she will sit where she is until you see her."

"Dare I ask?"

"On the floor, outside your office."

She rubbed her temples as she stood. "We'll talk later about how she got that far in the first place. I'll get her." Opening her office door, Elodie was already standing.

Rune swallowed her heart and emotions as she gestured the lithe elf in. "Still as stubborn as ever I see."

"It's the only way I know how to be." Elodie entered and sat in the chair across from Rune's desk. "Makeda—"

"No." Rune shook her head. "You don't get to call me that. Makeda is long gone. She left when she thought you died in that explosion. I'm Rune. Miss Red to you. And you are Miss Sud to me."

"I'm sorry—"

"Sorry's not good enough. I looked for your body, for *any* sign of you for months. I couldn't find anything. I had no choice but to think you were dead. Makeda died when I left Belgium."

Elodie grimaced, then nodded. She bit her lip. "Well then, Miss Red, I need to do business with you."

Rune took her seat behind her desk again. "What may I do for you?"

"Renart and I need to leave Morocco as soon as possible. There's a price on our heads." Elodie clasped her hands together. "It's bad this time."

"I'm sorry for you, but why come to me?" Rune shook her head. "I run a hotel and entertainment complex. Nothing more. Nothing less."

Elodie's gaze narrowed. "I'm not some slot off the street. Everyone who knows anything knows that if you need something in a hurry, Rune's Avatar Café is where you go."

Rune shook her head again. "Don't know who you've been talking to, but—"

"I can pay." Elodie dropped an ebony credstick on the desk. "Please."

The color of the credstick stopped Rune's rejection in her throat. "Hoi, chummer.... Maybe you need to tell me who or what you're running from." Now her eyes narrowed. "What did you bring down on my place?"

"Short version? Every merc unit from here to the border, the police, and every loyal Alliance and Federation member. It's in your best interest to help us." Elodie raised a slender hand. "Renart has some information on—"

Rune shook her head. "No. Don't tell me. The less I know, the better. He's got paydata that's enough to kill for, I'm sure." She pressed her lips together in a thin line, considering the amount of nuyen that could be on that credstick.

Elodie nodded. "We need to get to either Denver or Seattle as soon as possible."

"Not Tir Na nÓg? It's closer."

"No. There are problems there. Tir Tairngire would be better, but Denver or Seattle would be easier. I'm not kidding, there's multiple black market bounties on our heads."

Rune stood and paced around the room for several silent rotations. If nothing else, Elodie was right. She needed the Suds out of her establishment, or it was going to become a smoking crater. But probably not in the way Elodie wanted. "Why isn't he hiding? Why did you come here?"

"He was. Then he wasn't because...because I told him you would be able to *fix* things."

"You were wrong." Rune put her hand on the doorknob. "I can't help you. Things have changed. I'm not the woman you remember."

Elodie picked up the credstick, but didn't put it away. "Yes, you are. I know you still are."

There was a knock on the door.

Rune signaled Elodie to stay silent. "What?"

"It's Fatima. LongJack is waiting for you at your table."

Rune closed her eyes briefly. "Dammit." She opened the door and pulled a startled Fatima into the room. She gestured at Elodie. "Take her through the back way to the penthouse. Don't let anyone see you. Double security. Who's on shoot duty?"

Fatima's surprise shifted into the non-expression of all business. "Schism's in the nest and Bishop's on lead. I'll get it done. Do we need to lock it down?"

Rune shook her head. "Just the penthouse. Things are going to be hot for a while."

Elodie stepped up to Rune and pushed the credstick into her hands. "You *can* help us. Please. We're dead without you. *Fix* this." Then she stepped out of the office and into the hallway, waiting for Fatima there.

Rune nodded at Fatima's quizzical look. "You've got your orders. Also, have beef soycakes and a bottle of Hurlg sent to my table."

After the two of them left, Rune looked down at the credstick in her hands. *I can't do this. I can't give up everything I've made here. I'm going to have to tell the Mister himself that they came to the wrong girl.* Shoving the credstick into a hidden pocket, she took a quick look in the mirror, deemed herself presentable, and put on her usual saunter.

LongJack already had a mug of the dark, thick ale in hand. He looked like the typical bruiser ork but Rune knew better. Behind the tusks and skin the color of dying moss lay a keen mind. LongJack was the best decker she knew—white hat, black hat, and merc alike. He was also in charge of the Afzalat, the most powerful merc unit in

Rabat. Rumor had it that while he and his people could be bought by the highest bidder, they preferred to be hired by the Alliance.

Rune put on a wide smile as she approached the table. LongJack stood and nodded. "Rune. A pleasure. Thank you for seeing me on such short notice."

"You are always welcome here." She watched him sit after she'd taken her seat. No smile. Stiff posture. This was business, and it wasn't going to be pleasant.

The ork nodded. "I know. But..." He pulled himself together and gazed at her. "You have people here that cannot be here. I'm coming to ask that you remove them from your place."

She shook her head, frowning. "I'm not sure what you mean." They were silent for the moment it took for the beef soycakes, a house specialty, to arrive. "I'm afraid I need a little bit more information."

"We know that Renart Sud is here. There's a bounty on his head. I'm sure you are aware." He pushed on as she watched him. "I am getting much pressure from my superiors to acquire this man. He has crossed lines he should not have crossed."

"Rune's Avatar Café is a safe place for everyone. I pay a lot of money to make sure this is so."

"I know. It's why I'm asking you to tell Renart he is no longer welcome. I don't care about the woman. But Renart needs to go. What happens to him afterwards is my business."

"Someone's trying to hack our system." Walid's voice chirped over her comm link. *"They're good, but we're better."'*

"Acknowledged." Rune said *sotto voce*. Her smile turned brittle. "If you want your hacker to survive, tell them to withdraw now. We will kill to protect our own."

LongJack gave her a half-smile and a nod. "We had to try."

"No. You didn't. Not in my place. Don't ever mess with me again." Rune stood. "This place is safe for everyone—remember that."

LongJack stood and gripped her arm to keep her from leaving. "Don't be so sure of that." He nodded to the main entryway, where Captain Belali and two uniformed police officers stood.

"What are you doing?" Rune's stomach dropped in fear as she jerked her arm out of LongJack's grasp.

"Showing you just how important this is."

As Rune watched, the two officers walked to a table indicated by the Captain. They leaned over, speaking quietly to the man eating alone there, then picked him up bodily, slapped cuffs on him as he started struggle, and tazed him when he wouldn't calm down. The officers carried the unconscious man out of the Café.

Captain Belali walked over to her and removed his hat. "My most sincere apologies, Miss Red. That man was a wanted criminal. Very dangerous. You know how much I dislike interrupting the course of your business, but when duty calls, what can you do?" He gave her an apologetic smile and a half bow before following his men out.

LongJack kept his voice low. "You have twenty-four hours to turn Renart out. After that, we will come in and get him. No one will stop us."

"*We* will stop you." Rune felt the rush of rage flush her cheeks. "With deadly force."

He nodded. "I know. I am sorry for the damage we will do to the Café. I really do like this place." He straightened. "Twenty-four hours."

Rune watched him leave, her stomach in knots. If she wanted to protect what was hers, she was going to have to do something she did not want to do. She hated being pushed and she was getting it from all sides. There was only one thing to do now.

"Please! You can't do this to us. Rune, please."

Rune ignored Elodie's plea as she escorted Renart and Elodie to the front desk. She gestured to the valet to take their bags. "I'm sorry it has come to this, Mr. Sud. Your credstick was found to be a forgery. I understand this isn't your fault but, as you cannot pay, you and your wife cannot stay. You understand."

Elodie, once again dressed in her teal and gold abaya and niqab whirled on Rune, stepping between her and Renart. "We trusted you."

"You should've found a better banker." Rune kept her voice mild. She shot out a hand and caught Elodie's wrist before the furious woman slapped her. "Don't press your luck."

Walid coughed into his fist. "Pardon me. Your car has arrived."

Renart gently removed Rune's hand from Elodie's wrist and pulled his wife to his side. "She's doing what she needs to do, Elodie. I understand it all too well. We will make do." He escorted his wife outside to the car without looking back.

Rune shook her head and walked to the bar. "Whiskey, Sasha. Make it a double." She took the glass of amber liquor and warmed it between her palms.

"That was faster than I expected you to move. I expected them to be here in the morning."

She scowled into her drink before tossing it back in two long swallows. Then she turned to face Belali. "I wasn't given a choice. I didn't want another example or a firefight in my place."

The man had his hat in his hand and glanced at the floor for a moment before he looked up again. "I wasn't given much of a choice either. My orders came from above." He leaned forward and took one of her hands in his. He pressed a credstick into it. "I've been asked to give you this from LongJack. Since you did what he asked, he thought you should be paid for your effort."

She glanced down at the silver credstick before making it disappear. "The Café is safe, but my reputation is in ruins, I'm sure. This might cover what I'm going to lose in business."

Belali straightened. "Business is business, and that is all this was. People will forget." He shrugged. "Such is the price of doing business in Rabat."

"What will happen now?" Rune gazed over the emptier than usual main dining hall.

"Oh, well. My people will keep watch on Mr. Sud and his lovely bride. We will know where they are at all times. LongJack will call me. I will tell him what I know. I will be paid. And then..." He shrugged again, looking away. "I suspect that Renart Sud and his wife will no longer be wanted by the powers that be."

She shook her head. "You're a piece of work."

"We all do what we need to do to survive." He bowed his head to her. "And now, duty calls."

Rune returned to her office, keeping her gait steady and her face neutral. When she was safely behind closed doors, she paused long enough to take a steadying breath but didn't stop. Walking to the back part of her office, she opened a hidden door and stepped inside a very small elevator.

Waiting for her at the bottom was Fatima. "All is well?"

Rune nodded. "As well as can be. At least Belali took the bait. You?"

"No problem. Oded owed me a favor. He got me two stage kits in short order. They're being coached now."

The two of them walked through the hidden passageways underneath Avatars and the Café until they reached one of the safe havens. There, two human men—both redheads—were being coached how to speak, hold themselves, and walk by Saladin. Rune watched for a long couple of minutes before she nodded. "Renart. Elodie."

Only one of the men twitched in her direction, then stopped and made an attempt to cover his mistake by studying his nails.

"Not bad. Which one are you?"

The man who had twitched hung his head. "Renart."

Rune nodded. "You'll need to do better if you want to survive."

"I know."

"What happens now?" Elodie, the shorter of the two men, asked.

"Now, we hand you over to the team I've hired who will get you to where you're going. I'll pay them half upfront, and half after one of you contacts me. Then the two of you will be on your own. Remember, those nanopoly masks will only last twenty-four hours. That's all your money gets you."

"What do you get out of this?"

Rune gazed at her, looking for the woman behind the mask. She couldn't see Elodie's delicate elven features at all. "Besides my nuyen?

The knowledge that both of you owe me. I suspect favors from you two will come in handy in the future. Also, I know where you are and how you got there. That's enough for me this time around."

"Thank you for doing this for me."

Rune shook her head. "I'm not doing it for you. This isn't some old-time romantic movie. I'm doing it for me."

Elodie looked away, then returned to Saladin and Renart.

"We'll always have Belgium." Rune murmured, smiling a soft, sad smile as she turned to Fatima. "Is the team here?"

"Yes. Waiting in the garage." Fatima glanced at Saladin. "He got them fake SINs that match their masks."

"What about their regular gear?"

"Silent mode or stored."

Saladin lifted his head and called. "We're ready here."

Rune straightened her shoulders. "Time to fix things for everyone."

Rune sat at the bar of the closed dining hall. Avatars, below them, was still going strong, but the Café always shut down at 0200, and all diners were out of the hall by 0300. She stared at the empty place.

"Can I get you anything?"

Saladin and Fatima had returned with her to the dining hall to make sure everything was set for tomorrow. Rune knew it was because they thought she needed babysitting. Maybe she did. "Double whiskey. Real. Not colored water."

"You want me to play something for you?" Fatima brought her music deck over to the bar.

Rune smiled. "Yeah. Something sad and sweet. But not The Song."

"I can manage that." Fatima let her fingers dance over the keyboard in a modern ballad.

"What are we going to do when they discover the fake Renart and Elodie?" Saladin slid a glass of real alcohol to her.

"Nothing. The runners I hired know nothing of the other team. They thought Renart and Elodie hired them to cover for the 'forged credstick,' but were too young, dumb, or desperate to check their credstick during the deal."

"It wasn't forged, was it?"

Rune shook her head. "Of course not. So, either they'll escape or they won't. If they do, they do—and a job well done. I might use them in the future. If they don't, they'll tell the truth or die."

"And we're still in the clear, either way." Saladin nodded.

"Speaking of which, everyone involved gets a bonus. LongJack paid for my acquiescence. I figured I should share the bounty."

Fatima and Saladin grinned at each other. "I hope he never finds out."

"Such is the price of doing business in Morocco." Rune raised her glass to her employees and friends. "Here's looking at you, kid."

ABOUT THE AUTHOR

Jennifer Brozek is a multi-talented, award-winning author, editor, and tie-in writer. She is the author of *Never Let Me Sleep*, and *The Last Days of Salton Academy*, both of which were nominated for the Bram Stoker Award. Her *BattleTech* tie-in novel, *The Nellus Academy Incident*, won a Scribe Award. She continues to write tie-in fiction with her most recent *Shadowrun* novella, *DocWagon 19*, and her YA *BattleTech* novel, *Iron Dawn*, the first of the Rogue Academy trilogy.

Her editing work has netted her a Hugo Award nomination, as well as an Australian Shadows Award for the *Grants Pass* anthology. Jennifer's short form work has appeared in Apex Publications, Uncanny Magazine, and in anthologies set in the worlds of *Valdemar*, *Shadowrun*, *V-Wars*, *Masters of Orion*, and *Predator*.

Jennifer has been a freelance author, editor, and tie-in writer for over ten years after leaving her high paying tech job, and she's never been happier. She keeps a tight schedule on her writing and editing projects and somehow manages to find time to volunteer for several professional writing organizations such as SFWA, HWA, and IAMTW. She shares her husband, Jeff, with several cats and often uses him as a sounding board for her story ideas. Visit Jennifer's worlds at jenniferbrozek.com or follow her on Twitter: @JenniferBrozek.

LOOKING FOR MORE SHADOWRUN FICTION, CHUMMER?

WE'LL HOOK YOU UP!

Catalyst Game Labs brings you the very best in *Shadowrun* fiction, available at most ebook retailers, including Amazon, Apple Books, Kobo, Barnes & Noble, and more!

NOVELS

1. *Never Deal with a Dragon* (Secrets of Power #1) by Robert N. Charrette
2. *Choose Your Enemies Carefully* (Secrets of Power #2) by Robert N. Charrette
3. *Find Your Own Truth* (Secrets of Power #3) by Robert N. Charrette
4. *2XS* by Nigel Findley
5. *Changeling* by Chris Kubasik
6. *Never Trust an Elf* by Robert N. Charrette
7. *Shadowplay* by Nigel Findley
8. *Night's Pawn* by Tom Dowd
9. *Striper Assassin* by Nyx Smith
10. *Lone Wolf* by Nigel Findley
11. *Fade to Black* by Nyx Smith
12. *Burning Bright* by Tom Dowd
13. *Who Hunts the Hunter* by Nyx Smith
14. *House of the Sun* by Nigel Findley
15. *Worlds Without End* by Caroline Spector
16. *Just Compensation* by Robert N. Charrette
17. *Preying for Keeps* by Mel Odom
18. *Dead Air* by Jak Koke
19. *The Lucifer Deck* by Lisa Smedman
20. *Steel Rain* by Nyx Smith
21. *Shadowboxer* by Nicholas Pollotta
22. *Stranger Souls* (Dragon Heart Saga #1) by Jak Koke
23. *Headhunters* by Mel Odom
24. *Clockwork Asylum* (Dragon Heart Saga #2) by Jak Koke
25. *Blood Sport* by Lisa Smedman
26. *Beyond the Pale* (Dragon Heart Saga #3) by Jak Koke
27. *Technobabel* by Stephen Kenson

In the year 2079, shadowrunners do the jobs no one else wants. There's plenty of work to do, and plenty of obstacles to overcome. Backstabbing corporate pawns, aggressive law enforcement, and other shadowrunners angling for your payday can get in your way. Your job is to beat them to the punch and make the big score before they can stop you.

Shadowrun: Sprawl Ops puts players in control of their own team of shadowrunners, selecting who they'll hire and then building up the cash, gear, and abilities the runners need to survive the streets. Only one team will complete the final mission that scores a huge payday and wins the game. Do you have the guts, wiles, and treachery it will take to make it to the top? Time to find out.

WWW.CATALYSTGAMELABS.COM/SHADOWRUN